THE **SAS** IN ACTION

Peter Macdonald served with the British Army and Rhodesian Security Forces during the 1970s. He is now a full-time photo-journalist specialising in military matters and is the author of *The Special Forces: A History of the World's Elite Fighting Units*, *Soldiers of Fortune: The Twentieth Century Mercenaries* and *US Elite Forces*.

To my good buddy JJ

Peter Macdonald

PETER MACDONALD

THE SAS IN ACTION

PAN BOOKS

First published 1990 by Sidgwick & Jackson

This revised edition published 1998 by Pan Books
an imprint of Macmillan Publishers Ltd
25 Eccleston Place, London SW1W 9NF
and Basingstoke

Associated companies throughout the world

ISBN 0 330 35392 6

1 3 5 7 9 8 6 4 2

A CIP catalogue record for this book is available from the British Library.

Typeset by SetSystems Ltd, Saffron Walden, Essex
Printed and bound in Great Britain by
Mackays of Chatham plc, Chatham, Kent

Contents

Preface

In the poem-play *Hassan*, written by James Elroy Flecker, the Master of the Caravan questions a group of travellers thus:

> 'But who are ye, in rags and rotten shoes,
> You dirty-bearded, blocking up the way?'

The reply, given by Ishak, the minstrel to the Caliph, is inscribed on the SAS memorial at Hereford:

> 'We are the Pilgrims, master; we shall go
> Always a little further: it may be
> Beyond that last blue mountain barred with snow
> Across that angry or that glimmering sea . . .'

The information for this book has come from a multitude of sources. The book is not an official SAS Regimental history, for there is no such animal. Nor does it express the views, official or otherwise, of the Regiment, the British Army or indeed the British Government. *The SAS in Action* describes the operations and training of the SAS – any views expressed are mine alone.

Acknowledgements

If this book is dedicated to any group of people, it is dedicated to the wives and families of the SAS Regiment, both regular and TA, who suffer loneliness and uncertainty, and without whom the men would not be able to do what they do best.

CHAPTER ONE

Raiders and Misfits

One day in July 1941, a tall, dark-haired man in the uniform of a junior officer in the Scots Guards approached the checkpoint outside Middle East headquarters in Cairo. When stopped by the sentry he attempted to bluff his way through, but without success. Then, while the guard's attention was momentarily distracted by the arrival of a staff car, the subaltern slipped past and into the building. His disappearance did not go unnoticed by the sentry, who realised that he had just been outmanoeuvred by a young lieutenant on crutches.

Once inside the headquarters building, the lieutenant entered the office of a major on the Adjutant-General's staff and identified himself. He said he needed to speak urgently with the Commander-in-Chief, General Sir Claude Auchinleck. The major was unimpressed. He recognised his visitor as an officer who had fallen asleep during one of his tactics lectures; he did not like him and refused to listen to his request. The telephone rang; it was the sentry reporting the intruder. While the major was otherwise engaged, the young officer slipped out of the office and into the corridor.

The next room he encountered was the office of the Deputy Chief of Staff, Major-General Neil Ritchie. The lieutenant entered uninvited, apologised for his unconventional arrival and told the general he had matters of great operational importance to discuss. Impressed by the young man, despite, or perhaps because of, his daring approach, the senior officer invited him to sit down. The subaltern outlined his plan: to destroy Axis aircraft in the Western Desert while they were still on the ground. He would achieve this with a small team of hand-picked men who would parachute behind enemy lines before the next Allied offensive. General Ritchie listened attentively and with growing interest. The concept seemed sound and the young officer seemed convinced he could carry it off. The general approved the scheme and gave permission for the subaltern to raise his force. It would be known as L Detachment, Special Air Service Brigade. The name of the lieutenant, now promoted to captain and given charge of the new unit, was David Stirling.

Stirling was not a professional soldier but had joined up at the beginning of the war. At school and later at Cambridge, there was little to distinguish him from his contemporaries, apart, perhaps, from the fact that he stood six feet five inches tall. His major interest had been climbing; his ambition, to conquer Everest. When war broke out, Stirling returned from the Canadian Rockies, where he had been training, and immediately joined the Scots Guards, a regiment with which he had a family connection. The following year he transferred to No 8 (Guards) Commando and at the beginning of 1941, sailed to the Middle East with 'Layforce', a combined force of three commando units, named after the founder of No 8 Commando, Brigadier Robert Laycock.

'Layforce' comprised a total of 2,000 men. Its objective was originally the capture of the Greek island of Rhodes, but in February 1941 Rommel arrived in North Africa with the Deutsches Afrika Korps (DAK) and turned the tide of war against the British in the Western Desert. The Rhodes operation was scrapped and 'Layforce' was dispersed throughout the eastern Mediterranean theatre. No 8 Commando was based initially in Mersa Matruh, Egypt, from where it conducted a small number of unsuccessful commando operations against the Germans in Cyrenaica (the eastern portion of modern-day Libya).

Among the officers of No 8 Commando were a number of enterprising individuals, including J.S. 'Jock' Lewes, an Australian-born officer serving with the Welsh Guards. Together with his colleagues, including Stirling, Lewes began parachuting with some 'acquired' parachutes unloaded by mistake at Alexandria. If parachuting was in its infancy back home in Britain, it was nonexistent in the desert. There were no instructors and no properly rigged aircraft, but, undeterred, Lewes and his fellow officers began training. Stirling was the first casualty. Jumping from a Valentia, an aircraft ill-designed for parachuting, Stirling's chute caught and ripped on the plane's tail assembly. He landed heavily on hard ground, severely damaging his back and suffering temporary paralysis of the legs. It was during the two months he subsequently spent in hospital that Stirling hatched the plan he presented to Major-General Ritchie in July 1941.

L Detachment SAS Brigade began life at Kabrit in the Suez Canal Zone with three tents, a placard proclaiming the new unit's identity, and a three-ton truck. There was of course no brigade; the title was used in an attempt to convince enemy intelligence that there was a parachute formation at large in the Middle East. Nevertheless, it was an independent command for the newly promoted captain (he reported directly to the Commander-in-Chief) and he immediately set about recruiting the six officers and sixty men he was allotted, drawing mainly on No 8 Commando. He soon raised his quota, but not without encountering some difficulty, as commanders were reluctant to lose good men.

From the beginning L Detachment attracted a high calibre of volunteers: experienced men who saw the chance to get to grips with the then rampant enemy. Stirling's first recruit was the parachuting Jock Lewes; the other officers were Bonnington, Fraser, McGonigal, Thomas and Blair Mayne, a well-known Irish rugby international who, at the time of his recruitment, was under close arrest for striking his commanding officer. Stirling also recruited soldiers and NCOs, among them Bennett, Cooper, Lilley, Rose and Seekings – names which would become synonymous with acts of daring and feats of endurance.

Now that he had the cadre of L Detachment, Stirling set about training them. Although many of the men had previously undergone commando training, they found Stirling's regime exceptionally hard. Forced marches through the desert at any hour of the day or night were standard; distances of 65 kilometres or more with weights of over 30 kg were not uncommon. The ability to navigate was vital for all ranks and great emphasis was placed on endurance and willpower. Indeed, the early selection process of L Detachment bore a strong resemblance to that undertaken by prospective SAS members today. The skills and personal characteristics required have changed very little over the years.

Parachute training followed; the candidates practised jumping from scaffolding platforms, from grounded aircraft and off the back of moving trucks before graduating to the real thing. L Detachment had the use of a Bristol Bombay aircraft, a more suitable machine than the Vickers Valentia, but despite this advance two parachutists were killed on the first jump when their chutes failed to open. The problem was traced to the clip that connected the static line to the anchor rail inside the aircraft. In certain conditions the clip could slip off the rail; without an anchor, the static line could not tauten and open the chute. A different clip was substituted and Stirling was the first to jump the following morning. His chute opened safely.

While training was in progress, Jock Lewes worked on developing a bomb suitable for the type of operation L Detachment would be carrying out. Stirling's concept involved inserting small groups by parachute onto a dropping zone (DZ); from here they could move forward and attach explosives to enemy aircraft while they were on the ground. Therefore the explosive had to be light, as it had to be carried, but powerful enough to destroy an aircraft. After testing various mixtures, Lewes eventually came up with the combination of explosive, incendiary, oil, plastic and thermite, which became known as the Lewes bomb.

L Detachment's first mission was timed to coincide with Operation Crusader, the offensive planned by General Auchinleck to begin on 18 November 1941. The enemy had a new type of ground-attack fighter – the Me 109F – based at the coastal airfields around Maleme and Tmimi. The plan was to drop the force onto two separate DZs from which it would launch its attacks on Tmimi and Maleme, and on a third airfield at Gazala. L Detachment was to approach the airfields, lie low and observe during the day, then mount its attack the following evening – 17 November. The two parties were to move in under cover of darkness, plant their Lewes bombs on the aircraft, and move back inland to rendezvous (RV) with the Long Range Desert Group (LRDG). In the event, any chance the force may have had of accomplishing the mission was wrecked on landing.

On the evening of 16 November, despite severe weather conditions, sixty-four officers and men from L Detachment boarded five Bombays in Cyrenaica for the flight to the DZs. During the journey, the weather deteriorated still further: dense cloud obscured the DZs and the aircraft became lost. One plane, flying under the cloud in an attempt to get its bearings, had to land after being hit by ground fire; the remaining aircraft dropped their parachutists miles off course.

The situation was no better on the ground, however. Wind speeds at ground level averaged 70 k.p.h., with gusts of up to 140 k.p.h., and on landing the men were dragged off across the desert by their parachutes, some never to be seen again. Most of the supply containers were lost; those that were found contained some Lewes bombs but no fuses. Without these vital components the bombs were useless. The attack was called off, and in rain that turned the dried-up wadis into fast-flowing rivers, the survivors of the aborted mission made their way to the LRDG rendezvous. Out of the sixty-four that started out on the raid, only twenty-two survived.

Despite its disastrous start L Detachment was allowed to soldier on, and the men learned from their mistakes. It was obvious that the weather had played a decisive part in the failure of the operation by making accurate parachuting impossible. Parachuting could therefore not serve as the sole means of getting to a target area, and an alternative way of infiltrating behind enemy lines had to be found. The obvious choice was to adopt the LRDG approach and use vehicles.

The LRDG was equipped for its long-range reconnaissance role with stripped-down 30 cwt trucks, modified for desert use and with a range of over 1,600 kilometres without refuelling. Its commander, Major R.A. Bagnold, whose vehicles had already ferried the SAS back from the failed Gazala raid, very graciously offered his unit's assistance in getting the SAS into target areas; Stirling gratefully accepted, realising that L Detachment could learn much from these veterans of desert travel.

Cooperation between the two units worked well from the start, and from their base at the Jalo oasis in the Libyan desert, patrols struck out at German airfields. Two operations were planned for 14 December. Sirte airfield, which lay to the west of Benghazi, would be attacked by troops led by Stirling and Mayne, while a force commanded by Lewes would strike at Agheila airfield situated between Benghazi and Sirte.

Escorted by S1 Patrol LRDG, Stirling and Mayne, together with ten men, set off for Sirte, about 560 kilometres away. They travelled in seven 30 cwt trucks, painted a dull pink to make them more difficult to spot from the air. The first 480 kilometres passed uneventfully; then, on the third day the convoy was spotted by an Italian reconnaissance plane. The patrol's gunners engaged the aircraft but it got away. The combined LRDG/SAS patrol then had just enough time to camouflage their vehicles in an area of scrub nearby before they found themselves being strafed by three Italian warplanes. Both men and transport escaped unscathed, but within 6 kilometres of the target they were again spotted and Stirling, reckoning that the enemy was now prepared for an attack, divided his force in two. One party, led by Mayne, would go on to raid the airfield at Tamit, about 50 kilometres to the west, while Stirling would lead the remaining men to Sirte on foot.

Stirling's group moved up to Sirte that night, walking right onto the airfield before they realised where they were. Escaping undetected, they moved to a ridge on the far side of the airfield. The plan had been to observe their target from this point throughout the following day and then move down during the evening and place charges on the aircraft. But the following afternoon, Sirte was evacuated, leaving them no target to attack.

Mayne's team were more successful, destroying twenty-four aircraft with Mayne himself adding to his growing reputation. Having run out of bombs, he removed the instrument panel of one aircraft with his bare hands. The team also gatecrashed an aircrew mess party, engaging those present with small arms at close quarters, and blew up the fuel dump before they left. The raid lasted fifteen minutes.

The airfield at Agheila, the target for Lewes's patrol, proved to be in use at that time only as a staging post and on the night of the SAS visit there were no aircraft on the ground. Not to be denied, Lewes switched his attention to a nearby house, which he understood was used as a conference centre by the enemy. Unfortunately the group's vehicles were identified as British before they got close enough to attack the building and Lewes and his men came under heavy fire. Leaving half his force to return the fire, Lewes led the remainder to a nearby vehicle park where they placed thirty charges to good effect. In the resulting confusion, he and his men retired to safety.

The SAS had struck their first blows against the enemy, and were now, without a shadow of a doubt, operational. On 21 December one raid led by Bill Fraser on Agedabia airfield resulted in the wrecking of thirty-seven enemy planes; two were left intact, causing Fraser to apologise for this 'failure'! By the end of 1941 the SAS had nearly a hundred enemy aircraft to their credit – all destroyed on the ground – plus a number of vehicles and petrol stores.

But the detachment had also lost good men in the past two months, including Jock Lewes, gunned down by an Italian aircraft as his patrol were on the way back from a raid at Nofilia. It had also nearly lost a whole patrol. Returning from a fruitless attack on an airfield at 'Marble Arch', a group led by Fraser missed their RV and found themselves marooned in the desert over 300 kilometres from home. Marble Arch was a nickname given by British troops to a large arch erected by Mussolini to mark the border with Tripolitania. They had no option but to walk and must surely have perished but for their seemingly bottomless reserves of cunning and sheer nerve. When they were recovered over a week later, they had raided two enemy trucks, hijacked a German Army car and its crew, and rigged up a do-it-yourself water desalination plant into the bargain. This was by no means the only occasion on which SAS men were rewarded for their daring. In other cases individuals or even complete patrols disguised as Arabs or as Germans or Italians succeeded in deceiving the enemy.

Auchinleck's Operation Crusader had succeeded in driving Rommel back out of Cyrenaica and at the beginning of 1942 Tobruk and Benghazi were once again in Allied hands while the Axis forces were regrouping at Agheila. Stirling, mindful of the fact that Rommel was resupplied by sea, temporarily switched his sights from airfields to ports and presented Auchinleck with a plan for an attack on the harbour at Bouerat, a town on the Libyan coast, west of Sirte. The Commander-in-Chief, impressed by L Detachment's achievements, granted Stirling permission to recruit a further six officers and between thirty and forty men, and gave him access to No 8 Commando's recce unit, the Special Boat Section (SBS). A little later L Detachment was further reinforced by a

Free French parachute squadron of some fifty 'air commandos'.

Although the LRDG was still responsible for inserting L Detachment patrols, the SAS were quickly gaining experience and beginning to acquire their own identity. Until now each man had worn the badges and accoutrements of his parent unit, except on operations when the majority of SAS men sported Arab headdress in the manner of the LRDG. Nevertheless the SAS needed a trademark of their own and a new badge was designed, a winged sword above a scroll bearing the unit motto 'Who Dares Wins'. Popularly known as the 'winged dagger', the device is believed to represent sword Excalibur. The badge was first worn on a white beret, which was soon replaced by a sand-coloured one. In addition to the cap badge, the SAS adopted their own parachutist brevet, comprising a parachute in the centre of the outstretched wing of the sacred ibis – a bird revered by the ancient Egyptians. A custom grew up surrounding the positioning of the 'Sabre' wings, as they became known. Newly parachute-qualified personnel wore them on the upper right arm, in the same position as the men of The Parachute Regiment and Airborne Forces wore theirs; once the wearer had distinguished himself on operations, however, the wings were transferred to the left breast. This tradition has been discontinued, although the wings themselves and the beret and badge are still in service.

The SAS operation against Bouerat took place in late January 1942. A raiding force consisting of two SBS, fifteen SAS and two RAF personnel was transported by the LRDG across the desert to the coast with the intention of attacking enemy shipping. This time the operation did not go according to plan. The force had its transmissions picked up by German DF (direction finding) units, was harassed by Italian warplanes and lost its radio vehicle. Shorn of communications, it now had no idea what awaited it in Bouerat. To make matters worse, one of the trucks now had a chance encounter with a pothole and the force's only canoe was damaged beyond repair. Unable to mine oil tankers in the harbour even had there been any (in the event there were not), the SAS party divided into two to assault secondary targets. One group, led by Stirling, located the petrol storage depot, which it blew up, together with a number of petrol tankers and other supply vehicles. The second group, under Captain Duncan of the SBS, destroyed the port's radio station. Both parties returned intact, despite the fact that Duncan's group ran into an ambush and had to fight its way clear.

As its experience and reputation grew, the detachment became larger and better equipped. Although the LRDG was still relied on for many things, including its specialist knowledge and the training of navigators, L Detachment was developing towards its full potential. One area in which it was becoming increasingly independent was that of mobility. On a visit to Cairo in June 1942, Stirling managed to lay his hands on some twenty three-tonners; he also obtained an item of equipment which was to change the face of SAS operations in the desert: the US-made Willys jeep. The SAS acquired fifteen of these amazingly versatile four-wheel-drive vehicles and they were adapted to become agile, cross-country gun platforms. They were fitted with twin Vickers K.303 machine-guns which in an earlier life had been mounted on RAF biplanes. Each vehicle carried two pairs – one in front of the navigator's seat and one in the rear of the vehicle – and certain SAS jeeps carried a Browning 0.5in machine-gun, in addition to the Vickers and the crew's personal weapons. With their own jeeps and four-wheel-drive three-ton trucks, the SAS were now capable of transporting their own supplies and equipment. The new transport also allowed the SAS to extend their operations and conduct patrols which lasted several weeks.

The start of SAS jeep-borne operations roughly coincided with the withdrawal of the Eighth Army to the defensive line of El Alamein as Rommel thrust his way back through Cyrenaica. The first patrols were carried out at the start of July 1942; the targets were the enemy airfields at Daba, Bagush, Matruh, Sollum and Fuka. On the raid at Bagush, charges were placed on the aircraft as usual, but only twenty-two of the forty Lewes bombs exploded. Quickly rallying his men, Stirling led them across the airfield and shot up the remaining planes with eight Vickers, mounted variously on his staff car (the 'blitz-wagon'), a jeep and a three-tonner. The new technique worked well and Stirling wasted no time in trying it out again.

The next operation was against the Junkers Ju 52 airfield at Sidi Haneish, one of the Fuka aerodromes, and for this raid Stirling employed a fleet of eighteen jeeps. Approaching in line abreast, the raiders were about a kilometre from the airfield when the runway lights were switched on for a returning aircraft. With the element of surprise still with them and the target well illuminated, Stirling opened up with his Vickers; the others quickly followed his example.

On Stirling's command the patrol switched from line-abreast to arrowhead formation and the vehicles raced between rows of Heinkel, Junkers and Messerschmitt transport and combat aircraft. The runway landing lights had been switched off, but the whole area was clearly illuminated by scores of, by now, burning planes. Stirling's vehicle was knocked out by enemy mortar and machine-gun fire, but, transferring to another, he led his patrol in a circuit of the airfield during which they destroyed further transport aircraft parked on the perimeter. The SAS then broke off the engagement and headed out into the desert. In two raids that evening L Detachment had destroyed between forty and fifty aircraft, bringing its total 'kills' in the year since it was formed to around 250; a higher figure than that achieved by the RAF in the same period. L Detachment's achievement was not merely the destruction of enemy aircraft, which in itself contributed handsomely to the Allied effort, but to divert Axis troops from the front to guard the desert airfields; Auchinleck's faith in the SAS concept had paid off.

CHAPTER TWO

Professional Warriors

In the struggle to eject the Axis from North Africa, the SAS established themselves as a force to be reckoned with, continuing their raids on airfields and harassing the enemy in support of Monty's push west. Nevertheless, they were still not universally accepted by the more orthodox soldiery and when victory was finally achieved in the desert in May 1943 and the Allies turned their attention to Sicily and Italy, the fate of the SAS seemed to be in the balance. In the end there was a role for them, but not before they had undergone considerable reorganisation.

By the start of 1943, the Special Air Service had come a long way from their small beginnings at Kabrit. In October 1942, the month in which the battle of Alamein began, L Detachment had been accorded regimental status as the 1st Special Air Service Regiment (1 SAS) and with the addition of the remaining elements of No 8 Commando and the SBS and volunteers from the Greek 'Sacred Squadron', the SAS continued to expand. With a second regiment (2 SAS), to be commanded by his brother William, in the pipeline, Stirling, now a lieutenant colonel, was well on the way to realising his current vision of three SAS regiments, one for each operational theatre. But no sooner had these forces come together than his own capture at the beginning of 1943 by a German counter-insurgency patrol (he was subsequently incarcerated in the maximum-security prisoner-of-war camp at Colditz) took him out of circulation at a critical time. This, combined with the end of the desert campaign, thwarted his plan for a full-scale SAS brigade. Indeed as operations closed in North Africa, the SAS became fragmented: the French SAS Squadron detached itself from the British Army and joined the Free French, laying down the foundations for the future 3 and 4 SAS; the 'Sacred Squadron' returned to Greek control. Stirling's old command, 1 SAS, was seemingly earmarked for disbandment but was reprieved. A and B Squadrons were renamed the Special Raiding Squadron (SRS) with Major Paddy Mayne, Stirling's natural successor, in command. Mayne was promoted lieutenant colonel and took the 250 officers and men of the SRS to Palestine for training. At the same time D Squadron SAS, a unit of similar strength under the command of Earl Jellicoe, also went to train in Palestine and became the Special Boat Squadron. Up to this time, Special Boat teams had been part of the SAS; this reorganisation signalled the parting of the ways. Meanwhile 2 SAS moved to Algeria where it began recruitment and training.

The landings in Sicily went ahead in July 1943 and the Special Air Service were involved in tackling a number of targets in advance of the main force. In one action alone the SRS captured three coastal batteries, killing over a hundred enemy and taking a further six hundred prisoner – all at a cost of only one man dead and six wounded. But these were tactical, rather than strategic, operations, more suited to commando or parachute units than the SAS. What is more, during the preceding months, the Special Raiding Squadron had been training in Palestine and the Lebanon for mountain and ski warfare with a view to possible deployment in the Balkans. Despite the fact that elements of 2 SAS parachuted into the north of Sicily during the 380-day campaign, the SAS were generally deployed out of role – not the first, nor the last, time they would be misused in this fashion.

Although David Stirling's capture had proved a great blow to the SAS (his powerful personality had dominated and controlled the organisation he had created), his loss was not as catastrophic as some have suggested. The SAS continued to evolve, with Bill Stirling originating many new and successful concepts. At his suggestion 2 SAS became heavily involved in the strategic battle for Italy which followed the Italian capitulation in September 1943. Operations in the Western Desert had proved that the SAS were at their most effective when operating behind enemy lines. Therefore when the Allies moved to drive the Germans from the Italian mainland, the SAS were once again sent to cause havoc at the enemy's rear.

One SAS operation which began right at the start of the Italian campaign was Operation Speedwell. The aim of Speedwell was to destroy railway lines between Genoa and Spezia; Bologna, Pistoia and Prato; and the line from Florence to Arezzo. Two SAS parties were parachuted in. One, under the command of Captain Pinckney, dropped to the south of Bologna; the second, led by Captain Dudgeon, was to destroy the lines between La Spezia and Genoa. The operation began on 7 September 1943 and both patrols had mixed fortunes. Pinckney was lost on landing, but two of his teams destroyed a total of four trains. One of Dudgeon's teams succeeded in wrecking a further two trains, although Dudgeon himself, together with an SAS trooper called Brunt, was captured and murdered after a contact with Germans; two NCOs who went missing are believed to have met the same fate.

The murder of captured SAS men was in accordance with a personal directive issued by Hitler. In it he stated that 'captured special forces troops must be handed over at once to the nearest Gestapo unit . . . these men are very dangerous, and the presence of special forces troops in any area must be immediately reported . . . they must be ruthlessly exterminated'. The directive, initially issued because of SAS successes in the Western Desert, had not been implemented by Rommel. In Italy the situation was very different and SAS officers and men, once caught by the enemy, could expect only torture and death. Nevertheless, the tragic losses apart, Operation Speedwell was a success. The two SAS patrols had succeeded in hampering the movement of German reinforcements to southern Italy at a time when they were urgently needed, although whether Allied planners took advantage of the situation is open to debate.

Other operations in which the SAS took part during September 1943 included a landing by the SRS at Bagnara on the toe of Italy and a pathfinder operation carried out by 2 SAS at Taranto for the 1st Airborne Division; in

October both units were involved in the successful battle for the Adriatic port of Termoli. But by this point SAS involvement in Italy was drawing to a close, at least for a time. After deploying small groups to attack German lines of communication and recover POWs released after the Italian capitulation, the SAS retired to Britain for reorganisation before the D-Day landings.

In January 1944 the SAS Brigade was formed under the command of Brigadier Roderick (later General Sir Roderick) McLeod. Comprising the SRS (now once again under the title of 1 SAS), 2 SAS, the 2nd and 3rd Free French Parachute Battalions (later 3 and 4 SAS), the Belgian Independent Parachute Squadron (later 5 SAS), and F Squadron GHQ Reconnaissance Regiment (Phantom), the brigade had a strength of around 2,500 all ranks. HQ SAS Troops came under the direction of Lieutenant General Frederick 'Boy' Browning, commander of the 1st Airborne Division, and a liaison section was created within the division to co-ordinate SAS activities.

Heading the liaison staff was Lieutenant Colonel I.G. Collins, an experienced special-operations planner who was responsible for liaising between the SAS and other groups, including the SOE (Special Operations Executive). He had a difficult task, for although by this time the majority of British military commanders had realised that special forces such as the SAS and SBS had an important role to play in modern warfare and original misgivings about the relative values of 'private armies' had been shelved by all but the most obstinate, few people understood the effective use of SAS troops. A number of suggestions for their possible employment bordered on the suicidal. In fact the proposed misuse of the SAS in a purely tactical capacity in the Normandy invasion prompted Bill Stirling to resign as commanding officer of 2 SAS. He was replaced by Lieutenant Colonel Brian Franks and the role of the SAS in the battle for north-west Europe was eventually worked out.

Although they were not directly involved in the D-Day landings, the SAS did go to war in France and Belgium in a strategic role. They were under the control of the 21st Army Group for operations around the Loire, Paris and Abbeville and were directed by Supreme Headquarters Allied Expeditionary Force (SHAEF) for operations in Belgium and the remainder of France. Dropped into occupied territory, reconnaissance teams contacted local resistance organisations and evaluated the general situation. If an area seemed ripe for exploitation, reinforcements were brought in and a base established.

Once in position, the SAS advised, and on occasion trained, the local resistance fighters; they also conducted their own guerrilla war against the occupying forces, usually within a radius of up to 80 kilometres from each base. Bridges were blown, railways destroyed, trains derailed and roads mined. Enemy convoys were attacked and bases targeted for RAF bombing missions.

The RAF (38 Group, 46 Group and the Special Duty Squadron) were responsible for the insertion and resupply of the SAS operating in France and Belgium. Although the role was a new one for them they carried it out with great skill, often overcoming difficulties imposed by the lack of effective communications. Besides the normal supplies of arms, ammunition and explosives, the RAF brought in jeeps. These vehicles, similar to the ones used in North Africa but without the desert adaptations, were partially fitted with armour plate. They were to prove of great value to the SAS and a real menace to the Germans.

One of the SAS missions launched in support of the Allied invasion of north-west Europe was Operation Houndsworth. Inserted into eastern France just before D-Day, the SAS, with the help of a three-man team of guides (a so-called 'Jedburgh' team), set up a base from which they carried out a series of successful attacks over a three-month period. Apart from earmarking targets for the RAF, this group, which eventually comprised around a squadron of SAS officers and men, blew up the Dijon, Lyons and Paris railway lines a total of twenty-two times, caused over two hundred enemy casualties, and took over one hundred prisoners.

A similar operation conducted over a two-month period during the summer of 1944 was Operation Gain. A party of around sixty men, this time of D Squadron 1 SAS, was tasked with, among other things, disabling the railway system in the area of Rambouillet, Orléans and Chartres. This jeep-borne squadron, commanded by Major Ian Fenwick, operated with great flair, and nowhere is this better illustrated than in their methods of attacking German supply convoys. Finding that the enemy moved at night with lights on, Fenwick ordered his detachments to do the same, and on occasion SAS vehicles actually travelled unidentified within German convoys. By the time they withdrew to Allied lines towards the end of August, Fenwick's party had scored a number of notable victories at a cost of ten men. One of these casualties was Fenwick himself, who was killed trying to crash through a German ambush. Gain, like Houndsworth, made an impact out of all proportion to the size of the force involved and caused severe disruption within the enemy's rear echelon.

Apart from these operations carried out from established bases, the SAS were also sent in to conduct a series of assaults on specific targets in the enemy rear areas in the lead-up to the invasion. Thus on D-Day minus one, eighteen SAS teams were dropped into France to attack enemy lines of communication in support of the Allied advance from the bridgeheads. As the invasion progressed and the Allies broke out from the Normandy beaches and began to push inland, the SAS were ordered into northern France. A series of operations was conducted during this phase of the advance, including Operation Loyton, under the command of Lieutenant Colonel Franks.

The aim of Loyton was to locate suitable targets for the Allied air forces, at that time enjoying air superiority, and generally to harass the enemy with a view to preventing free passage of reinforcements to the front line. After gleaning as much information as possible from SOE and MI6, Franks sent in a reconnaissance party under Captain Henry Druce. However, on his arrival Druce was disturbed by the attitude of the Maquis with whom he was supposed to liaise in organising the DZ for Franks and the main party. Ten days afterwards his fears about the reliability of the local resistance group were confirmed when one of their number turned informer.

The result of this treachery was the seizure of the Maquis's radio. Druce had been forced to rely on the resistance for communications because his own wireless set had been damaged during the drop; he now found himself without access to a radio. Nevertheless he found other means of getting his message through and managed to bring in the remainder of the SAS group, but as Franks and his men dropped onto the DZ on the night of 31 August/1 September, small-arms fire suddenly broke out on the ground. Apparently, one of the Maquis, already suspected of being a traitor, had opened up with a sub-machine-gun (SMG) while attempting to escape. Other resistance fighters opened fire in the confusion, which only ceased when Druce shot the suspect dead.

With the arrival of Franks and his group, Operation Loyton got under way. The SAS commander had only eighty-seven men at his disposal as he preferred to avoid contact with the unreliable local resistance wherever possible. This small force executed a number of successful actions and were responsible for the diversion of two German divisions from the front. Tasked solely with eliminating the SAS, these troops were prevented from joining the battle and were instead forced to roam the countryside hunting an elusive enemy.

But these victories were not achieved without loss. When the survivors of Loyton exfiltrated through to the Allied lines between 9 October and 12 October, more than thirty men were missing. Of these, twenty-eight were known to have been captured alive and were subsequently tortured and killed by the Gestapo. After the war it was discovered that these men had gone to their deaths bravely and a number of their murderers were apprehended and brought to justice, but at the time it was a high price for the SAS to pay despite the success of the operation. SAS activity throughout France continued in a similar vein until the end of 1944 when the Allies reached the borders of Germany. At this point, 3 Squadron 2 SAS, commanded by Major Roy Farran, was despatched to Italy to fight alongside the partisans.

The squadron arrived in Italy in December 1944 and their area of operations was the north of the country. Although untried, 3 Squadron was highly trained and raring to go. Volunteers were continually being selected, many with a wealth of previous experience in other fields of warfare and eager to prove themselves within the SAS. Farran himself was a career officer but he was as capable of the unorthodox as the most flamboyant wartime volunteer. Indeed when the unit began Operation Tombola in March 1945, the squadron commander, ordered by 15th Army Group not to accompany his unit, contrived to 'fall' from one of the Dakotas while despatching his men. It was no accident.

Tombola was conducted in the area between Spezia and Bologna – the same area in which Pinckney and Dudgeon had operated the previous year. The aim of the operation was to train Italian partisans and direct their activities against German occupying forces in the Tuscan Apennines. Up until this time guerrilla operations in the area had been co-ordinated by SOE under the command of Captain Mike Lees. The guerrillas themselves were a mixed group comprising Italians and Russians, communists and republicans, deserters and escaped prisoners of war. On his arrival, Farran inspected these men, some of whom were still in their early teens, and decided that something drastic would need to be done to turn them into a fighting force. He immediately submitted a long list of supplies, including a 75mm howitzer, interpreters in Italian, Russian and German, khaki berets with coloured hackles – and a Scottish piper. The latter, along with the berets, was intended to inspire the Italians. These supplies plus arms and ammunition were dropped in shortly afterwards and training began. Within a fortnight Farran's guerrilla battalion was ready for its first operation.

The area of operations for Tombola was bordered to the north by the River Secchia and close to Mount Cusna; it was highly suitable for guerrilla warfare. Farran's force based itself in a remote valley high in the mountains where they used the 75mm howitzer as the basis for a defensive position known as the Cisa Box. Towards the end of March, the squadron put into action an idea originally conceived by Captain Lees when they carried out an attack on the headquarters of the German LI Corps at Villa Rossi. The Germans occupying the building put up heavy resistance and despite all attempts by the partisans remained in control of the upper floors. Meanwhile, an assault on the Villa Calvi, timed to coincide with the Villa Rossi assault, was more successful.

Nevertheless the assault party lost the element of surprise early on in the operation. As they attempted to gain entry to the Villa Calvi, after inadvertently crossing a minefield, but without mishap, they encountered and were forced to engage a four-man German patrol, alerting the

Germans inside the building, who opened fire. However, the attackers still managed to break in and kill the occupants of the ground floor, among them Oberst Lemelson, the German chief of staff. Under cover of Bren-gun fire laid down by men outside the villa, the partisans set fire to the house and made good their escape, heading in the opposite direction to the way they had come and away from their hide-out in the mountains to a rendezvous with the remainder of the Tombola base group.

The link-up was achieved after twenty hours of marching over rough country and a night crossing of the River Secchia. The attackers' progress was initially slowed by two men who had been wounded by a grenade during the final assault, and the party's leader, an SAS officer named Harvey, called for volunteers to take care of the most severely wounded man. Two men remained with the casualty and nursed him back to the hide-out while the rest withdrew to the RV at a quicker pace. Here they lay up for a few hours to recover from their ordeal before setting off to the Cisa Box shortly after daybreak.

The partisans' first action had been a considerable success, despite the fact that a signal had been sent by 15th Army Group to prevent it going ahead. Farran, aware of the adverse effect that a last-minute cancellation would have on morale, conveniently managed to 'have left' before the message arrived. Estimated enemy casualties of the operation were around sixty, including a large number of German officers, while Farran's group lost three killed and fourteen wounded or missing.

There followed a number of actions around the River

Secchia, while the Germans made repeated attempts to track the guerrillas down. The SAS sent out fighting patrols, usually half British and half partisan in make-up, and a number of pitched battles took place in which the Anglo-Italian force usually emerged the victors despite the enemy's numerical superiority. The fortunes of war were rapidly turning against the Germans and they were dispirited. The advancing American 1st Armoured Division began to push the remaining three German divisions back across the River Secchia and towards the Po. All the time they were constantly harassed by the combined SAS and partisan force. By the time Farran received orders to exfiltrate his squadron, the war in Italy had only a fortnight to run.

While 3 Squadron 2 SAS was on operations in the Tuscan Apennines, the remainder of the SAS Brigade had been busy conducting reconnaissance missions for the British and Canadian armies advancing into Germany. In April 1945, with the end of the war in sight, the SAS were active in Holland, Belgium and Norway. They were in at the kill in north-west Europe, but ironically the demise of the Wehrmacht, once the world's most effective war machine, heralded their own disbandment – for a time at least.

CHAPTER THREE

Outposts of Empire

The SAS Brigade, like so many wartime special operations forces, was disbanded in 1945; only one small unit remained and that was 'semi-official'. In the postwar chaos that followed the Allied victory in Europe, a six-man team began investigations into the murder of captured colleagues. A mass grave had been discovered at Gaggenau, near Baden-Baden, which contained the bodies of some of the twenty-eight SAS men captured on Operation Loyton. The War Office was making no effort to investigate the disappearance of SAS men on active service, and there was no concerted effort to bring German service personnel to justice for carrying out Hitler's infamous 'Commando Order'. This prompted Lieutenant Colonel Brian Franks to pursue the murderers himself.

There were a number of reasons for this seeming apathy on the part of Allied governments. One was the political embarrassment caused by the fact that the Vatican was linked with a major Nazi escape line. The second was that both British and American intelligence organisations were recruiting former SD and SS officers for operations in Eastern Europe. Concerned that the perpetrators would escape, Franks set up his own investigations unit under the command of Major Eric Barkworth, who, together with Company Sergeant Major (CSM) 'Dusty' Rhodes and four others, continued the chase after 2 SAS was disbanded. Reporting back through the Phantom signals set-up to HQ SAS, the team was responsible for the capture of a number of Gestapo officers involved in the murder of captured SAS personnel and SOE agents – all this despite attempts to prevent it operating in the British sector of occupied Europe.

Although the British SAS ceased to exist with the end of the Second World War, abroad the situation was very different. The French and Belgian SAS units became established in their respective countries' armed forces. France's 3 and 4 SAS became 2e and 3e Régiments Chasseurs Parachutistes (RCP); the latter still retains the SAS Sabre wings as the predominant feature of its unit emblem with below it the words 'Who Dares Wins' in English. Meanwhile the 1st Battalion Belgian Para-Commandos retained the 'winged dagger' as its cap badge, and continues to maintain the traditions of 5 SAS. Nevertheless, within two years of the war's end there was once again a British unit wearing the insignia of the SAS – albeit not a regular one. In 1947 a Territorial Army – that is, a volunteer – unit known as the 21st Special Air Service Regiment (Artists' Rifles) was formed with none other than Lieutenant Colonel Brian Franks as its first commanding officer. The Artists' Rifles was a London-based TA unit originally raised in 1860 and known for providing 'officer material' for other arms and corps in wartime. This 'marriage' between the SAS and such a unit was to prove productive: the formation of 21 SAS (Artists) reintroduced a number of former wartime SAS officers and men back into the military system. Four years later a squadron from 21 SAS was on its way to take part in the Malayan Emergency – the conflict which was to bring about the rebirth of the SAS as a full-time British Army regiment.

Since 1948 ethnic Chinese communist terrorists (CTs) had been engaged in a campaign of terror in the rural areas of Malaya; they were experts at jungle warfare. One of the communist leaders was Chin Peng, who had been awarded the MBE for his services to the Crown during the Japanese occupation of Malaya. Together with a number of his former comrades from the SOE-sponsored Force 136, Chin Peng conducted a campaign of violence against the authorities. With arms, ammunition and explosives supplied by the Allies during the war and afterwards secreted away in jungle caches, the CTs were adept at striking vulnerable targets before disappearing back into the impenetrable jungle. To combat this, in 1950 the British raised a counter-insurgency unit – the Malayan Scouts – which specialised in extended jungle patrols and locating and ambushing the elusive CTs. The unit was commanded by its creator, Major J.M. 'Mad Mike' Calvert, a jungle warfare veteran of the Burma campaign who had commanded the SAS Brigade in Europe towards the end of the war.

Calvert started recruiting his force of jungle fighters locally from British forces stationed in the Far East. One of the problems he faced was that his somewhat easy-going unit did not always attract the right sort of volunteer. While many, including a number of National Servicemen, were skilled soldiers, there were some who chose the Scouts as a way of avoiding the discipline of more conventional areas of the Army. It took some time before this 'undesirable' element could be weeded out and they were to colour military opinion against the Malayan Scouts, and subsequently against the SAS, for some time to come. But Calvert was aided in his task of selecting more suitable volunteers by Major John Woodhouse, who went on to create an SAS selection programme which remains the basis for the one now in use. The one hundred men raised in the Far East became A Squadron Malayan Scouts (SAS). Two further squadrons were recruited from totally different sources. B Squadron, which arrived in Malaya in 1951, was drawn wholly from the ranks of 21 SAS and included many wartime veterans (although they had no experience of jungle operations they had the 'flexible approach' so often associated with the SAS and were eager to learn); C Squadron, on the other hand, was the result of a recruiting drive carried out by Calvert in Rhodesia.

One of the major problems faced by all the squadrons was the lack of qualified instructors and the lack of adequate training in jungle warfare techniques. The jungle, with its inherent dangers and diseases, was a difficult place to survive, let alone conduct successful counter-insurgency operations. Yet under pressure from senior military commanders Calvert was forced to deploy his troops with the minimum of training. The Rhodesian squadron, for example, had only three weeks of jungle training before being set to work, and this was given by Woodhouse and an NCO with less than a year's in-theatre experience between them.

Despite the early problems of indiscipline, and the fact that training was primarily conducted while on operations, the Malayan Scouts (SAS), renamed the 22nd Special Air Service Regiment (22 SAS) in 1951, achieved a number of successes. They proved the viability of extended jungle operations at a time when it was generally considered that Europeans were incapable of surviving the hostile environment for long periods. One patrol spent a total of 103 consecutive days on operations, its only contact with the outside world during this period being aerial resupply and radio communications.

The central pillar of British policy in Malaya was the 'Briggs Plan', a campaign to win the 'hearts and minds' of the local population. The CTs faithfully followed Chairman Mao Tse-tung's philosophy of using the peasant population as a source of food, shelter and potential recruits. The plan, named after the Director of Operations in Malaya, General Sir Harold Briggs, was designed to prevent this idea of guerrillas moving among peasants like 'fish in a sea' from working. Thousands of locals were relocated in safe villages (kampongs): with the 'sea' drying up, the 'fish' would be forced to head for deeper water; that is, retreat further into the jungle.

By 1952 22 SAS was on the offensive. The CTs, lacking the support of the local population, withdrew still further into the jungle. Once totalling more than 10,000 men, the terrorist army had dwindled to less than 5,000, and the CTs were forced to operate in small bands for fear of detection. The Regiment itself began to develop a unit identity during the campaign, but also underwent a number of changes. Mike Calvert was invalided out in 1951 and was replaced by Lieutenant Colonel John Sloane, a more orthodox soldier who introduced more traditional military discipline to the SAS. In 1952 Oliver Brooke took over and did much to further the growing relationship between the Regiment and the Malayan aboriginals. When Brooke was seriously injured during a parachute descent his place was taken for a short period by Mike Osborne who, in turn, was replaced by George Lea. Lea had much to do with shaping the SAS, in particular building up a strong cadre of officers.

A number of squadron commanders also left their mark on the Regiment, among them John Edwardes, Harry Thompson, Peter de la Billière and John Woodhouse. Indeed it was the latter who suggested employing aboriginal tribesmen in the war against the CTs. Before the aboriginals could be expected to cooperate, however, a rapport had to be built up between them and the Regiment. The way in which this was achieved became almost a blueprint for later SAS 'hearts and minds' campaigns.

To begin with, a number of jungle forts were established by the Regiment. Attracted by free food, medical treatment and protection from the CTs, local tribesmen would trickle into the forts and set up their 'bashas' next to those built by the SAS. Eventually these jungle forts became permanent, defended encampments – a safe haven for the local tribes for miles around. Once a fort had been established, its running would be handed over to the police or Malayan security forces and the SAS would go and build another. In this way a chain of forts was constructed down the centre of the country, effectively controlling the area and denying it to the terrorists.

The medical help played an important part in building confidence between the troopers and the tribesmen, many of whom were suffering from easily cured diseases. Doctors and Royal Army Medical Corps (RAMC) NCOs attached to the SAS held sick parades for the natives; the RAF dropped medical supplies and, on occasion, arranged a helicopter ride for the local headman, thus demonstrating both British strength and a genuine interest in the welfare of the local population. The 'hearts and minds' policy paid off, and the aboriginals responded by passing on information on the whereabouts and movements of CT groups. In this way the 'eyes and ears' of the security forces were extended into the most inaccessible areas of the 'ulu', as the jungle was known.

Woodhouse returned to Britain in 1953 and set about developing a standard selection programme. A number of new faces were recruited into the Regiment, and a number of familiar ones returned. Men who had served with the LRDG and the wartime SAS volunteered, and some of them were to have a marked influence on the SAS in years to come. One such officer was Dare Newell, a former SAS officer with experience in guerrilla warfare gleaned from wartime operations in Albania and Japanese-occupied Malaya. Dare Newell went on to become Regimental Adjutant, while Woodhouse eventually took command of the Regiment.

The SAS, first as the Malayan Scouts and then as 22 SAS, spent a total of nine years on operations in the Malayan jungle out of a campaign which lasted eleven years in all. During this period the SAS perfected the techniques and tactics demanded by jungle operations and, from the experience, learned a great deal which would stand them in good stead in the campaigns to follow. Navigation over the often hilly terrain, in hot and humid conditions, had initially proved almost impossible. However, the SAS perfected the use of the prismatic compass, a skill which had to be mastered by all volunteers who sought to gain entry to the Regiment. In addition much was also learnt about the art of jungle survival. Living in primitive conditions the SAS troopers acquired new skills from the aboriginals and from Iban trackers brought to Malaya from Sarawak. They learnt preventative medicine from the RAMC medics, signalling from attached signallers, and a host of other technical skills associated with patrol operations.

One such technique perfected by the SAS during their time in Malaya was parachuting into primary jungle – a highly dangerous activity. SAS men were dropped into the jungle canopy with the expectation that their chutes would become caught up in the trees as they fell. Once securely snagged the parachutists lowered themselves to the jungle floor by means of a rope. This method could be employed only in primary jungle, where there was sufficient strong foliage to support a man long enough for him to make his way down to earth under his own steam.

Jungle DZs were only used on operations. They were

located and marked out by Auster pilots (the Auster was a light observation aircraft flown by the Army Air Corps) and a number of successful airborne insertions were conducted during the Malayan campaign. In 1953 a total of 177 men from the three squadrons were dropped into the jungle for Operation Termite, with only four minor casualties.

Using this method of insertion, patrols were able to extend their area of operations further than conventional troops. Food and other supplies proved a limiting factor initially, but the Regiment devised and introduced a special seven-to-fourteen day SAS patrol ration, allowing men to operate for up to two weeks without resupply. Nevertheless patrols relied heavily on air support for insertion, resupply and casualty evacuation.

Aerial resupply was not always easy as is evident by the casualties incurred by 55 Company Royal Army Service Corps (RASC). Responsible for despatching supply containers to the ground forces from RAF aircraft, 55 Company lost over a hundred men killed when planes crashed into the jungle. As helicopters were scarcely out of their infancy, fixed-wing aircraft had to be used, including Hastings, Valettas and, towards the latter stages of the campaign, Beverley transports. Stores and equipment were parachuted down onto the jungle canopy and collected by troops on the ground. However, as helicopters became capable of carrying a greater payload and operating at higher altitude, the reliance on fixed-wing aircraft lessened. Towards the end of the conflict both Royal Navy and RAF helicopters were used increasingly and a number of injured SAS soldiers owe their lives to the skill and dedication of the pilots.

The structure and organisation of the SAS evolved and became established during the Regiment's time in Malaya. The original three squadrons (A, B and C) that had formed the Malayan Scouts had been augmented by a fourth (D Squadron) before Calvert left for the UK. Then in 1956 a further squadron, the Parachute Regiment Squadron, was raised from volunteers drawn from the Paras and commanded by Major Dudley Coventry. That same year C Squadron returned to Rhodesia to become the Rhodesian SAS and was replaced by a New Zealand squadron under Major Frank Rennie. This Kiwi connection meant that a number of Fijians joined the Regiment. These men were excellent soldiers and many were to spend their entire service life with 22 SAS.

By 1958, the year in which 22 SAS became established in the British Army ORBAT (order of battle), the war in Malaya had turned in favour of the security forces. The communist groups became more fragmented, many of their leaders being killed or captured. Food was scarce outside the forts and protected kampongs and recruits were difficult to come by. When propaganda failed, the CTs resorted to terror.

One of the last of the communist leaders to be rounded up was Ah Hoi, also known as the 'baby killer', after the gruesome disembowelling of an informer's pregnant wife. Local villagers had been forced to watch this atrocity as Ah Hoi tried to prevent further cooperation with the security forces. After the killing Ah Hoi took his small band further into the jungle and sought shelter in the Telok Anson swamp, to the south-west of Ipoh. The British administration, determined to kill or capture him, selected the SAS to go in after him and his men. In February 1958 D Squadron HQ and three troops, thirty-seven men in all, parachuted into the swamp, about five kilometres from its western edge. During the descent into the heavily forested area, one soldier, Trooper Mulcahy, severely injured his back when his canopy collapsed as it hit the treetops. D Squadron's initial task on landing therefore was to clear a number of trees to create a helicopter landing zone (LZ) from which Mulcahy could be 'casevaced'. In an impressive display of flying, the pilot brought the helicopter into the small clearing and hovered just above the swampy ground while the casualty was loaded aboard.

After the successful evacuation of the casualty the squadron fanned out to search for CTs. Various deserted camps were found, but the enemy managed to evade the SAS until a young aboriginal with one of the patrols spotted a couple of terrorists on the bank of the Tengi River. Two members of the patrol, Sergeant Sandilands and Corporal Finn, crossed the river behind a log, opening fire on the two terrorists when they came within range. One was killed outright but the second, a woman, made off at speed and was soon lost in the dense jungle. Following up the track made by the fleeing woman, the troop found a recently deserted camp. The CTs were on the run, and D Squadron responded by placing a cordon around the area. Two days later a small, emaciated woman came out of the jungle to negotiate surrender terms. The terms put forward by the female CT, whose name was Ah Niet, included a general amnesty for all jailed communists and a large sum of money for the CT team. These unrealistic terms were immediately rejected and Ah Niet was released to inform Ah Hoi that he either brought his band out, or the RAF would conduct a bombing raid on his hiding-place. Faced with this choice, Ah Hoi and the remnants of his group gave themselves up over the next forty-eight hours.

Morale among the communists was at an all-time low. Before his surrender Ah Hoi had been forced to move his hiding place eighteen times over a period of three months, because of aggressive patrolling by the security forces. In addition he had lost two of his men in contacts with SAS patrols. Other CT bands were in a similar position and over the next few weeks further terrorists surrendered, sometimes alone but occasionally in groups. The Malayan Emergency was drawing to a close.

The 22nd SAS Regiment left Malaya with three major achievements under its belt. First it had proved that European troops could operate in a hostile environment for months, when previously the maximum duration for an infantry patrol was considered to be seven days. As a result of these patrols, the security forces had been provided with intelligence, considered by many to be more important than the 108 confirmed CT kills in nine years. Secondly, the SAS had proved the value of the 'hearts and minds' concept in modern COIN (COunter-INsurgency) operations and had lived for long periods with the natives, winning them over to the administration's cause and gaining valuable allies. These lessons were used to advantage by the SAS in their later campaigns in Borneo and Oman, and in South-east Asia by their American Special Forces counterparts. Finally the SAS had won from Whitehall the right to exist as a regiment. This was a victory well deserved and perhaps the greatest single achievement of their campaign in Malaya.

Four years after the success in Malaya, the SAS found itself committed to a very different type of war, in the barren mountains of southern Arabia and backstreets of Aden city. In 1964, situated at the south-western corner of the Arabian peninsula, dominating the southern entrance to the Red Sea, was the British-ruled Federation of South Arabia. It is now known as Yemen. Britain had ruled the territory since 1839, but, except for Aden city, it was a backward and underdeveloped place. The mountainous interior was populated by wild tribes, who were all heavily armed and only nominally loyal to the British crown. Egyptian-backed radical Arab nationalists took part in an uprising, in what was then North Yemen, during late 1962 and their agents had begun to ferment unrest in British-ruled territory.

In just over a year the Radfan region was slipping from British control so a force of the locally recruited Federal Regular Army was sent into the mountainous Radfan region to sort out the rebellious Queteilbi tribe during January 1964. When the troops withdrew a month later, the rebels came down from their mountain hide-outs to re-establish their rule.

April 1964 saw a British brigade of paratroopers, Royal Marines, East Anglian Regiment and supporting armour and artillery, nicknamed Radforce, dispatched from Aden city to restore the situation. A Squadron, of 22 SAS, was due to travel to Aden for a training exercise but its commander volunteered his men's services to Radforce. Relatives were told the squadron was going on exercise to Salisbury Plain. The squadron was quickly moved up country to the forward air strip at Thumier, ready to support the brigade advance into Radfan. The initial plan called for the SAS to infiltrate into rebel-held territory to act as pathfinders and mark a drop zone (DZ) for the paratroopers to jump into, before they moved out to take on the enemy. On the night 29/30 April, eight men of 3 Troop, led by Captain Robin Edwards, moved off on a 10-kilometres march to the drop zone, which was codenamed Rice Bowl. The mountainous terrain proved tougher going than expected and the troop signaller Trooper Warburton began to go down with severe stomach cramps. It was starting to get light so Captain Edwards decided to lay up on high ground overlooking the drop zone until the following night, when they would complete the marking of the DZ.

Down the hill from the hide was a rebel village and after sun-up herdsmen started to appear around the SAS men. A pair of locals found them and raised the alarm. Within minutes dozens of heavily armed tribesmen were swarming around the SAS hide. A fierce firefight developed around the rocks on the hillside. Trooper Warburton was recovered enough to use his radio to call in wave after wave of RAF Hunter strike aircraft to strafe the rebels with rockets and cannon. This heavy firepower kept the rebels at bay during the daylight, but the SAS men decided to escape from the trap under the cover of darkness.

The night move over the mountains turned into a running fight as the tribesmen closed in for the kill. Captain Edwards was shot and killed. His comrades had to leave his body behind in the confusion. Next to be picked off was Trooper Warburton. Twice during the withdrawal the SAS staged successful ambushes on their pursuers, killing several of them. By dawn the SAS men had shaken off the rebels and were picked up by British troops and returned to base.

The incident was not closed until the news broke in the British newspapers that the severed heads of the two dead SAS men were on display in the Yemeni capital. This was the first the dead men's families knew of their deaths.

Britain was now involved in a major commitment to contain the rebellion. The three SAS sabre squadrons set up a regular roulement to ensure one of them was always on the ground in Aden. During the remainder of 1964, A Squadron continued to be heavily involved in Radfan supporting British troops sweeping through the mountains. The SAS was sent out to set up covert observation posts to track rebel movements. For days on end the SAS men would lie in their positions, sending sighting reports back to headquarters so that strike aircraft and artillery fire could be brought down. SAS teams were inserted by helicopter or marched over the mountains to reach their positions.

The mountainous terrain and hot desert sun made life

in the observation posts unbearable. Exposed metal parts of weapons and radios became too hot to touch. Water was at a premium and once in position it was almost impossible to resupply the men in daylight. Covert night-time resupplies were the only way to get in new water, otherwise the troops had to collect water from the streams.

In the mountains, the SAS and rebels fought a cat-and-mouse game. SAS patrols had to stay in their hides during the day to watch for anything suspicious. When targets were located the SAS men walked artillery on to them, adjusting the fall of shot until it was spot on. Rounds had to be literally 'walked' on to the targets quickly, before the rebels could escape. If the rebels were experienced they would soon realise they were being watched and go hunting for the SAS. Fast-moving firefights would then ensue in the rocks between the SAS men and the rebels.

The war in the mountains continued in much the same way for three years until the British withdrew in the summer of 1967. As the war escalated it started to spread to Aden city, where it took on a very different character. By Middle Eastern standards Aden was a relatively modern city, but its old quarter still contained the traditional souk (market-place) and alleyways. Arab guerrillas became expert at close-quarter assassinations, with pistols, knives and grenades. Dressed in civilian clothes they were indistinguishable from the rest of the local population and they could split away undetected after killing their unsuspecting victims. Senior British politicians, generals, off-duty soldiers, service families, foot patrols and locally recruited policemen all fell victim to the Arab guerrillas.

To counter this growing threat, Major Peter de la Billière formed the first SAS Keeni-Meeni unit to specialise in close-quarter urban warfare. 'Keeni-Meeni' is a Swahili phrase, which describes an undulating snake in long grass, and aptly described the mission of the SAS to merge in with the local population. Operating in local clothing, the SAS patrols skulked around the Arab neighbourhoods watching for guerrilla activity. The SAS teams would then draw concealed pistols and dispatch the guerrillas to Allah.

Highly accurate handgun shooting was then a new skill for the SAS and a special close quarter battle (CQB) school was set up to teach the new arrivals the essentials. Dark-skinned Fijian SAS soldiers were particularly suited for this work because they blended in more easily with Aden's Arab population.

For the last year of British rule in Aden, the SAS Keeni-Meeni teams waged a bloody backstreet war. Success or failure depended on the ability of SAS men to draw Browning pistols from under their Arab robes.

With the British Government committed to withdraw from Aden, come what may, the supply of intelligence from friendly natives dried up. This meant the SAS often went in blind on its undercover patrols, just hoping for something to turn up. On a number of occasions, the SAS men's disguises let them down and they came under suspicion from guerrilla supporters. Here the skills taught on the CQB range came into their own. Invariably the

SAS was able to shoot its way out of a tight corner. Four SAS men were killed and many wounded in 1966 and in the run-up to the June 1967 British withdrawal.

As the war in southern Arabia was hotting up in the summer of 1963, the SAS became involved in the war just across the border in Yemen. This country was known for most of the 1970s and 1980s as North Yemen, before it was 'united' with South Yemen, which was formerly the old British colony of South Arabia. Pro-Egyptian Arab nationalists seized power and overthrew the pro-western Royalist regime. The British and Saudi governments were horrified and put together a scheme to help the Royalists wage a guerrilla war against the nationalists and the 50,000 Egyptian troops that had arrived to shore up their allies. Due to opposition from the US Government, this had to be a 'black' or deniable covert operation, so the first SAS team to be inserted to assist the Royalists had to be officially discharged from the Regiment and recruited as 'mercenaries' by civilian supporters of the Royalists. However, the men were paid directly by the British Foreign and Commonwealth Office, operated from British bases in Aden and Cyprus, and coordinated their operations with the SAS in Aden.

Dressed as Arabs, the first four-man team made its way on a camel train into Yemen in June 1963, and made contact with the Royalists. The SAS men found the locals to be badly organised and equipped, so a major covert arms supply programme was set up. Aircraft flew black-market arms from Europe, Israel and French-ruled Djibouti which were parachuted into mountain drop zones manned by the SAS. It was then necessary to teach the guerrillas how to use the heavy machine-guns, mortars and other sophisticated weapons they had just received. This campaign bore a close resemblance to the Partisan campaign in Yugoslavia during the Second World War because the driving force behind it was the Conservative MP for Inverness, a certain Billy McLean, who was a Special Operations Executive (SOE) veteran from the Balkans. The operation grew in size during 1964 and around thirty French mercenaries were hired to help the SAS.

By October 1965 the SAS efforts were starting to show fruition when a major Egyptian offensive was halted with heavy casualties near Haradh. During the winter and spring the SAS-backed guerrillas started to harass Egyptian supply convoys. In April 1965 a large convoy was destroyed near Hazm, which forced the Egyptians to rely on aircraft to supply their remote garrisons. The Egyptians were starting to pay a heavy price for their Yemen adventure and in 1966 the first moves were made to negotiate their withdrawal.

Egyptian aircraft made a gas attack on a Yemeni village in January 1967 and at first they were thought to be using a new chemical nerve agent. The SAS brought out samples from the contaminated region and, much to the embarrassment of the British Government, it turned out that the Egyptians were only using CS riot control gas.

The Israeli victory in the June 1967 'Six Day War' meant the Egyptians had to withdraw their troops hurriedly to defend the Suez Canal so the 'secret' Yemen war began to wind down and the SAS was quietly withdrawn.

At the same time British troops were leaving Aden and South Arabia to its fate, so ending the involvement of the SAS in this bloody and ultimately futile conflict.

From the point of view of the SAS the conflict was very frustrating because they were unable to influence the strategic result, but it did provide useful experience in urban counter-terrorist operations. Its Keeni-Meeni tactics would soon be resurrected when the Regiment was called in to provide Britain's hostage-rescue capability and take the war to the IRA in the backstreets of Northern Ireland.

CHAPTER FOUR

Looking after our Friends

The SAS Regiment's performance in Malaya ensured that it survived the reorganisation of the British Army in the late 1950s. Nevertheless sacrifices had to be made and 22 SAS was reduced in size to two operational squadrons – A and D. It was already in this streamlined state when an emergency arose in late 1958. That November, D Squadron departed from the Far East, bound for the Middle East and war in an environment as different from the jungle of Malaya as it was possible to be.

During the 1950s, anti-government guerrillas under Talib ibn Ali began a long and bloody struggle for control of Muscat and Oman (the Sultanate of Oman since 1970) on the Arabian Gulf. Although the Sultanate was a backward country and its people were poor, it dominated the Straits of Hormuz, the major sea route for oil leaving the Gulf for the open Arabian Sea. For this reason, it was a traditional ally of Britain, so when the Sultan could no longer cope, it was to Britain that he went for help.

By 1957 the rebels had been driven back by a joint British–Omani force to Jebel Akhdar, a mountainous area rising to 2,440 metres and surrounded by a fertile plain; it was a seemingly impregnable stronghold. The British decided to use airpower to try to dislodge the insurgents, but this failed, and a conventional infantry assault against such a target was deemed out of the question. There was nothing for it but to send for the SAS, who arrived at the end of 1958. Even for the Regiment it was not all plain sailing and D Squadron – the first to arrive – took losses as it adjusted to the terrain, the weather and the new enemy. But a quick result was wanted before the campaigning season ended and so in the new year A Squadron arrived as reinforcement and the final assault on the mountain was planned.

The climax to the campaign took place at the end of January 1959 and was in true SAS style. Diversionary attacks were made to disguise the main assault, which took the form of an amazing ascent up onto the plateau at the base of Aqbat Dhafar, the rebel stronghold. The SAS men took a seemingly unclimbable route and their arrival at the top took the insurgents by surprise; in fact the rebel machine-gunners were not even manning their weapon on that side, so safe did they feel. The 'impregnable' Jebel Akhdar was taken and victory soon followed.

On its return from Oman, the Regiment passed through a period of operational inactivity. Advantage was taken of the lull to brush up individual and troop skills. Troopers were sent on outside training courses, exercises were conducted overseas and in 1960 22 SAS moved its HQ from Malvern to Hereford where it established itself at Bradbury Lines. It was almost four years before the SAS received their next operational assignment.

In December 1962 there was an internal rebellion in Brunei, a British protectorate, which, together with Sarawak and Sabah, formed the northernmost third of Borneo, an island to the east of Malaya; the remaining two-thirds of the island belonged to the independent state of Indonesia. The 'Brunei Revolt', as the localised rebellion was known, was organised and led by a young Brunei sheikh named Azahari, who wanted to unite the three dependencies. It was short-lived but dramatic. Small parties of armed guerrillas simultaneously attacked a number of strategic targets, including police stations, government buildings and a power station. Britain responded quickly. Troops stationed in Singapore, including Gurkhas, Royal Marine Commandos and soldiers of the Queen's Own Highlanders, were rapidly deployed to Brunei to suppress the revolt. Eight days later the rebellion was over and the thousand or so guerrillas who had taken part had disappeared into the jungle.

Nevertheless the situation on the island of Borneo was still unstable. An expansionist Indonesia under President Sukarno was seeking to acquire further territory in the region and regarded the rest of the island of Borneo with covetous eyes. It was into this scenario, with Indonesian-backed guerrillas poised just the other side of the 1,100-kilometres frontier, that A Squadron 22 SAS, at its own request, was propelled in January 1963.

At that time the Director of Operations in Brunei was Major-General Walter Walker, an officer who appreciated the value of the SAS and was pleased to have their assistance. Walker had five infantry battalions under his command and they, together with a single SAS squadron, were expected to secure the far-reaching frontier, an apparently impossible task. The terrain was varied and difficult: primary and secondary jungle, hills and mountains, swamps and fast-flowing rivers. The latter were the main arteries of communication in the thick impenetrable jungle. Along them, in longhouses built on stilts, lived the majority of the local population. Walker realised that the Regiment had experience in conducting long-range patrols and so he immediately deployed A Squadron into the jungle. He reckoned that the skills learned in Malaya, the SAS's familiarity with the 'ulu', and their ability to cooperate with local natives, would provide him with a vital asset in the coming struggle. He was right.

Shortly after its arrival A Squadron fielded a total of twenty-one patrols along the frontier. Although the border with Indonesia was ill-defined the SAS had two distinct advantages over the rebels when it came to locating crossing-points and mounting ambushes. Firstly, because of the nature of the terrain there were only a limited number of crossing-points and the SAS were professional soldiers, better at concealing their whereabouts than partially trained guerrillas. Secondly, the local tribes could probably be persuaded to provide them with advance notice of enemy movement. During its time in Malaya the SAS had come close to perfecting the 'hearts and minds' technique and they set about employing it again during the Borneo 'Confrontation'.

After keeping a village under observation, to establish where its allegiance lay, a patrol would pay a visit to the headman. Depending on how friendly the village was, they would either sit around and talk or, if things went well, eat and drink with the villagers. Once initial contact had been made, they would then withdraw to their jungle hide-out, and lie up for anything up to a week before returning to pick up where they had left off.

Visits to the villages were never hurried affairs and the SAS never forced themselves on the natives. Before long the visits became longer, perhaps with a patrol spending first one night, then another in 'their' particular village. In this way a relationship was established and soon there were a number of patrols operating out of the villages. The tribespeople provided food and accommodation, trackers if the village was in the jungle, transport and guides if it was on a river. The SAS in return brought gifts, provided medical care for the sick, and in some cases carried out building work. Unknown talent began to emerge. One NCO, 'Gypsy' Smith, manufactured an improvised hydro-electric generator but is perhaps better known in Regimental folklore for his alcohol still. Smith is reputed to have made the still using the frame of a bergen rucksack, but the exact details of its design remain a secret to this day.

Through this and other means a bond of mutual respect and admiration was forged between the natives and the troopers. The tribesmen supplied the patrols with information which they in turn passed on to their brigade HQ. One tribe, the Iban, had supplied trackers for the SAS in Malaya; old acquaintances were renewed and a number returned to work for the Regiment.

An old Borneo hand describes Iban proficiency:

> They were state of the art at tracking and trapping. On one occasion their skill even boggled my mind. We were moving towards an enemy force and the (Iban) tracker, who had been following the tracks of three or four people all morning, returned and said, 'One of the patrol is an officer and he is wearing brown boots, carrying a pistol, has an assault rifle, a bush hat . . .' I said, 'Hold on, wait. I mean I know you're very good at tracking and I know that you're much better at reading signs than we are but how, in the name of Christ, do you know what sort of hat he's got on, what sort of weapons he's carrying?' And the tracker said, 'Oh, he's over there.' And through a thin screen of trees there was a clearing in which stood an [Indonesian regular army] officer.

At the end of April, D Squadron replaced A Squadron and spent much of its tour training locally raised scouts together with the Gurkha Independent Parachute Company. Although there was no common language the Border Scouts learnt quickly and became both efficient and effective. The SAS were greatly helped in their training of the locals by attached specialists, including linguists from other units.

The Regiment had its first casualties of the campaign in May 1963 when a helicopter crashed in bad weather. Among the nine people on board were: Major Norman MBE, MC, second-in-command of 22 SAS and, like Dare Newell, a veteran of the guerrilla war against the Japanese; Major Harry Thompson MC, the man behind the capture of Ah Hoi in the Telok Anson swamp; and Thompson's signaller Corporal 'Spud' Murphy. Aircraft crashes caused almost as many casualties as did contacts with the Indonesians, and this loss was a particular blow to the Regiment. Thompson had been due to take over command of 22 SAS the following year.

Tension along the border with Indonesia was increasing and more casualties were to follow. A United Nations team visited Borneo during 1963 to assess the feelings of the local population. That summer the Federation of Malaya accepted Sarawak and Sabah into what then became the Federation of Malaysia, while the Sultanate of Brunei chose to remain a British protectorate. As the politicians made their plans the Indonesians acted and in August 1963 launched a major cross-border offensive. According to General Walker, the rebellion in Brunei ended in 1963 and the war then began.

Indonesia's first major incursion into Borneo came just as D Squadron was leaving and A Squadron was returning for its second tour. As the conflict escalated the decision was taken to re-form B Squadron and training was underway by December. The following October B Squadron was manned and ready, and, supported by a cadre of NCOs from A and D Squadrons, it deployed to Brunei for the first time. Despite the additional manpower the Regiment was fully stretched. To ease the pressure, it was augmented by the Guards Independent Parachute Company, a unit of the Household Division, which was later to become G Squadron 22nd SAS Regiment, and SAS selection courses were run in-country.

By the end of 1964 there were eighteen British infantry battalions on active service in Borneo, a total which included eight Gurkha battalions. In addition there were three Malaysian Army battalions bringing the number of troops deployed to 14,000, including supporting arms and services. Most of these men were deployed in the jungle and some were better suited to operations in this strange environment than others. A former SAS NCO, who now runs a survival school, explains: 'A lot of soldiers from other units found the jungle in Borneo very disturbing, and some soldiers in regular infantry units actually died of shock. This is one of the reasons, apart from the type of action fought in Borneo, why the Gurkhas, Paras, Marines and SAS were involved so heavily.'

The sergeant goes on to describe his first experience of the jungle and the effect it had on him:

> I was very keen to see the jungle and the animals and the birds, so psychologically I was looking forward to it. However, nothing prepared me for the first few steps through the foliage. It was like leaving a room with a 1,000-watt bulb and entering a room with a 20-watt bulb. It was dark and gloomy. Instead of seeing the animals and being surrounded by them, as they sensed you coming and heard the sound, they would move off. So you were immediately surrounded by a zone of silence instead. Often, when you made contact with the enemy, it would be because you weren't moving at a time when he was moving past

> you. You could actually hear this zone of silence move towards you, or move parallel to you, more than you could hear the enemy patrol.

In the late summer of 1964 the SAS established a number of training camps for Border Scouts in northern Borneo and western Sarawak. From among those trained the SAS selected forty Iban Dyaks for cross-border operations. The Iban were just one of the Dyak tribes living in Borneo; there were also Land Dyaks, Muruts and Punans – all with their own customs and way of life. Until fairly recently some of these tribes had been headhunters (some still were according to some sources) and most were deadly accurate with blowpipes which could fire a poison dart up to 50 metres. The Dyaks were a very introverted people and given to killing trespassers, rather than warning them off. A number of Indonesian soldiers who strayed into Dyak territory did not live to regret their intrusion. It paid to have them on your side.

The situation in Borneo continued to hot up and the SAS were authorised to patrol up to 25 kilometres into Indonesia. These operations were codenamed 'Claret' and a brief summary of one such cross-border patrol gives an idea of what these missions could be like, and an insight into the make-up of the SAS soldier.

In February 1965 a patrol was approaching what appeared to be a long-vacated guerrilla camp when the lead scout, Trooper Thomson, saw an Indonesian soldier just as the latter opened fire. Hit in the left thigh, Thomson was flung to one side and landed in a clump of bamboo, next to a second Indonesian whom he promptly shot dead. Meanwhile the patrol commander, Sergeant Lillico, returned fire despite also having been hit in the initial burst. The remainder of the patrol immediately dispersed and laid down a barrage of fire. The Indonesians, perhaps under the impression that reinforcements had been brought up, apparently withdrew. Lillico, himself unable to walk but believing Thomson capable of doing so, ordered the lead scout back to bring forward the remainder of the patrol. Thomson crawled onto a nearby ridge, put down some fire in the direction of the guerrilla camp and, after applying a tourniquet and shell dressing to his shattered leg and taking a dose of morphia, continued his crawl towards the patrol's ERV (emergency rendezvous). The remainder of the patrol meanwhile had decided to withdraw to a nearby infantry position to raise a force to return and sweep the contact area.

The sergeant was now alone in the jungle. He dragged himself into the shelter of a clump of bamboo, bandaged his wounds and injected himself with morphia. He then passed out and remained unconscious until awoken by a helicopter hovering over the jungle canopy. Lillico reckoned that he must be invisible among the bamboo and so resolved to crawl to the ridge, where the foliage was less dense, the following morning.

By late the following afternoon, as Thomson was being recovered by the follow-up patrol, having dragged himself 1,000 metres, Lillico had reached the ridge as planned. He fired a few shots to attract the attention of the search party he knew would be out looking for him, but his attempts to signal for help were answered by bursts of automatic fire from close by and he was forced to remain silent while the Indonesians carried out a search of the area. The enemy failed to find him, but his position was now overlooked by an Indonesian soldier up a tree 40 metres away. This meant that Lillico could not signal to his would-be rescuers and he had to watch as a friendly helicopter came and went. Fortunately, just before last light the helicopter returned; this time the sergeant managed to attract the crew's attention and was winched to safety. For his part Sergeant Lillico was awarded the Military Medal and Trooper Thomson received a Mention in Despatches.

In the summer of 1965 the British battalions in Borneo were reinforced by the arrival of Australian and New Zealand forces from the 28th Commonwealth Brigade, Malaysia. These included two SAS squadrons, one from New Zealand and one from Australia. Activity in the border areas increased and patrols often faced large groups of Indonesian regulars, often paratroopers or marines. Reconnaissance and ambush patrols were sent out to cover rivers and trails used by the Indonesians, enemy bases were attacked and the SAS acted as guides for larger infantry formations. The Regiment remained closely involved in the conflict, with its squadrons serving four- to five-month tours on rotation.

Singapore opted out of the Federation of Malaysia in August 1965 and two months later there was an appallingly violent coup in Indonesia. After some months of bloodletting during which there were an estimated 600,000 deaths, Sukarno, the Indonesian leader, was replaced by General Suharto. A peace agreement was signed in August the following year, and the 'Confrontation' came to an end. It had been one of the least publicised campaigns since the Second World War, lasting four years and costing the lives of 114 British and Commonwealth soldiers. Of these, three were from 22 SAS, which also lost two men wounded in the nine operational tours it completed during the conflict. Borneo had been difficult, but it had also been successful, and the SAS had played an important part in the victory.

At the start of the 1970s the Regiment was once again back on Oman. Sultan Qaboos was fighting overthrow by rebels in Dhofar, a region of Oman which bordered the Marxist People's Democratic Republic of the Yemen (PDRY), to which the rebels could turn for aid and shelter. Qaboos turned to Britain for support and it was decided to send in the SAS, who were not only trained in counter-insurgency operations but also capable of providing medical aid to the Dhofaris. It was hoped that the SAS 'hearts and minds' approach developed in Malaya and Borneo might succeed where other methods had failed. The first squadron arrived in February 1971, and until September 1976 the Regiment maintained at least one squadron in Oman on a four-month operational tour.

The SAS troops which deployed to Dhofar were split into groups known as BATTs (British Army training teams). These raised and trained units of varying size called *firqat* units, which contained local men, many of whom were former guerrillas (*adoo*). The SAS also established CATs (civil action teams), comprising a medic, a vet and at least one Arabic speaker. Both BATTs and CATs did much to win over the local Dhofaris.

However, following a series of successful SAS/*firqat* operations between March and October 1971, the *adoo* decided to strike back and on the night of 18 July 1972 250 *adoo* attacked the town of Mirbat. Supported by heavy machine-guns, mortars, 75mm recoil-less rifles and one Carl Gustav anti-tank weapon, the *adoo* were fortunately spotted by a patrol of the Dhofari Gendarmerie and the element of surprise was lost as the sound of small-arms fire alerted the eight SAS soldiers within the perimeter. Their commander, Captain Kealy, immediately made his way up to the roof of the 'BATThouse', as the SAS quarters were known, to assess the situation.

About 100 metres to the north-west was a small fort defended by some thirty askars (armed militia from northern Oman). These, together with about twenty-five gendarmes holding a larger fort 700 metres to the north-east, were now returning the *adoo* fire. Instantly, on the 'BATThouse roof, Corporal Chapman and Lance Corporal Wignall took up position behind a 0.5in Browning machine-gun and a General Purpose Machine-Gun (GPMG), while Lance Corporal Harris set up a mortar at the foot of the building. Nevertheless the defenders were outnumbered and outgunned; their only heavy weapon was an ancient 25-pounder field gun at the Gendarmerie Fort. Acting purely on instinct, a Fijian, Trooper Labalaba, raced across to the gun pit to assist the Omani gunner.

Kealy had only recently joined the Regiment and, at twenty-three years old, was relatively inexperienced. He nonetheless quickly realised that the key to Mirbat's defence was the Gendarmerie Fort and the gun. If the guerrillas were denied this position, there was a chance that the defenders could hold out until air support could be called in. Informed by his radio operator, Savesaki, that Labalaba had been wounded, Kealy agreed to the former's request that he be allowed to go over to the gun pit. The second Fijian covered the 700 metres to the fort under heavy enemy fire and, by some miracle, made it unscathed.

Concentrating their fire on the fort and 25-pounder position, the *adoo* stepped up their attack and some guerrillas managed to break through the camp perimeter despite the accurate fire being laid down by Chapman and Wignall on the BATThouse roof. The situation was becoming increasingly desperate. Kealy got on the long-wave set and radioed for an airstrike and helicopter casevac. Then, unable to reach the gun pit on the shortwave, Kealy, together with an SAS medic named Tobin, raced across to the Gendarmerie Fort, leaving Corporal Bradshaw to direct fire from the BATThouse.

In the gun pit both Fijians were badly wounded but were still firing at the enemy closing in on their position. Captain Kealy and Savesaki engaged the advancing *adoo* at close quarters with small arms and grenades, while Labalaba continued to operate the 25-pounder until he fell. The Fijian was quickly replaced by Trooper Tobin, who managed to fire one more round before he himself was fatally wounded.

Kealy radioed Bradshaw, telling him to aim the mortar rounds closer to the gun pit, and was informed that the air support was on its way. Soon after, Strikemaster jets arrived and, directed by Bradshaw, engaged the guerrillas with cannon, driving them back with heavy casualties. Further sorties were directed against the rebels' heavy weapons on Jebel Ali while a relief force, comprising members of G Squadron 22 SAS and led by the squadron commander, was brought in by helicopter. These twenty-three men, who had been training at Salalah when the attack began, carried nine GPMGs between them. They were landed to the south-east of the BATThouse and fought their way to the SAS at the gun pit. The battle for Mirbat was over.

The successful defence of Mirbat against a well-equipped, brave and determined enemy was in many ways the turning point of the campaign. Although Kealy's detachment lost two men dead and two more were seriously injured, the guerrillas lost over thirty men and many more later died of their wounds. But more important than the figures is the fact that this victory did much to rob the *adoo* of their influence over the Dhofaris – influence which increasingly accrued to the SAS and the *firqat*.

In his book, *SAS: Operation Oman*, General Tony Jeapes, an SAS squadron commander in Oman, describes how the success of the *firqat* led to the eventual victory. The Regiment must take much of the credit for this success for it remained the backbone of the *firqat* despite the fact that there were often fewer than fifty, and rarely more than one hundred, SAS personnel deployed to Dhofar at any one time. In 1974, the Sultan had 15,000 troops deployed fighting the *adoo*; a year later these forces were augmented by 1,600 men from 21 separate *firqat* units, all trained and administered by the SAS.

The campaign did not end until 1975, by which time the *adoo* had lost their support both inside and outside Oman. In the five years of fighting, the Regiment had lost just twelve men killed, including the two who died at Mirbat.

CHAPTER FIVE

Fighting the IRA

From the covert observation post (OP), it was possible to detect almost any movement in the surrounding fields and along the narrow tarmacadam road that reached across the border. The border itself seemed more imaginary than real – there was nothing obvious to indicate the divide between Northern Ireland and the Irish Republic. The local civilian population on both sides of the border knew exactly where it was, as did the men who manned the OP. The difference was, the locals could cross it with impunity.

Inside their camouflaged hide, which was totally concealed from the outside world and formed part of a natural hedgerow, four men lay in cramped conditions. Two of them were resting in the two green sleeping bags. The third maintained a radio watch on the set strapped to the top of his bergen, while the fourth scanned the surrounding countryside slowly through a pair of high-power, fixed-focus binoculars, while making occasional entries in a brown, plastic-backed notebook.

Ready to move at a moment's notice should their position be compromised, the men spent their time in alternate states of bored lethargy or slumber, and constant alertness. At pre-set intervals, the 'watchers' rotated with the 'sleepers' in a system known as 'hot-bedding', squirming into the warm, recently vacated sleeping bags as the others took over the observation duties.

The patrol manning the OP had been in position now for three nights and two days, and would remain there until they either saw what they had come to see, or were recalled or replaced by another team. All four men belonged to an SAS squadron deployed to Northern Ireland as part of the British Army's counter-terrorist campaign in the Province. Although not unaware of the policies and politics involved in the conflict, the men maintained a 'professional' detachment from everything but the job in hand. Above all, they were experienced, extensively trained professional soldiers, not the 'hit squad' that their enemies, mindful of their many successes, tried to maintain they were.

SAS counter-terrorist and intelligence-gathering operations in the Province usually, but not always, pass unnoticed by all but the most ardent speculators. Unseen by enemies and friends alike, the SAS in Ulster wage an unrelenting war against an experienced foe. It is a war that, for the British Army as a whole, has dragged on since 1969 when troops were deployed to Northern Ireland as the latest round of sectarian troubles broke out. Troops were sent to the Province in 1969 to protect the Catholic community from violence at the hands of the more prosperous and powerful Protestant population. Faced with the task of maintaining law and order it was inevitably not long before the Army succeeded in alienating both sides. The Catholics turned to the Irish Republican Army (IRA), but the latter were without weapons and experienced men. Further, there was a split occurring in the ranks between those who held to the IRA's socialist ideology (the line of what was to become the Official IRA) and those who favoured direct action. The result was that a new organisation emerged – the Provisional IRA (PIRA), the 'Provos' – and went to war on the Protestant paramilitaries, and eventually against the British Army. In the early period stones and petrol bombs were the main weapons used against the soldiers, but in the end these gave way to firearms and in February 1971 a British soldier was killed – the first since the 1969 deployment.

In the ensuing months, the violence turned from rioting to terrorism: innocent civilians on both sides of the sectarian divide were picked up and murdered in gangster-style executions, bombs exploded in shops and public houses, and off-duty soldiers were targeted for assassination. On the one side were the Protestant Orange paramilitaries; on the other, nationalist republicans. The latter were particularly strong in Belfast and Londonderry and in the border areas of Tyrone, Fermanagh and Armagh; the southern section of the last mentioned – South Armagh – was the major stronghold in what became known as 'Bandit Country'.

The British Government responded to the escalating violence by adopting the techniques that had proved successful in counter-insurgency operations in Malaya and Kenya. Intelligence units were formed to take the war to the terrorists. They were given the task of capturing IRA men and turning them back on the enemy as informers. On 22 June 1972, one such unit came to light when soldiers in civilian clothes opened fire with a Thompson sub-machine-gun within the republican Andersonstown district of Belfast. Four civilians, including a republican politician, were wounded. One of the soldiers, charged with attempted murder, identified his unit as the Mobile Reconnaissance Force (MRF). The soldier was acquitted, and an angry Northern Ireland Civil Rights Association (CRA) claimed that this had been but one of many such attacks on non-military republicans, and they issued a pamphlet advising the public 'What to do if the SAS/MRF shoot you'. Among other things, the document instructed the wounded to lie still and pretend to be dead until the squad left. The Civil Rights Movement – and some journalists – believed that the MRF were waging a 'Phoenix-style' assassination programme; that is, similar to that operated by the Central Intelligence Agency (CIA) in Vietnam. The aim, it was suggested, was to eradicate the republican political infrastructure.

The SAS, however, was not even in the Province in 1972, and so was unable either to operate on its own or to serve with the MRF. Elements of D Squadron had been sent to the Province for several weeks in 1969, during which time they maintained an unusually high profile; they even laid a wreath on the grave of Lieutenant Colonel 'Paddy' Mayne at Newtownards cemetery. In addition, senior SAS officers were undoubtedly rotated through intelligence posts in the Province during the early 1970s, although some of them had already completed their tour of duty with the Regiment and had returned to their parent units by the time of the republican allegations. In fact it took a series of grotesque acts of terrorism before British Prime Minister Harold Wilson took the controversial step of ordering the Regiment into the Province in 1976.

After a bloody 1974, talks between representatives of the Foreign Office and the IRA in January 1975 resulted in a temporary halt to hostilities between the latter and the Army. But sectarian violence continued and indeed some of the most appalling episodes of the 'Troubles' took place during this year. One of the most notorious incidents occurred on 1 August, when Orange paramilitaries, wearing the uniform of the Ulster Defence Regiment (UDR), murdered three members of the popular Irish group, the Miami Showband. The IRA later responded by bombing a Belfast bar and killing five people. Altogether 1975 turned out even worse than the previous year, for although the actual number of terrorist attacks went down, the number of deaths from sectarian violence rose from 216 in 1974 to 247 in 1975. The IRA were assessed as being responsible for 60 per cent of these deaths.

The cease-fire with the Army came to an end in November 1975 and at the start of 1976 came the series of events that precipitated the arrival of the SAS in the Province. On 4 January five Catholics were killed in two separate shooting incidents. The following day six IRA men stopped a bus in South Armagh. After releasing the Catholic driver, they machine-gunned the Protestant passengers: ten were killed, only one survived. Two days later, a squadron of the SAS was deployed to the Province, with eleven soldiers being immediately despatched as the squadron's advance party. Within a year, a second squadron followed, together with signals support. The initial brief of the SAS was to destroy the PIRA leadership in South Armagh.

Never again were the gunmen to feel safe in Bandit Country, where the kill ratio had formerly been fifty to one in favour of the terrorists. The fields and hedgerows of South Armagh were a far cry from the jungles of South-east Asia and the deserts of the Middle East. For a start, the population of the area was not obviously susceptible to a 'hearts and minds' approach. However, there were similarities: the border – marked by lane, hedgerow and stream – was easily crossed, particularly at night, and the isolated farmhouses on the Republican side of the border provided a sanctuary from the British Security Forces. An SAS sergeant describes how operations were carried out in early 1976:

> Our four-man patrols were put out on two types of operation. Firstly, we set up OPs to watch areas associated with terrorist activity or individuals known to be active with the local PIRA unit. It was difficult country to infiltrate, since there wasn't much cover. We would walk in at night, sometimes two weeks before we expected activity. The second sort of patrol went out in response to intelligence reports of arms finds or IRA sightings. These were the most dangerous,

as we would have to move in fast, day or night, making the best use of available cover.

The OPs used in the first type of operation were carefully concealed hides, often located underground and with the top sealed with turf. In the second type, OP concealment relied on whatever was available, which was often only a bush or wall. If an OP was compromised, the discovery resulted in a dash to the landing zone (LZ), where the patrol would be extracted by helicopter.

One of the Regiment's first successes in this new campaign came on 11 March 1976. Acting on a tip that Sean McKenna, a twenty-three-year-old suspected PIRA member, was hiding in the South – in Edentubber, County Louth – a four-man patrol slipped across the border to arrest him. Two members of the patrol secured the outside of McKenna's rented cottage, while the remaining two entered the building. McKenna awoke to find the SAS in his bedroom. Marched across the border, he was handed over to the Royal Ulster Constabulary (RUC). He was tried on twenty-five charges and sentenced to 303 years in prison.

The same style of operation was used to capture Peter Joseph Cleary, a PIRA staff officer posing as a scrap-metal merchant. Cleary was in the habit of visiting his fiancée's house at Forkhill, just inside the Northern Ireland border. An OP was set up to watch his movements, and a patrol snatched him on the night of 15 April 1976. They bundled him across the fields to the helicopter LZ but, as the aircraft approached, shots were heard. As the smoke cleared, Cleary was dead, hit by three bullets to the chest. At the subsequent inquest, an SAS soldier – wearing dark glasses, a navy-blue anorak and a polo-necked sweater – told the court that, as the patrol was lighting the landing lights for the aircraft, Cleary had attempted to overpower the soldier guarding him, who then fired three rounds into Cleary, killing him instantly.

A year after arriving in the Province, the Regiment once again demonstrated its value in Bandit Country. On 12 January 1977, PIRA men ambushed a patrol of the Royal Highland Fusiliers (RHF) at Crossmaglen, killing Lance Corporal David Hinds. A description of the car in which the gang made its escape to the Republic was logged into Security Forces computer files. Instead of abandoning the vehicle PIRA continued to use it for operations. On 19 January, it reappeared in the district, and an SAS patrol laid an ambush further along the road. As darkness fell, a young man carrying a sawn-off shotgun approached the ambush position, whereupon a sergeant, covered by a trooper, rose from cover and gave a challenge. The gunman raised his weapon, and was instantly shot by the trooper. The rest of the PIRA Active Service Unit (ASU) had been walking in parallel behind the other hedge, and they immediately opened fire on the SAS. In the resulting firefight, more than forty rounds were exchanged. The body of the young man with the shotgun was identified as that of Seamus Harvey, a local PIRA volunteer. He had been hit by thirteen bullets, two of them from his own men. Behind the hedgerow, the SAS found spent cartridge cases and a pool of blood.

As a result of these incidents six PIRA leaders had

been forced south and another four captured or killed. For its part, the PIRA propaganda machine was working overtime to convince the Catholic population that the SAS were acting as death squads. Nor was the leadership slow to seize the propaganda initiative and turn it to their own advantage. When they executed a suspected British informer, Seamus Ludlow, as he was leaving a pub in the Republic, they claimed that he was an innocent civilian murdered in the Irish Republic by the SAS, who had mistakenly identified him as an IRA man. PIRA did not have to admit to an informer in its ranks, while the authorities were reluctant to identify Ludlow as an intelligence asset.

In subsequent years, there were other incidents that gave the IRA propaganda gifts. These largely resulted from mistakes made by the SAS while adapting to the new type of war they had been asked to fight in Northern Ireland. But whatever the circumstances they are nonetheless still indelible blots on the copybook of the Regiment – one particular occurrence caused deep embarrassment; another family heartbreak. The first such incident resulted in a diplomatic row. On 5 May 1976, a Triumph Toledo saloon car, containing two SAS men on a snatch operation, blundered into a Garda (police) checkpoint about 500 metres inside the Irish Republic. Two hours later, a rescue party of six SAS men, travelling in two cars and looking for their colleagues, also crossed the checkpoint. When the Garda men searched these vehicles, they discovered an assortment of weapons, including Browning pistols, pump-action shotguns, Sterling sub-machine-guns and various knives. The soldiers were taken to Dundalk, where they were charged with the illegal possession of firearms with intent to endanger life and released on bail of £40,000 sterling. At their trial in Dublin, however, they were convicted of the lesser charge of possessing unlicensed firearms and fined a nominal sum of £100.

A far more serious and distressing incident occurred in July 1978. John Boyle, sixteen, who worked on his family's farm in County Antrim, wandered into the local graveyard to search for some family headstones. There, concealed under a fallen headstone, he discovered a plastic fertiliser sack containing a paramilitary uniform and weapons. The boy's family informed the RUC, who quickly notified the Army. In turn the SAS was briefed to set up a covert surveillance position and to apprehend any terrorist that returned to the cache. The briefing stated that 'a child' had made the discovery, and so the Regiment requested that the RUC should warn the family not to return to the cemetery. But the warning, not delivered until the next morning, came too late to avert a tragedy.

A four-man patrol had moved into the area overnight, two soldiers taking up position in an old barn overlooking the graveyard, from where they could provide covering fire for Sergeant Bohan and Corporal Temperley, who were concealed in a hide close to the weapons. Early the next morning, they saw a young man enter the graveyard and approach the concealed weapons. He opened the bag, pulled out the rifle, and inadvertently pointed it towards the hidden SAS men. Without issuing a warning, the two men in the hide opened fire, killing John Boyle.

It can be assumed that, like many boys of his age, John was fascinated by guns, and had returned to look at his find. Both soldiers were charged with murder and, in a controversial trial, evidence was presented indicating that the bullets had struck John Boyle from behind. Despite the acquittal of the SAS soldiers, the judge delivered a scathing criticism of the operation. The IRA had been presented with a major propaganda triumph.

Not all the IRA's victories against the SAS were to be won by words alone, however. In the area in which the SAS operated, there were some highly dangerous and experienced terrorists. Among them were confederates of Dominic McGlinchey, a renegade IRA man who was believed to be responsible for over thirty murders. McGlinchey had become the leader of the self-styled Irish National Liberation Army (INLA), a small splinter group containing some of the most hardened terrorists. In March 1978, Intelligence identified a house in a small hamlet outside Londonderry as a terrorist safe house. The Regiment was detailed to set up an OP in a nearby lane in order to keep the house under observation. On the night of the 16th, two SAS soldiers in the hide heard movement along the hedgerow to their rear. Through their starlight 'scopes they saw, walking towards them, two figures that appeared to be wearing UDR uniforms.

As regular units were not always informed of SAS operations, Lance Corporal David Jones stood up to identify himself, and immediately received a fatal bullet wound to the chest. The other SAS man, also wounded in the contact, returned fire. The Security Forces were quick to react. After the two soldiers had been evacuated, dog teams and heavily armed troops followed a trail of blood that led away from the hedgerow. They found a prominent INLA terrorist, Frank Hughes, hiding in a gorse bush and nursing a wounded leg. A man infamous for the murders of two policemen had proved himself faster than the SAS men. The Regiment, dependent for the success of its operations on stealth, surprise and speed, would not easily forget their mistake.

Among the most demanding, dangerous and difficult duties a soldier can be asked to perform are operations in built-up areas, and the risks are multiplied when the operation is undercover. In the labyrinths of the Falls Road area of Belfast and the sprawl of Andersonstown, surveillance was a dangerous occupation. Cars and pedestrians were being checked at barricades set up by paramilitaries, and the passage of an Army foot patrol was habitually accompanied by the cacophony of dustbin lids being banged together by local women as a warning of the soldiers' arrival.

When an excellent reason arose for the establishment of an OP within the sectarian ghettos, troops in armoured personnel carriers (APCs) would arrive in the streets. An SAS trooper, who was on service in the Province at the time, describes the routine:

> The recce unit, which might be as few as two men, would be hidden among the troops detailed to 'search' the area. A house would be chosen at random in the terrace opposite the target we wanted to watch. Ten or so troops would pile into the building and distract the occupants, while the recce team entered the loft.

> Once inside, they would 'mouse-hole' along the terrace until they were in front of the target. A slate pin would be replaced with an elastic band, providing a movable peep-hole, the radio would be checked, and then they were on their own. When it was time to come out, the unit would raid the street again and we'd just reverse the process.

One such operation was compromised when a plastic bag that was being used by the SAS as a latrine leaked excreta into the rooms below. The house was emptied as a PIRA hit squad prepared to attack the men in the OP. Fortunately, the senior SAS soldier realised that the operation had been blown and radioed for help. The Army arrived in the nick of time. On 2 May 1980, such patient surveillance paid off when a house in Antrim Road, East Belfast, was identified as an IRA arms dump. An eight-man SAS team arrived outside number 369 in two unmarked cars. Operating in a potentially dangerous area, the SAS were armed with Colt Commando 5.56mm automatic rifles and Heckler and Koch MP5 9mm machine pistols. One patrol of four men was briefed to cover the rear of the building, while the second patrol would burst in at the front.

However, as the car stopped outside the door of number 369, the team came under fire from a window somewhere on the top floor. One of the soldiers also saw breaking glass and muzzle flashes from a window to the left of the front door. As the SAS stormed number 369, Captain Westmacott was killed by fire from number 371. The SAS had been given faulty intelligence: number 369 was empty, and the arms dump was situated next door. Eventually, Regular Army units and the RUC surrounded the area and the terrorists subsequently surrendered.

This action, though ultimately successful, shows the importance of accurate intelligence, and how dangerous it can be to get it only slightly wrong. The gathering of such information through surveillance and reconnaissance is an SAS speciality. They were far from being the only unit active in their field in Northern Ireland, but they did help in the work of other organisations. The senior intelligence agencies in the Province were the Security Service (DI5), which was involved under a mandate to 'defend the realm', and the Secret Intelligence Service (DI6), which ostensibly concerned itself with overseas aspects of the war. The latter was to achieve great success in disrupting arms shipments from Libya after the interception of the Panamanian-registered freighter the *Eksund* on 27 October 1987, and the massive follow-up operation by the Irish Security Forces and the Garda. Another body running covert operators was the RUC, which maintained a foothold in the intelligence empire with the Special Branch unit E4A and their own Special Support Unit (SSU): E4A gathered the intelligence that the SSU (now disbanded) then acted upon. The RUC units, accused during the John Stalker affair of implementing a 'shoot-to-kill' policy, were trained by 22 SAS at their base at Hereford, but were manned by ordinary policemen and operated under the direction of the RUC and, possibly, the Intelligence Services.

Military Intelligence was also active in the Province.

14 Intelligence Company (14 Int) was part of their operation as was Brigade Intelligence (Bde Int). It was with the latter that Captain Robert Nairac was serving at the time of his torture and murder by PIRA in South Armagh in 1977. His killers believed him to be not a soldier, but a member of the Official IRA with which they were on bad terms. Like the men in 14 Int, those with Bde Int were seconded from other regiments of the British Army (Nairac was Grenadier Guards) and were trained, in part, at Hereford.

By 1987, PIRA had started to direct its campaign towards 'soft' targets. That year, there were twelve attacks on undermanned rural police stations, the better-defended being mortared from a safe distance. One tried-and-tested technique used by PIRA was to breach the outer defences of a police station with a heavy vehicle. When this machine, laden with explosives, reached the walls of the station, the bomb would be detonated, destroying the building; the PIRA Active Service Unit would then lay down a heavy barrage of fire onto any survivors in the ruins. When, in April 1987, a JCB mechanical digger was reported missing in East Tyrone, the RUC went on alert. A watch was set up on various PIRA members believed to have taken part in previous attacks, and surveillance on the East Tyrone PIRA Brigade's quartermaster was increased. The JCB was eventually discovered at a remote, derelict farm. The nearest police station was at Loughall, less than 16 kilometres away. A surveillance team was inserted into the area.

The explosives were ferried into the farm in broad daylight; the operation was being watched by RUC officers. As the actual date of the attack was still unknown, the ever-patient SAS moved into Loughall. Setting up a 'box-type' ambush, men were positioned in the isolated police station and also concealed in hides in the hedgerow opposite. Other teams built hides on the road at a distance either side of the police station, effectively closing the box. On Friday 8 May, the terrorists were watched preparing for the attack and the police station was consequently evacuated. Shortly after 19.00 hours, an eight-man PIRA ASU drove into the area in stolen cars. Lining up in the road, they laid down a barrage of fire on the police station to cover the entry of the digger, which ploughed through the perimeter fence and continued towards the police station. As the explosive charge was detonated, destroying half the building, the SAS commander gave the order to open fire. It was all over in less than a minute. The JCB driver, along with other survivors of the initial SAS fusillade, attempted to escape in a stolen Hiace van. Within seconds, however, it was riddled with high-velocity rifle bullets; all inside were killed. The PIRA East Tyrone Brigade had been wiped out.

However, like so many other operations fought among a civilian population, Loughall was marked by tragedy. As the charge exploded at the police station, a white Citroën attempted to leave the area, and drove past the SAS 'stop group'. Believing the car to contain escaping terrorists, the SAS opened fire, killing Anthony Hughes and badly wounding his brother Oliver. The operation at Loughall was but one example of the new, streamlined operations being run by the Intelligence Services, the police and the Army. Similar success came in early 1988, when DI5 received information that a former UDR soldier living in mid-Tyrone had been targeted for assassination. The RUC immediately stepped up surveillance on the Harte brothers, who led the mid-Tyrone Brigade. But, once again, the time of the proposed attack was unknown.

On 20 August 1988, while the investigation was proceeding, the Harte brothers and another PIRA man, Brian Mullen, detonated a bomb that destroyed a coach carrying the 1st Battalion The Light Infantry to their barracks in Omagh. The ASU fled south, tracked by the Security Forces. When Gerald Harte unexpectedly recrossed the border in late August, the RUC reckoned that an assassination attempt on a UDR man was imminent. The suspected target was removed to safety and a member of a four-man SAS patrol replaced him. During the night, the other three SAS men began a long walk into an agreed ambush position.

The next morning, 30 August, the target's Leyland truck was driven by his impersonator to the ambush point, where a breakdown was faked. The patrol began its vigil. It was hoped that when the man failed to arrive at his place of work, the terrorists would come to look for him. The death squad arrived six hours later in a stolen car. After cruising past the UDR man's truck, they disappeared, only to return later in a second stolen vehicle and open fire immediately. Taken by surprise, the SAS man acting as decoy jumped clear and the SAS directed a sustained stream of automatic fire into the stolen car, killing the Harte brothers and Brian Mullen.

During the 1990s the SAS staged three more high-profile ambushes that resulted in the deaths of eight terrorists caught in the act, armed with weapons. By 1994, when PIRA and the loyalists declared their cease-fires, the Security Forces had built up a large and highly effective undercover surveillance operation. However, by this point the SAS had begun to take a back seat to the 'Operators' of 14 Int. They ran the Province-wide surveillance operations of terrorist suspects, in conjunction with the RUC Special Branch, so the SAS presence in Northern Ireland was steadily reduced to only a troop-sized unit for offensive operations. If a large body of troops was needed they could be flown over from Hereford at a few hours' notice.

The ending of the PIRA cease-fire in 1996 meant the war against PIRA was back on. For the covert warriors of the SAS and 14 Int, the war had not stopped. They had conducted business as usual and were taking no chances. A new PIRA cease-fire in July 1997 has brought fresh hopes for a lasting peace. But Sinn Fein's refusal to decommission a single piece of its arsenal before talks begin has meant that fighting IRA terrorism remains a top priority for the SAS.

CHAPTER SIX

Fire against Fire

For the fourth time that day, he crouched, waiting for the earpiece of his headset to crackle into life with the controller's command to move. Both the rubber face-mask of his respirator and his headset were hot beneath his anti-flash hood, and sweat coated his face and trickled down his nose. He was uncomfortable and felt mildly claustrophobic, and his view of the outside world was restricted to what he could see through the respirator's eyepieces and what he could hear through his head-phones. He waited, pent-up, for the order to move in.

Suddenly the crackle of static erupted in his ears, followed by the command 'Sections One and Two, Go! Go! Go!' Still he waited. There was a pause, and he could easily and accurately visualise the two four-man teams springing into action and abseiling off the top of the neighbouring roof, then sliding quickly down the side of the building. 'Section Three, Go! Go! Go!' On the first 'Go!', he pressed the button on the small metal box he was holding, detonating a charge that exploded with a mighty bang. Although knocked backwards by the blast, he was up and moving towards the wall before the plaster dust even had a chance to settle. Debris filled the room, but close-to he could clearly make out a hole in the wall about a metre in diameter and around a metre up from the floor. He gave a signal to one of the three other soldiers with him. The man moved forward quickly, and lobbed a stun grenade through the opening. Less than three seconds later, there was an almighty flash and bang, and the building shook.

A second or two later, the first man was through the hole and halfway into a forward roll on the other side. He came up in a crouch, weapon held directly in front of him. There was only one target in the room – a terrorist. The soldier fired three well-aimed bursts down the central 'killing' line before moving off across to the far side of the room. The other three men had now tumbled into the room and one joined him by the door. Pausing slightly, they sighted their Heckler and Koch MP5s and fired through the closed door and into the corridor. A second later the second man yanked the battered door backwards while the first tossed a stun grenade into the corridor. While he made the obligatory count of three, he cast his gaze high into one corner of the room. There, mounted close to the ceiling, was a video camera. Aware that both his actions and his words were being monitored, he thumbed his mike, 'OK lads, a big smile for the controller. And let's clear the corridor quickly, or he'll have us here all f***ing day!'

The exercise described above is one that is practised relentlessly by the SAS at their headquarters in Hereford as part of their role as Britain's main counter-terrorist force, a role that daily is becoming more important.

There are now over 1,200 terrorist groups according to the files of the world's intelligence services. Some groups struggle for control of individual countries or provinces; others, caring little for national identities, are committed to the overthrow of 'World Capitalism'; others attempt to install right-wing dictatorship by means of 'death squads'. The modern era of terrorism began when the Popular Front for the Liberation of Palestine (PFLP) commenced a series of aircraft hijacks in July 1968. New, highly trained military and paramilitary forces needed to be raised to combat terrorism. They would need to be prepared to launch operations anywhere in the world in order to protect their nationals. Furthermore these organisations would, irrespective of national considerations, need to cooperate with each other, sharing intelligence, counter-terrorist technology and expertise.

While other countries created new groups to combat the terrorists, Britain already had units trained in the guerrilla/counter-guerrilla role. The most adaptable of these was the 22nd SAS Regiment.

The steady decline of Britain's overseas commitments during the 1960s had left the Regiment with the increasingly narrow task of training for special operations in an East–West conflict. The Regiment's commanding officer at the time, Lieutenant Colonel John Waddy, prepared a situation paper for the Ministry of Defence, which he hoped would secure a future role for 22 SAS. He suggested that the Regiment could have three roles in combating terrorism. These were: intelligence-gathering, responding to specific threats, and pre-empting planned terrorist actions.

The Regiment's early ventures into counter-terrorism were in the field of VIP protection. With its long involvement in Britain's 'colonial wars', it was ideally suited to provide protection for those friendly overseas heads of state who felt vulnerable to assassination. To meet this challenge, the Regiment created a Counter-Revolutionary Warfare (CRW) Wing whose staff could train elite 'Praetorian Guards' or, with such forces as could be raised and trained locally, provide protection themselves. The CRW Wing was also tasked with the collection of intelligence on insurgent groups and on all aspects of counter-terrorist technology.

As the use of terror increased, so the CRW Wing was enlarged to provide instructors in all aspects of close personal protection and hostage rescue. All SAS squadrons were rotated through the CRW school between tours in Northern Ireland and overseas operations and exercises. During its period on CRW, a squadron would be expected to undergo training in all facets of the work and to provide 'Special Project Teams' for counter-terrorist operations, either in Britain or in support of overseas forces. For the purposes of a hostage-rescue operation each Special Project Team is divided into two groups: one group is a team of marksmen, whose task is to maintain perimeter security around the target; the other is the assault team, which executes the actual rescue. Training at the CRW school lays great emphasis on close quarter battle (CQB) skills. This is a field in which all infantry soldiers in the British Army receive instruction – indeed the development of CQB skills is essential for fighting in built-up areas (FIBUA). A standard

British Army CQB range is a sophisticated set-up and contains remote-operated, pop-up targets designed to develop quick reflexes and to produce an overall awareness of the fast-moving battlefield. Using live ammunition, the individual soldier (or sub-unit) advances through the range, covering a 360-degree arc of fire. As the soldier engages one target, others are triggered to appear to his right, left, or even behind him. But the Regiment was not satisfied with these standard arrangements. An SAS instructor gives an example of how they can be modified:

> The range is very stressful and tiring, and once you have been round it a couple of times, there is a tendency to switch off. Having engaged a target successfully, some of the lads would forget to check their rear. So we had this idea of concealing a machine, opposite the targets, that fired high-speed tennis balls at head height seconds after the target had been engaged. If, after firing on the target, you spin round in a crouch to check the area to your rear, you don't get a clout on the head. It does tend to focus one's concentration.

It was soon realised, however, that rescuing hostages held by heavily armed terrorists in, for instance, the cabin of an airliner called for more refined skills in close quarter battle. Therefore a building known as the 'Killing House' was constructed at SAS HQ at Hereford. The Killing House can be laid out and furnished to look like any of the vast array of targets the Regiment may be called upon to assault, from a government building to a suburban 'semi'. Here SAS soldiers learn how to terminate a hostage situation in the fastest, most efficient way. Exercises take place under conditions which are as realistic as possible, down to the use of live rounds and pyrotechnic devices. The assault team – the team which carries out the rescue attempt – is split into pairs which strike simultaneously at different points of the house.

A set procedure is used for entering rooms. The pair first take up position either side of the door. Then one man will force an entry, using a shotgun, while the second throws in a stun grenade, or 'flash-bang'. This device is 15 cm long and 10 cm wide and contains a mixture of magnesium powder and mercury fulminate.

When the grenade is thrown, the mercury fulminate, a percussion explosive, detonates with a very loud bang; the magnesium then ignites, generating a 50,000 candle-power flash. The noise and brilliant light released by the 'flash-bang' serve to disorientate the room's occupants totally for up to 45 seconds, thus making the rescue that much easier to achieve. A modified version, the Harley and Weller E182 stun grenade, produces multiple bursts.

The SAS assault team enters the room immediately after the explosion. Until recently in Killing House exercises, it would have contained a group of SAS troopers playing the role of the hostages, mixed with 'terrorist' dummies. The assault team had to identify hostage from terrorist immediately, and instantly take out the 'bad guys', while leaving the 'good guys' unharmed. Cameras inside the room filmed the assault and provided material for the debrief. A competent pair was, and still is, expected to be able to enter a room and neutralise any terrorist inside within four seconds. This system worked well until an SAS sergeant, acting in the role of a hostage, moved unexpectedly and was accidentally shot and killed. An inquiry was held into the NCO's death and the Killing House was redesigned. The hostage-rescue area now consists of two rooms: one containing the 'terrorists' and 'hostages', and one which the assault team attacks. The rooms are connected by a sophisticated camera system, which instantly and simultaneously projects the events taking place in one room to a life-size wraparound screen in the other, and vice versa. So, when the assault team bursts into the target room, it 'sees' the terrorists and hostages, and can respond immediately, firing at the images of the terrorists projected onto the soundproof, bullet-absorbent walls. At the same time, of course, the terrorists are responding to a projection of the SAS entry, and shooting back.

One obvious bonus of this new, safer system is that the terrorists no longer have to be played by dummies, and SAS men can perform the task instead, so contributing to a far more realistic scenario. After the exercise is completed, the films are rerun and, using time comparisons, the success or failure of the rescue can be judged. In an average training week, each man will fire approximately 5,000 live rounds in the Killing House. The majority of these end up in the walls, which are coated with a material that prevents ricochets. For added safety, special 'frangible' rounds are now used which have less than a quarter of the range of a normal round, and are designed to disintegrate into powder upon impact. Tra-

David Stirling, the creator of the SAS (centre), flanked by his brother Bill (left) and Randolph Churchill (right), in North Africa in 1942. Stirling recognised the value of sending a number of small teams behind enemy lines, as opposed to just one or two large formations. (TRH PIctures)

'Paddy' Blaire Mayne, the 'wild Irishman' who was one of the first recruits to L Detachment in 1941. Totally fearless in battle and a superb leader of men, he went on to command 1 SAS in Italy and northwest Europe in 1943-45. His bravery won him an amazing four Distinguished Service Orders. (TRH PIctures)

A column of heavily armed SAS Jeeps in Germany in 1945. Despite David Stirling's capture in 1943, by the end of World War II the SAS had shown itself to be a unit that could operate successfully in any terrain. In France in 1944, for example, it had conducted dozens of operations behind German lines. (TRH Pictures)

Left: 'Mad Mike' Calvert, who fought with the Chindits against the Japanese in Burma and commanded the SAS Brigade from March 1945. His ideas on how to defeat the Communist Terrorists (CTs) in Malaya led to the reaction of the Malayan Scouts in 1950, which led on to the reformation of the SAS in 1952. (TRH Pictures)

Below: Malayan Scouts on operation in Malaya. The Scouts' first mission was in Perak province, and despite problems with discipline and poor training, Calvert's ideas regarding using small teams for extended jungle operations and winning over the locals proved to be correct. (TRH Pictures)

Above: SAS soldiers with local Aborigines in northern Malaya. Winning the 'hearts and minds' of the jungle inhabitants was crucial to achieving victory in the counter-insurgency war. This involved the troopers living among the locals and patrol medics administering treatments – which paid great dividends. (TRH Pictures)

Below: The SAS experimented with dropping men onto the thick jungle canopy in Malaya. It was called 'tree jumping', and involved each man landing among the trees and then lowering himself to the floor by rope. It was not a great success: in January 1954, during Operation 'Sword', three men died after smashing into trees. (TRH Pictures)

Above: In late 1958, the SAS was called upon to mount a campaign against rebels fighting the Sultan of Oman in the north of his country. The insurgents were confined to the Jebel Akhdar, a barren and mostly inaccessible granite plateau. It was a far cry from the humid jungles of Malaya, and involved a different kind of warfare. (TRH Pictures)

Below: SAS troopers being briefed prior to A and D Squadrons' final attack to take possession of the Jebel Akhdar in January 1959. The assault involved a ploy to deceive the rebels as to the exact route of advance, and a nine-hour climb with full kit in the dark. The operation ran faultlessly, and was a complete success. (TRH Pictures)

Above: Lieutenant-Colonel Anthony Deane-Drummond, commander of 22 SAS, on the Jebel Akhdar after its fall to the SAS, February 1959. In the foreground are some of the weapons captured from the rebels. For his planning of the final assault and his overall leadership during the campaign, Deane-Drummond was awarded the DSO. (TRH Pictures)

Below: Back to the jungle: an SAS patrol near the Kalimantan border in 1963. A Squadron had arrived on Borneo in January, and was immediately deployed along the border with Indonesian Kalimantan to provide early warning of Indonesian incursions. (TRH Pictures)

Left: An SAS trooper with Iban tracker in Borneo. As in Malaya, the Regiment 'hearts and minds' strategy was integral to its campaign. This involved gaining the locals' trust by sharing their hardships and providing medical assistance. It was usual for patrols to live with villagers for up to three months at a time. The intelligence they gleaned regarding enemy movements from the local grapevine was invaluable. (TRH Pictures)

Right: Jungle operations are physically and mentally taxing. SAS troopers serving in Borneo in the 1960s went into the jungle well fed and fit, but came out with long hair, emaciated bodies and threadbare clothing. Nevertheless, with the cooperation of the locals they had defeated the Indonesians by March 1966. (Soldier magazine)

Right: The tactics in the Radfan involved SAS teams being inserted into high observation posts to keep watch for enemy movements; they would request air strikes and reinforcements when they were detected. However, the political decision to withdraw from Aden turned the military campaign into nothing more than a strategic rearguard action. (private collection)

Below: Trucks and Land Rovers of Radforce in the Radfan, Yemen, April 1964. The operation was designed to interrupt rebel supply routes, but went horribly wrong. A Squadron's Captain Robin Edwards and his troop were cut off and surrounded by rebels and forced to retire with casualties. Edwards himself was killed and his severed head put on display. (private collection)

Above: A makeshift SAS surgery in southern Oman during the Regiment's war in Dhofar in the 1970s. The campaign in Dhofar was essentially a counter-insurgency war, in which the SAS implemented its 'Five Fronts' effort. Devised by Lieutenant-Colonel Johnny Watts, it provided medical assistance to the locals and their livestock, and disseminated information concerning the SAS's policies. (TRH Pictures)

Below: SAS soldiers with SAS-trained Dhofari irregulars in southern Oman. Originally in the service of the communist rebels, the adoo, these deeply religious men had been alienated by the Marxist ideology of the People's Front for the Liberation of the Occupied Arabian Gulf (PFLOAG). Following the Sultan's amnesty, they were formed into groups of fighters called firqats. (TRH Pictures)

ditional techniques for assaulting buildings call for soldiers to use grappling hooks or ropes to enter through second-floor windows, or make use of window ledges and drain pipes to climb onto the roof. Entering from the roof allows the attacking soldiers to fight 'from the high ground', and grenades, explosives and automatic firearms can be used to clear the rooms below. The building can then be cleared floor by floor, starting at the top.

These techniques, suitable as they may be for FIBUA, are often too slow, noisy and dangerous for a hostage-siege situation. The safety of the hostages is paramount and it is crucial that this phase of the rescue operation be achieved quickly and without the terrorists' knowledge. A less obvious approach than direct frontal assault must therefore be employed. For example, should the target be one of a row of terraced houses, the SAS could gain access to the roof via the building next door, or blow a small entry hole in a communicating wall – less subtle but still fast and efficient. The Regiment's training is not, however, confined to assaulting buildings. With the advent of attacks on commercial aircraft, several airlines gave the SAS CRW Wing modern passenger aircraft for use as training aids, and a mock-up of an airliner interior has also been constructed at the Killing House. In addition, the Regiment has developed techniques to end hostage sieges on London Underground trains.

Whatever the target, the SAS must have the equipment they need to stay a step ahead of the terrorists. The latest technology went into developing the special protective uniform worn at Princes Gate in 1980. It consists of a black fire-retardant suit, ceramic-plate body armour, and a combined respirator/Davies communications CT-100 system that allows for constant communication with the other members of the assault team and with control.

The SAS CRW Wing is always on the lookout to improve the armoury. For example, in the wake of the Mogadishu incident in 1977 the standard British Army 9mm Sterling sub-machine-gun was replaced by the more accurate Heckler and Koch MP5 sub-machine-gun used by the West German anti-terrorist squad, GSG-9. Indeed their special role means that the Regiment has been given considerable scope to choose weapons outside the range normally available to the British Army. Other weapons selected by the Regiment for their ease of concealment, fire-power or accuracy include the Israeli 9mm Uzi sub-machine-gun, the 5.56mm Cold Commando assault rifle and the Remington 870 pump-action shotgun. Interestingly, the standard 9mm Browning High Power semi-automatic pistol is still preferred by the Regiment for close-quarter work and is used as a backup weapon on hostage-rescue missions.

Transport for the CRW Wing is provided by a fleet of fully equipped Range Rovers on permanent standby for counter-terrorist duties. In addition, C-130 Hercules transport aircraft, as well as Lynx and Puma helicopters, are maintained on constant alert for Regimental support by a Special Forces Flight of 47 Squadron RAF. The Wing also has its own satellite communications systems maintained by 264 Signal Squadron (SAS), which allow soldiers in the field to stay in immediate and constant contact with Hereford from anywhere in the world. To support them in their CRW work, the SAS maintain a computerised database containing information relating to potential targets, such as architectural plans showing wall construction, window positions, passages and service conduits. From this information, all arcs of fire and assault routes can be computed using three-dimensional graphic images. The database can be accessed from the site of a terrorist incident by means of secure telephone lines, once again maintained by 264 Signal Squadron.

A 'Special Project Team' is on permanent standby at Hereford, waiting for the telephone call that will have it speeding to the scene of an incident. When the Wing was first set up, there were many in the Regiment who thought that the special situation which would necessitate their intervention would be long in coming – if, indeed, it came at all. But in 1974, terror arrived on the streets of Britain of a ferocity not seen since the Blitz. In August 1974, the PIRA General Army Council sent a new ASU to 'strike at economic, military, political and judicial targets' in Britain. The gang members interpreted their orders as instructions to create panic among members of the British Establishment. Their first attacks were directed at London clubs, Harrow School, and public houses frequented by soldiers. As time went by, however, the ASU became less discriminating, and bombs began to explode at offices, restaurants and Underground stations. Then, two weeks after two diners had been killed in the bombing of Scott's Restaurant in Mayfair, the terrorists inexplicably returned to the scene of the outrage.

On the evening of Saturday 6 December, a police surveillance team stationed near Scott's watched as a car containing the four men slowed down in front of the restaurant. To the police officers' surprise, a machine-gun appeared and sprayed the front of the building. As the car accelerated into nearby Carlos Place, the two policemen sent out a radio alert before commandeering a passing taxi and giving chase. After a running gun battle with the police units that had moved in to try to block their escape, the four PIRA men tricked their way into 22B Balcombe Street, Marylebone, the home of a middle-aged couple, John and Sheila Matthews. As the Special Patrol Group (SPG) surrounded the house, the police negotiation team was alerted.

The police were reluctant to hand over operational control to the SAS, and for two very good reasons: the hostages had not been harmed, and there was a strong belief within the police that military assistance should only be sought as a last resort. Nevertheless, it was thought that the mere threat of SAS intervention might have some effect on the gunmen, and so a report that operational control was to be transferred to the Regiment was leaked to the BBC and the *Daily Express* newspaper. The gang heard this story and it effectively ended the siege. The gunmen, if not the general public, knew that the SOPs (Standing Operating Procedures) for a hostage rescue were such that they would be very unlikely to survive an outright assault to release the hostages.

Thus the Regiment was only indirectly involved in the Balcombe Street siege. For its first major counter-terrorist assignment, it had to wait another three years – and then it was a foreign affair. On 13 October 1977, members of the notorious Baader-Meinhoff group hijacked a Lufthansa Boeing 737 en route from Majorca to Frankfurt.

For the next five days, the plane was allowed to refuel at airports in various Mediterranean and African countries while the terrorists publicised their demands: $15 million, the release from jail of Andreas Baader, one of the group's two founder members, plus the freeing of nine other activists held in German prisons and of two Palestinians held in Turkey.

The German Government put its own elite counter-terrorist unit, GSG-9, on alert. In the past, GSG-9 had conducted joint exercises with 22 SAS and shared information about anti-terrorist technology. Now, they requested support and, in particular, a supply of the SAS's own invention: the stun grenade. Two SAS men, Sergeant Barry Davies and Major Alastair Morrison, along with an ample supply of 'flash-bangs', joined the twenty-six-man German team in a converted Lufthansa Boeing 707 airliner as they followed the hijacked aircraft from country to country. Finally, the aircraft was forced to land at Mogadishu airport in Somalia – out of the reach, it was thought, of European security forces. There the gang, along with the eighty-six passengers and six crew, awaited the West German response. If such incidents were not to 'snowball', there could only be one response, particularly as the gang had already murdered the 737's pilot. The German Government instructed GSG-9 to plan an operation to free the hostages. At dusk on 17 October, using a large fire on the runway (caused by a blazing oil drum) to lure the terrorists onto the flight deck, the assault teams crept towards the plane. Rubber-coated ladders were placed at the emergency exits over the wings and at the front and rear of the aircraft. Then the aircraft doors were blown simultaneously by means of explosive charges, and the SAS men threw in stun grenades. GSG-9 men stormed into the passenger compartment; the gang opened fire, wounding four hostages and one GSG-9 operative, and two terrorist grenades were thrown into the passengers' cabin. Fortunately they exploded harmlessly under the seats, and with precision shooting, the Germans killed all the terrorists, with the exception of one, who was badly wounded but still alive when the shooting stopped.

At Mogadishu, the SAS had assisted in someone else's operation carried out on the other side of the globe. Within three years they were to occupy centre stage in the west end of London. The first hint that the SAS were about to face their first major test of the techniques practised in the 'Killing House' came on Wednesday 30 April 1980. A former SAS NCO, who had left the Army and was working as a dog handler with the Metropolitan Police, phoned SAS headquarters at Hereford and told them, informally, that terrorists had taken over the Iranian embassy in Princes Gate, London, and the Regiment might be asked to take control of the operation. Without waiting for the official call, the Special Project Team from the unit on rotation at the time, B Squadron, took the Wing's Range Rovers to London.

Earlier that day, five men calling themselves the Democratic Revolutionary Front for the Liberation of Arabistan had walked into the Iranian embassy and taken its occupants captive. The hostages included: twenty-two members of staff; Police Constable Trevor Lock of Scotland Yard's Diplomatic Protection Group, who was the embassy's police guard; and Sim Harris, a BBC sound recordist who was at the embassy to request a visa. The Intelligence Services soon discovered that the six terrorists – all from Arabistan, an Arabic-speaking area of Iran – were members of a Marxist–Leninist organisation based in Libya. It was believed that they were armed and supported by intelligence officers from Iran's old enemy, Iraq.

The Prime Minister, Mrs Margaret Thatcher, decided to put the Regiment on stand-by after discussions with representatives of the Ministry of Defence, the Security Service (MI5), the Foreign and Commonwealth Officer (FCO) and the SAS – known collectively as COBRA after the Cabinet Office Briefing Room in which it meets.

This recommendation was passed to the Joint Operations Centre (JOC) within the Ministry of Defence. This body is responsible for the actual deployment of the Regiment and is composed of representatives of the Home Office, the Foreign Office, the Intelligence Services and the SAS itself. JOC issued a formal authorisation the same day, 30 April; as it did so the Special Project Team had already been in London six hours. While the SAS retired to a London barracks to plan a possible assault, the police opened negotiations with the terrorists. Initially, the terrorist group's leader, Salim Towfigh (also known as Oan), demanded that the Iranian authorities release ninety-one Arabistani prisoners being held in jails in Iran. He also requested Arab ambassadors to act as mediators between the terrorists and the British authorities. The deadline by which these demands were to be met was set for 12.00 hours on Thursday 1 May. When it became plain that the government in Teheran would not free the prisoners, the terrorists demanded instead the provision of an aircraft to take them, the hostages and an Arab ambassador to an unnamed Arab country.

Police negotiators stuck to their task – managing to gain the release of a sick Iranian woman on the Wednesday night – and by Friday morning, two deadlines for the meeting of the terrorists' demands had passed without incident. At this point Security Service technicians tried to insert audio and visual (fibre-optic) bugs within the embassy walls in order to allow the SAS some idea of the layout of the building should an assault become necessary. They were unsuccessful. By late Friday, threats were starting to be made against the lives of the hostages. The terrorists were furious that their demands had not been fully reported by radio news and demanded that the request for Arab mediators be broadcast forthwith; it was. The next day British Government officials held talks with various Arab representatives to try to reach an agreement, but without success, and on Monday 5 May, the Iranian gunmen's patience finally ran out. Salim shot dead Abbas Lavasani, a member of the embassy staff. On the direct orders of Mrs Thatcher, the SAS were told to assault the embassy and free the hostages.

The assault plan was simple. Two four-man teams would abseil from the roof down the rear of the building to the ground-floor and first-floor balconies. A further team was to enter at the front of the building from a first-floor balcony which they would reach by crossing from the balcony at No 16 Prince Gate next door. At 19.26 hours on Monday 5 May, the rear-assault teams, dressed in their now-famous black counter-terrorist garb, started to abseil down the back of the building. Using frame charges, sledgehammers and brute force, the teams broke through the embassy's armoured windows and forced their way in, throwing stun grenades as they went. As these exploded, part of the building caught fire and one member of the assault team who had got tangled up in his abseiling rope was now in severe danger of being burnt to death. He was cut free and fell onto one of the balconies – bruised, scorched, but alive.

Meanwhile the assault team lost no time in starting to clear the building. The ground-floor group immediately despatched the terrorist guarding the front hall, but the first-floor group nearly ran into trouble. Salim, the terrorist leader, was lurking on the first-floor landing as the SAS entered. The gunman took aim but before he could fire, PC Lock was on him and had wrestled him to the ground. The police officer then drew the 0.38in revolver he had somehow managed to keep hidden throughout the siege, but decided not to fire. At that moment an SAS man shouted, 'Trevor, move away!' The policeman did as he was told and rolled to one side; Salim was machine-gunned by the SAS trooper.

As the struggle with Salim was taking place, Sim Harris, the BBC sound recordist, who had been with Lock and the terrorist leader on the first floor, made an attempt to escape from the building; he was told to stay put by an SAS man. But at this point a smouldering stun grenade set curtains ablaze in the room where he was, fire broke out on the first floor, and Harris, fearful of burning to death, struggled out onto a first-floor balcony, thus becoming the first of the hostages to be seen by the public. As he emerged an SAS man ordered him to cross to another balcony from which he was escorted back into the building until the operation was over.

Meanwhile in the telex room on the second floor, where the majority of the hostages were held, the terrorists began shooting. They had killed one of their prisoners and wounded two others when men of the frontal-assault team burst in. By now the atmosphere in the embassy was thick with noxious fumes of CS gas fired through the windows by the SAS backup team. Unable to decide instantly who in the room was captive and who was captor, the rescuers called for the terrorists to be pointed out. Two were indicated and two were shot dead.

Minutes after it had started the Princes Gate operation was over. Five terrorists were dead; the sixth was discovered trying to pass himself off as a hostage and was arrested.

The SAS's next hostage-release mission was quite different from these operations and involved assisting a foreign head of state whose family was being held by Marxist revolutionaries. Sir Dawda Jawara, President of Gambia, was attending the May 1981 London wedding of Prince Charles and Lady Diana Spencer when insurgents struck, taking over his capital, Banjul, and imprisoning members of his family in a hospital in the city. France called on neighbouring Senegal to despatch troops; the USA offered the assistance of their counter-terrorist unit, Delta, but later reneged; Britain sent in the SAS.

The mission was entrusted to the second-in-command of 22 SAS, Major Ian Crooke, who picked two men, packed bags with explosives, weapons and a satellite communications system, and flew post-haste, in civilian clothes, to Banjul. A contact enabled the group to miss out immigration and customs, and having located the Jawara family, the SAS set out to rescue them.

The first obstacle the SAS encountered was the security post outside the hospital, which was easily subdued, leaving Crooke and his team to deal with the guards keeping watch on the family. This they managed by enlisting the aid of a British doctor, who convinced the rebels to put their weapons down as they were worrying the patients. The guards thus disarmed, it was no problem for the SAS to remove the family to the security of the British embassy. With the President's wife and children safe, the SAS were free to organise a Sengalese push against the rebels that effectively ended the rising.

The Gambian episode received comparatively little publicity, while in contrast, events at Princes Gate were played out in front of television cameras and brought the Regiment much unwanted media coverage. They also brought controversy over whether it had been absolutely necessary to kill the terrorists. But if there was criticism of SAS methods at the Iranian embassy, it was light indeed compared with the storm of disapproval that followed the Regiment's next major counter-terrorist operation – Gibraltar. In the autumn of 1987, routine interceptions of mail to the homes of known Irish Republican supporters turned up a postcard sent from the Costa del Sol by Sean Savage, a member of PIRA. British intelligence circles were well aware that PIRA was seeking revenge for Loughall and that it was turning its attention to British military targets in mainland Europe. It was also known that a Belgian terrorist organisation, the Communist Fighting Cells, was providing PIRA with safe houses and logistical support. The IRA European intelligence officer was finally identified and put under surveillance. All the signs pointed to an imminent terrorist operation in mainland Europe, and in November signs began to emerge that a PIRA active service unit (ASU) was setting up a terrorist operation in southern Spain. PIRA operatives, Sean Savage and Danny McCann, were seen at Malaga airport and moving along the coast towards Gibraltar. McCann was an explosives expert with convictions for possessing explosives. They were members of an elite PIRA unit working for the terrorist group's general headquarters in Dublin.

In February 1988, the British asked the Spanish security services to monitor the movements of an Irish woman, using the name Mary Parkin on a false passport. The surveillance found that she was making regular trips across the border into Gibraltar. The authorities were able to deduce the target: the Royal Anglian Regiment band and guard, which took place as regular as clockwork at 11.00 a.m. every Tuesday.

Further deductions, taking into account the probable target and the location – Gibraltar town – led to the belief that the attack would be made by remote-controlled bomb.

In Gibraltar, a high-level security planning team was set up, led by MI5 – the Security Service – to protect the British colony. London decided to commit members of the SAS CRW Wing to the operation and they were in

Gibraltar by 4 March when McCann, Savage and Mairead Farrell were spotted getting off an aircraft at Malaga airport. Farrell had served a fourteen-year prison sentence for possessing explosives. What happened from this point is the subject of considerable dispute. The Spaniards say they kept the ASU under observation but the British maintain the trail of the PIRA team went cold. In Gibraltar, the security forces began preparing for the worst and expected an attack the following Tuesday, 8 March. On Saturday 5 March, Operation Flavius got underway, a joint police, SAS, MI5 briefing was held to coordinate the security forces' response, under the chairmanship of Gibraltar police commissioner Joseph Canepa. MI5 surveillance officers told the assembled anti-terrorist specialists that the PIRA team would be armed and equipped with a massive car bomb, triggered by remote control. The SAS operatives at the briefing were told the terrorists would detonate the bomb if they were confronted. The agreed plan was for the terrorists to be allowed across the border where they would be caught red-handed. The SAS troop commander, speaking under conditions of anonymity as Soldier E at the inquest into the terrorist deaths, said, 'I particularly emphasised to my soldiers . . . that at least one of the three terrorists, if not more, would in all probability be armed; and secondly, there was a strong likelihood that at least one, if not more, of the three terrorists would be carrying a "button job" device [to explode the bomb].'

The rules of engagement for the SAS were confirmed at the briefing. The overriding requirement was to do all in their power to protect the lives and safety of members of the public and the security forces. The SAS was under the command of the Gibraltar police commissioner and his subordinates for the duration of the operation. They were authorised to open fire if they had reasonable grounds for believing that the terrorists were currently committing, or about to commit, an act which was likely to endanger life and there was no way to prevent this. The SAS men could open fire without warning if the giving of a warning or a delay in firing could lead to death or injury to the soldiers or civilians, or if giving a warning was impractical. The SAS soldiers were armed with 9mm Browning pistols and each carried four magazines of twelve rounds each; they used a new propellant that made the rounds smokeless, wore casual civilian clothes and concealed their weapons in the smalls of their backs, tucked in their trouser waistbands. Each member of the SAS team, the police Special Branch and MI5 surveillance team, or 'watchers', wore a concealed radio to communicate with the Operation Flavius operations room. These had small ear pieces and microphones hidden in their users' jacket collars.

At 08.00 the following morning, the security forces began their surveillance operation on the border, using photographs supplied by MI5. At 12.30 a man was seen parking a white Renault 5 car near the Royal Anglian Band's assembly area. He was quickly identified as Savage. Around 14.30, McCann and Farrell were spotted crossing the border on foot and the three met by the car at just before 15.00. In the operations room, concern was high that an attack would be launched. The police handed over authority to the military but it was then returned to the police when the terrorists moved away from the car. One of the MI5 men told the inquest that tension was high among the security forces.

> When I came to Gibraltar I realised this was going to be a dangerous job. When I observed the three terrorists in the assembly area, they were observing the car. Nearby were some children. One of the three spoke to the other two, Sean Savage and Mairead Farrell. A few words were passed, maybe a joke. As they moved off there were smiles on their faces. I could not say what was said. It was a chilling moment as I felt that these were evil people who were prepared to spill blood.

An Army bomb disposal officer was now following the terrorists and he briefly examined the car after the terrorists had moved away from it. He concluded something was fishy because of an unusual radio antenna and declared it to be suspect. Soldier E said this soldier was 'able to confirm our suspicions that they were dealing with a car bomb'. One of the SAS men, Soldier A, told the inquest he was 100 per cent certain it was a bomb and the terrorists had a remote-control device and weapons. Subsequently, the police examined the car and found no bomb but 65 kg of powerful Semtex explosives was found up the coast in Marbella, in another car hired by the terrorists. It seems the terrorists' plan was to use the white Renault to keep the parking space and then replace it with the actual bomb vehicle just before their attack.

As the three suspects began to move back to the

border, Commissioner Canepa decided to hand the operation over to the military and at 15.40 he signed a form requesting the SAS to arrest them. When they got to Winston Churchill Avenue, the three stopped and Savage went off by himself into a side street, brushing past the two SAS men, Soldiers A and B, who were following them closely. McCann and Farrell continued walking until they reached the now famous Shell petrol station.

Soldier A said he was just about to shout the warning and arrest the terrorists. According to Soldier A, McCann began turning his head to look behind. The SAS men who were only a few metres behind the pair thought they had been rumbled and the terrorists were reaching for their remote detonating button. McCann was said to be smiling. Soldier A told the inquest: 'He [McCann] had a smile on his face ... he looked straight at me. We had literally eye to eye contact. The smile went off McCann's face and it's hard to describe, it's almost like McCann had realised who I was, or that I was a threat to him. The look on his face was one of alertness and he was very aware ...' In a split second, the two soldiers had drawn their weapons and pumped twelve shots into their victims. The SAS soldiers claimed they shouted a warning. Farrell and McCann were killed instantly.

A few hundred metres away in Corral Road, Soldiers C and D had Savage under surveillance; they saw him turn in the direction of the firing, and a police car with no connection with the operation drove by with its siren blaring. The SAS men immediately drew their 9mm Browning pistols and fired sixteen rounds into Savage. A pathologist described this as a 'frenzied' attack. A woman civilian was passing by and almost got in the way of the shooting, but the SAS men bundled her out of the way and continued shooting.

There is confusion about whether the soldiers issued a warning and the role of the police siren in the incident. Some witnesses said the siren went off before the shooting and triggered the whole incident. Several witnesses said the soldiers shouted warnings, even though they themselves could remember clearly what they said in the seconds before they opened fire. Some civilian witnesses claimed the SAS men had shot the terrorists when they were trying to surrender. At an inquest in Gibraltar a jury returned a verdict of lawful killing but only after the jury divided nine to two.

The incident became an ongoing legal problem for the British Government when the relatives of the dead terrorists took the case to the European Court of Human Rights, claiming unlawful killing. In 1994 the lower body of the court ruled in favour of the British but a year later the full court decided that more force than was necessary was used against the terrorists, saying those in charge of the operation made serious 'miscalculations' about the presence of a bomb in the car.

In Belfast, the killing of the three had more bloody repercussions. When the terrorists were being buried in the Republican section of Milltown cemetery, a Loyalist terrorist attacked mourners, killing three and injuring another fifty. Three days later at the funeral of one of these victims, two off-duty British soldiers strayed into the funeral procession. Their car was attacked and they were later murdered by PIRA gunmen in a backstreet.

Not surprisingly, the Gibraltar case has been the subject of much controversy. One area of discussion was the large number of rounds expended by the SAS in shooting the ASU. It seemed inconceivable that so many should be needed to stop three people. Some ex-members of the Regiment believe that certain pertinent facts about ballistics have been left out of the arguments. One ex-trooper explains:

> When we were training for our guerrilla role in Central Europe, the Regiment placed great emphasis on placing two quick shots on the target. This was called 'double-tapping'. With practice, it could even be achieved using an automatic weapon with a high rate of fire. The idea was to make the best use of the limited ammunition available, and it was more accurate. In the counter-terrorist role, though, you can't afford to 'double-tap'. The close-quarter conflicts are so intense, you must be sure that your first target is incapacitated before you switch to a second target.

In other words, even two shots may not be enough to stop a person. This is a point, often not appreciated by the media and the general public, which is further brought out by video training tapes produced by the Americans for their law enforcement officers. These tapes are freely available, and their contents well known to professionals whose work involves firearms. They make it clear that there is no firearm or bullet in existence that is guaranteed to incapacitate a person with only one shot and indeed a lethal wound will not necessarily incapacitate immediately. In support of the first point, the files of the Federal Bureau of Investigation (FBI) contain cases of felons being shot with more than forty rounds, over a period of several hours, before dying.

When this information is put in the context of the Gibraltar operation, it can be seen why the SAS expended so much ammunition. Implicit in the instructions given to the SAS team at Gibraltar was an understanding that the PIRA team should not be allowed to detonate the bomb. However distasteful it might seem, in counter-terrorist operations the legal necessity of catching the terrorist in the act, and the obvious need to prevent the crime, will always assume primacy over the humanitarian considerations of lawful arrest and trial. Hostage rescues and active CRW operations such as Gibraltar are the type of action which the public would perhaps most readily associate with the SAS in its anti-terrorist role. Yet in addition to all this, the CRW Wing still performs its original, much lower-profile task: that of training soldiers in the latest techniques of 'minding'; that is, guarding heads of state. In security circles this is known as Close Personal Protection (CPP) and SAS participation in this field can be traced back to the 1960s.

During the Aden conflict, Major Roy Farran (who had led Operation Tombola during the Second World War) and Major Peter de la Billière developed a close quarter battle school in order to select SAS operators for so-called Keeni-Meeni work. 'Keeni-Meeni' is a Swahili phrase used to describe the movement of a snake, and it became a synonym, in both Kenya and the Middle East, for under-cover work. To pass selection at Farran's school, the candidate had to remove a heavy Browning pistol from the folds of his native robe and fire six rounds into a playing card at 15 metres. Operators who passed the course were used to hunt Yemeni-trained assassins who were killing British Special Branch officers and their contacts.

In more recent times, CRW Wing has trained the units of the Metropolitan Police responsible for protecting the royal family, Government ministers and visiting dignitaries; the SAS has also replaced the police on occasions when specific threats have been identified. As the SAS became more engrossed over the years in internal security commitments inside Britain, groups of ex-SAS men formed private security companies to meet the demands of all the overseas countries seeking the Regiment's expertise. This was encouraged by the British Government, which saw in the scheme a further source of personnel for 'deniable' operations. The most notable of these private companies was the Guernsey-based Watchguard Company, set up by the Regiment's founder, David Stirling. Its clients were told that they would be buying expertise, not mercenaries. Subsequently, the firm worked in many African and Middle Eastern countries. However, when the British Government has considered a country's security too important to be left to a private firm, the task has been given to the SAS. This happened in Kenya in 1965, and in Abu Dhabi in 1968, much to Stirling's chagrin.

However, occasionally the activities of Watchguard have proved embarrassing for the Government. In 1969, shortly after Colonel Gaddafi seized power in Libya, Stirling organised a commando operation to free 150 political prisoners being held in Gaddafi's Tripoli prison, which was nicknamed the 'Hilton Hotel'. It was believed that these prisoners would form a credible opposition to Gaddafi's regime. In an attempt to maintain secrecy, Stirling employed ex-members of the French and Belgian para-commando regiments. However, the SIS (DI6) discovered details of the operation and, under pressure from the US (who at the time regarded Gaddafi as a bulwark against the spread of communism in the region), scotched it by making the details public. Another company that was run by ex-members of the Regiment was Keeni-Meeni Services Ltd, which provided a team of forty instructors to train the Sri Lankan police force's Special Task Force. It also supplied air crew to Lieutenant Colonel Oliver North (before his impeachment) to supplement the ex-CIA Air America crews who were running guns to the Contra rebels in Nicaragua.

More representative of the firms in the business of counter-terrorism than those so far mentioned is Defence Systems Ltd, run by Alastair Morrison, who was the SAS officer at Mogadishu. DSL has provided security for business interests in Angola and Mozambique, and it also provides guards for US embassies in high-risk areas. Control Risks Ltd, a subsidiary of London insurance brokers Hogg Robinson, employs ex-SAS officers as kidnap negotiators. Among other successes, the company obtained the release of two Lloyds Bank staff kidnapped by guerrillas in El Salvador, and that of George Curtis, vice-president of the American conglomerate Beatrice Foods, who was kidnapped in Colombia. The firm's 'kidnap-and-ransom' service is now being used by underwriters for Lloyds Insurance and many multinational companies. So be it officially, or rather more unofficially, the SAS continues to be of critical importance in the fight against terrorism worldwide.

In the post-Cold War world, a growing threat to Western societies is seen as coming from the illegal drugs trade, originating from the jungles of South America and Asia. The battle to stem the flow of cocaine and heroin into Britain has been described as the 'moral equivalent of war' and is taking on all the trappings of a military campaign. With billions of dollars at stake in the drugs trade, the drugs barons of Colombia, Pakistan and South-east Asia can afford to bribe their way past local police, military, intelligence agencies and governments. They can also afford to hire large and well-equipped private armies to protect their lucrative 'business' assets. Normal police methods just don't work against these people and therefore the British Government has increasingly turned to the SAS to do the job.

Assisting the foreign governments in counter drug operations is now a major commitment, which includes training for police and paramilitary forces, and planning and organising sweeps against drug plantations. SAS troops have been particularly active in Colombia and other South American countries, where the British police and customs need support and protection. When a British soldier working at the embassy in the capital Bogota was kidnapped, SAS soldiers helped in the effort to free him. Providing bodyguards for visiting British personnel is a key role for the SAS as the risk of assassination and kidnapping is considered to be very high.

Nearer to home, the SAS provides assistance to police and customs where drug dealers may be considered very heavily armed and dangerous. Assistance to the police is not unusual for the SAS. In the 1980s, before the Prison Service had developed its full hostage release capability, the SAS was called in to free Scottish prison officers being held hostage in Peterhead jail.

There are times when the SAS realises that some missions are just impossible. In 1993, when US peace-keeping troops in Somalia were trying to hunt down the local warlord, Mohammed Aideed, they asked the SAS to take on the job. After a reconnaissance trip to Mogadishu, the SAS politely declined the invitation. A few weeks later a US Delta Force team trying to snatch Aideed was ambushed in the backstreets of the city; eighteen soldiers were killed and eighty wounded.

The counter-terrorist capability of the SAS is proving to have more uses than were originally envisaged. However, the threat is evolving so the SAS must stay ahead of the game.

CHAPTER SEVEN

Ready for Action

In the early hours of 2 April 1982, from its position outside Port William, East Falkland, the MV *Forrest* reported surface contacts off Mengary Point and Cape Pembroke. These contacts were later identified as an Argentinian naval and amphibious task force, comprising the aircraft carrier *Veinticinco de Mayo* ('25th of May'); the destroyers *Hercules*, *Comodoro Py* and *Sequi;* the landing ship *Cabo San Antonio*; and three troop transports. The landing force included 600 Argentinian marines and a battalion of amphibious APCs (Armoured Personnel Carriers), supported by various army and navy personnel as well as special forces commandos.

Defending the British island was Naval Party 8901, a small Royal Marines garrison comprising sixty-seven all ranks, which would have been even smaller had it not been for the fact that it was in the process of being relieved. The Marines were armed with only standard infantry weapons, including 66mm and 84mm anti-tank missile launchers, and after a short action, they were ordered, on the morning of the 3rd, to lay down their arms by the governor of the Falkland Islands, Rex Hunt.

The governor, who was commander-in-chief of the Falklands ground forces under the Emergency Powers Ordinance of 1939, had decided to surrender rather than risk the possibility of civilian casualties. The first battle of the Falklands conflict was over.

The then commanding officer of 22 SAS, Lieutenant Colonel Mike Rose, first heard of the invasion on the morning of the Argentinian landings on East Falkland. His intelligence source on this occasion was reportedly, and some might say typically, a BBC radio news bulletin. Rose immediately set about informing the relevant authorities of his regiment's availability – and its ability – to carry out special operations in the Falklands. He also recalled men from leave and back from courses. While he set about convincing Army and Naval commanders of the benefits of SAS involvement in the South Atlantic, his men prepared themselves for the coming campaign.

22 SAS was admirably suited to the task that lay ahead. The Regiment's four 'Sabre' (operational) squadrons each had a boat troop and a mountain troop, specialising in skills which would undoubtedly be called upon during the campaign. In addition, one of the four squadrons was, at the time of the Argentinian invasion, serving its tour in support of British troops above the Arctic Circle.

On 5 April, D Squadron 22nd Special Air Service Regiment, which had been on standby at Hereford since the crisis first developed, flew out to Ascension Island. With them went Regimental HQ and supporting elements of 264 Signal Squadron (SAS). The following day they were joined by half of G Squadron so that by 6 April, the

SAS had the equivalent of six troops available for operations in the area. Ascension Island was to be Britain's staging post for Operation Corporate, as the campaign for the retaking of the Falklands was codenamed, and over the next fortnight the island was the centre of intense activity as vital supplies were flown in from the United Kingdom; stores were brought ashore from ships lying off the island; equipment was unpacked, checked and repacked.

Even as the SAS were en route for Ascension, Rear Admiral John 'Sandy' Woodward, the Royal Navy officer selected as overall commander of the British Task Force, was bearing down on the island with the advance group of ships, diverted from Exercise Spring Train in the mid-Atlantic. Simultaneously a carrier group, including *Invincible*, *Hermes* and the assault ship *Fearless*, had departed from Portsmouth and was chasing Admiral Woodward south across the Atlantic.

The Falkland Islands themselves were not to be the first target for the Task Force, however. This fate was reserved for South Georgia, an island which lay almost 1,300 kilometres to the east of the Falklands and had been taken by the Argentinians on 3 April. This decision to retake South Georgia from the occupying Argentinian garrison ran counter to the wishes of senior naval commanders. It was seen as a no-win situation. Firstly the risk of committing a large assault force to the open sea far outweighed any strategic gain to be made. But if a smaller force were sent in and defeated it would be just as damaging. Nevertheless there was a political requirement for action and Operation Paraquat to South Georgia was planned.

Before the attack on South Georgia could take place, however, Rear Admiral Woodward urgently needed information on the enemy's strength and deployment at the island's settlements of Leith and Grytviken. The estimated Argentinian force of around sixty all ranks were expected to be concentrated in one of these two locations, and D Squadron 22 SAS, among others, were tasked with carrying out the necessary reconnaissance. The plan was that as a naval task force group cruised off South Georgia, SAS teams would carry out reconnaissance in the areas around Leith and Stromness. Meanwhile Royal Marine SBS (Special Boat Squadron) parties would land and reconnoitre Grytviken and King Edward Point. It was estimated that these recce patrols would last five days.

On 9 April, with 3 Commando Brigade stiffened by 3 Para just leaving Southampton aboard Canberra on the long trip south, a party of SAS and SBS soldiers on Ascension Island embarked on the Fleet Stores Ship RFA *Fort Austin*, bound for South Georgia. The following day a task force group led by *Antrim* left Ascension carrying the remainder of the Operation Paraquat force; in addition, the submarine HMS *Conqueror* also deployed to the target area, with a party of No 6 SB Detachment, SBS.

Five days later, the *Antrim* group linked up with the ice patrol ship *Endurance* 1,600 kilometres north of South Georgia and started to close on the island. Cabinet approval for 'Paraquat' had still not been given at this point; in fact it was not forthcoming until 20 April while diplomatic moves were still being considered. Operation Paraquat began the following day.

Just before midday on the 21st, *Antrim*'s Wessex, a Mark 3 flown by Lieutenant Commander Ian Stanley RN, led the two Wessex Mark 5s being carried aboard the fleet oiler *Tidespring* through the steep-sided mountains of South Georgia and onto Fortuna Glacier. *Antrim*'s Wessex was the only one of the three helicopters fitted with a computerised navigational system and, in addition, the crews of the other two 'choppers' were inexperienced in arctic flying. The flight was not easy, but in spite of high wind speed, frequent squalls and poor visibility, the formation succeeded in landing the sixteen members of D Squadron's Mountain Troop, commanded by Captain John Hamilton, onto the glacier. Atop the windswept glacier, crevasses and deep snow hampered movement and the men managed only 500 metres before darkness fell on the first day and they were forced to 'bivvi up'. It proved to be a sleepless night for Mountain Troop. The lucky ones lay five to a tent, leaning against the sides to prevent collapse. The tents were ill suited to the task and at least once an hour, someone would have to go and dig away the built-up snow. The remainder of the troop remained outside, getting what little shelter they could beneath the equipment-carrying sledges, or 'pulks'.

The following morning, Captain Hamilton, realising the seriousness of the situation and aware of the danger of frostbite and hypothermia, signalled *Antrim* requesting helicopter extraction. After a number of attempts, the aircraft had managed to pick up the troops and get airborne, when one of the Mark 5s was hit by a sudden 'white-out'. This is a phenomenon experienced in arctic flying conditions: airborne snow produces nil-visibility, the horizon disappears and it becomes impossible to tell the ground from the sky. The helicopter crashed into the ice from a height of between 61 and 91 metres, the pilot managing to bring the nose up so that the tail rotor impacted first. The wrecked Wessex lay on its left side with its side door uppermost. The troopers and crew got out safely, the only casualty being one SAS man with a damaged back.

Recovered by the two remaining aircraft, the men were once again lifted off the glacier, only to have the same thing happen again. The second Wessex 5 crashed in a 'white-out', and the Mark 3, already overloaded, had no option but to leave the crash site and return to *Antrim,* where an emergency casualty room was hastily being set up. Once unloaded, the remaining helicopter returned to the site of the second crash, but was unable to land because of the weather. However, the crew did manage to make contact with the two RN aircrew on the ground, and confirmed that there were no serious injuries. By this time, the men on the glacier had erected a tent carried in the second helicopter and had recovered further equipment from the wreck of the first. The Wessex 3 returned to *Antrim* once more.

A second rescue attempt was made later that day; this time successfully. The stranded SAS troopers, together with the aircrew of the two crashed Mark 5s (a total of seventeen men), boarded the Wessex 3. The weather had barely improved, but in an amazing piece of flying, Lieutenant Commander Stanley managed to get his dangerously overloaded helicopter back to the Antrim. The Wessex, which because of its all-up weight was unable to hover, was forced to fly onto the deck of the ship in a manner which went against the normal rules of naval rotary-wing aviation. Ian Stanley was awarded the DSO for his part in the operation.

It was now 22 April, and D Squadron were no closer to getting onto South Georgia than they had been twenty-four hours earlier. Like David Stirling before him, Major Cedric Delves, officer commanding D Squadron, realised that there are times when insertion by air is not a viable option. An attempt had to be made by sea.

On 23 April, five Gemini inflatables, carrying members of D Squadron's Boat Troop, set off for the shore from *Antrim,* which had crept stealthily into Stromness Bay. Three of the small craft made it, but the other two developed mechanical problems with their outboard motors and, having no power, were swept away in rough seas. The occupants of the three boats that did make landfall established an OP on Grass Island in Stromness Bay, about 3 kilometres out from Leith. The following night they set out to get closer to their target, but in vain; their outboards failed and they were driven ashore by high winds. Ice splinters then damaged their Gemini craft beyond any immediate repair. Meanwhile, the men aboard one of the two Geminis that had been swept out to sea the previous evening had been recovered. They had drifted helplessly for some hours in a heavy swell before a strong wind, waiting until first light before activating a SARBE (Search And Rescue BEacon), a radio beacon onto which a helicopter homed for a successful rescue. The patrol in the second craft remained undetected for longer. After being blown towards Antarctica, the Gemini came close enough to a remote peninsula to make landfall. Rather than compromise the operation by sending an unnecessary request for extraction, the patrol whiled away five days practising their combat survival skills before eventually signalling for a pick-up.

The continuing bad weather also affected No 2 SB Detachment. They had air-landed on South Georgia by helicopter and then marched along the Sorling Valley, but once in the water at Cumberland Bay, the heavy Geminis that they had carried for eight hours suffered the same fate from ice fragments as those of the SAS. The SBS too had to ask for an extraction. A later attempt at inserting an SBS patrol was more successful; this party carried out a reconnaissance of Grytviken, while the SAS maintained observation on Leith. Both units reported that enemy activity was light, and that they seemed fairly lax.

Out at sea, Major Guy Sheridan RM, commander of the Paraquat force, was anxious to begin the assault on South Georgia as soon as possible. The incident which had hastened the decision to attack was the engagement and disabling of the Argentinian submarine *Santa Fe* on the morning of the 25th. Sheridan was in something of a quandary. The *Santa Fe* had been reinforcing the Argentinian positions ashore, thus strengthening the defenders' hand. The odds were further stacked in their favour because the bulk of M Company Royal Marines, the core of Sheridan's force, were aboard Tidespring, which had been moved to a position some 320 kilometres off shore when first reports of an Argentinian submarine nearby had been received. This left Sheridan with M Company HQ, the RM detachments on *Plymouth* and *Antrim,* and a section of 42 Commando's Recce Troop, together with SAS and SBS troops not otherwise employed. A grand total of around 75 men; the men landed from the *Santa Fe* had increased the opposition to around 140. Nevertheless it was decided that the demoralising effect of the submarine's demise outweighed the numerical disparity and the attack went in that afternoon.

The attack on Grytviken began with a naval artillery barrage directed by a gunnery officer put ashore with an SAS patrol. *Antrim* and *Plymouth* put down fire with their 4.5in guns, working a creeping barrage forward to within 800 metres of the enemy positions. The intention was to demoralise the Argentinians with a show of superior fire-power, rather than inflict damage on the buildings and cause casualties among the defenders. The scheme worked, and a heliborne landing 3 kilometres from the settlement by two troops of SAS further convinced the Argentinian commander there, Captain Bicain, that resistance was useless. The Grytviken garrison surrendered to Major Delves and Captain Young RN, the task force group's commander signalled the Admiralty: 'Be pleased to inform Her Majesty that the White Ensign flies alongside the Union Flag at Grytviken.'

The following day, 26 April, Captain Alfredo Astiz, the overall commander of Argentinian forces on South

Georgia, signed the instrument of surrender aboard *Endurance*. South Georgia was now back in British hands. The submarine *Conqueror* surfaced and transferred No 6 SB Detachment to *Plymouth* and later that day, the remaining SBS and SAS patrols were recovered from Leith harbour.

Paraquat had been a success and the first step on the road to the recovery of the Falkland Islands had been taken. It had been a remarkable triumph considering the unusual make-up of the force that carried it out: seamen, medics and aviators from the Royal Navy; marines from 42 Commando; gunners from the Royal Artillery; and soldiers from the SAS – all with their own way of doing things. In addition, the chain of command had been complex and unconventional, with Captain Young RN having soldiers under his operational control and Major Sheridan RM commanding Army personnel, including Lieutenant Colonel Keith Eve RA, a naval gunfire observation officer from 148 Forward Observation Battery RA.

But for the SAS the action had not been completely satisfactory, given the Regiment's high standards. First there was the near-disastrous landing on Fortuna Glacier. Feelings as to the wisdom of this operation had been mixed from the start, with at least two men with firsthand knowledge of the area, a scientist and an RN officer, advising the SAS to think again. Furthermore the Paraquat force commander, Major Sheridan RM, an expert skier and mountaineer, considered the 'natural' risks too great. He had recently returned from an arduous ski-mountaineering expedition in which he had traversed the

Himalayas. In the event his misgivings proved well founded.

But the SAS did not realise at the time that they were being advised by an authority; other voices deemed the mission possible and these and the SAS held the day. The result was a fiasco. It seems that the Regiment underestimated others' appreciation of the severity of the conditions while at the same time overestimating its own ability to deal with them – and almost paid the price. Yet it is to the credit of the SAS, and in particular to their fitness, endurance and training, that Mountain Troop managed to survive at all in conditions in which most non-special-forces personnel must undoubtedly have perished. And not only did they survive, they were still fit enough after their ordeal to take part in the main assault.

Boat Troop fared little better, but it is difficult to lay any blame for the problems encountered during the Gemini landings at the door of the SAS. The assault-force commanders needed intelligence on the Argentinian positions, and the Regiment, air insertion having been ruled out, had to go in to get it by boat. Atrocious weather and sea conditions combined with equipment failure to give the SAS little chance; once again they did well to stay alive, let alone reach Grass Island and report. At South Georgia the SAS took a battering from nature, not from the enemy; in the Falklands proper they would show what they could really do.

The moment Operation Paraquat was over, both the Army and the Royal Marines special forces were hastened back to the main Task Force. This force, now at full strength with the arrival of the carriers, immediately set sail for the Falklands, while the amphibious landing force, 3 Commando Brigade plus 3 Para, remained at Ascension pending the arrival of reinforcements in the form of 2 Para, currently en route to the island aboard the MV *Norland*. On 30 April the 320 kilometres maritime exclusion zone (MEZ) which had been declared around the Falklands on the 12th was upgraded to a total exclusion zone (TEZ). Within hours of this coming into effect the Task Force entered this area and an RAF Vulcan aircraft, flying from Ascension Island, bombed Stanley airfield. The same day SAS and SBS reconnaissance teams were 'choppered' onto East and West Falkland to report on the potential sites for an amphibious landing by 3 Commando Brigade.

The choice of a site for the amphibious landing was no easy task. The principal requirement was an undefended, sheltered anchorage with good routes out from a firm beach. Selection of a suitable site depended on accurate intelligence information, but the Task Force planners had an ace up their sleeve in the form of a highly experienced Royal Marine major, Ewen Southby-Tailyour, the commander of the Task Force Landing Craft Squadron.

While commanding NP 8901 (the RM garrison on the Falklands) from 1978 to 1979, Southby-Tailyour had pursued his passions of sailing, painting and photography. During voyages around almost 10,000 kilometres of Falklands coastline, he had drawn up about sixty charts, made innumerable sketches of the coastline, and taken hundreds of photographs. With his unique knowledge of the Falkland Islands, Southby-Tailyour was able to provide the military planners with specific, detailed information about possible landing sites.

Armed with this information, the amphibious force staff aboard HMS *Fearless* were able to reduce to five the nineteen landing sites initially identified as possibly suitable. After careful consideration and much debate, San Carlos Water on the west coast of East Falkland emerged as one of the favourites. Indeed it seemed the 'safest bet': intelligence reports suggested that there would be little or no opposition in the area, a vitally important consideration for an attacking force with almost no armoured support. The chosen site did have one major drawback, however: there were 80 kilometres of featureless terrain between San Carlos and Stanley – the ultimate target. No roads, no tracks, just difficult ground which would have to be covered on foot. The final decision would depend on whether detailed reconnaissance showed that San Carlos was indeed undefended. Such information could only come from men on the ground, and that is where the SAS came in.

The SAS patrols inserted on East Falkland by Sea King helicopter on 1 May comprised members of G Squadron 22 SAS, which had been hastily reinforced – even to the extent of taking men who had only just completed the jungle phase of their training. Their task, though not easy, was simple: locate the enemy's positions, discover his strength and disposition, ascertain his weapons and equipment, and assess his fighting ability. In order not to warn the enemy of their arrival, most patrols were dropped off around four nights' march from their respective target areas. Moving all night and lying up by day –

often in waterlogged shell-scrapes covered by chicken-wire and with an overlay of local vegetation – the men were exposed both to the elements and to the constant danger of being discovered by the enemy. The fact that no patrol was compromised before the main landings at San Carlos took place bears witness to the professionalism of the SAS.

Nevertheless there were a number of close calls. One soldier was lying up in a typical hide during the hours of daylight, when he became aware of a helicopter closing in on his position, which was situated in open, featureless ground on top of a ridge line. He remained motionless, face-down and unable to see upwards, while the Argentinian aircraft hovered close above him. The down-draught, caused by the main rotor at such low level, began to shred away the camouflage from the roof of his hide, leaving him exposed and feeling decidedly vulnerable. The next few minutes passed slowly for the uncomfortable trooper, but eventually the chopper moved off, leaving the soldier to re-camouflage his position quickly and reflect on his good fortune. Evidently the helicopter pilot had been checking his bearings during a cross-country flight, rather than looking out for an enemy patrol, and presumably had not glanced directly beneath his aircraft.

Once in their target areas, the G Squadron patrols set up OPs close to the Argentinian positions and lived cheek by jowl with the enemy, observing his movements. The information sent back to the Task Force and Amphibious Group was invaluable; indeed it showed that the Argentinian forces were greater in number than originally expected. The ratio of attackers to defenders in any action should normally be three to one in favour of the former. In the Falklands, the ratio was right, but it was the wrong way around. The Argentinians outnumbered the British forces by three to one: not good odds.

Meanwhile at sea in the South Atlantic, the Royal Navy was experiencing a period of mixed fortunes. On 2 May, the day after the SAS and SBS reconnaissance parties went ashore, the British submarine HMS *Conqueror* engaged and sank the Argentinian heavy cruiser *General Belgrano*. Two days later, however, the Task Force, indeed the whole British nation, was shocked to the core as a similar fate befell the Type 42 destroyer HMS *Sheffield*. On station some 65 kilometres off Stanley, the *Sheffield* was crippled by an Exocet missile fired from an Argentinian Super Etendard warplane; she sank six days later. Also in this time the first Harriers were lost – one to enemy fire; two collided over the sea. Nevertheless, the shortlist of landing sites was now down to three locations and on 8 May the amphibious landing group, now stiffened by the arrival of 2 Para, sailed south from Ascension. The following day the amphibious staff settled on San Carlos Bay as the target; three days later, 12 May, 5 Infantry Brigade – one battalion of Gurkhas and one each of Welsh and Scots Guards – departed from Southampton as reinforcements aboard the liner *QE2*.

So far the SAS ashore on the Falklands had been limited in their 'aggressive' activities to calling down airstrikes by ship-based Harriers onto Argentine positions and troop concentrations, and, in addition, to providing co-ordinates and correction for the naval bombardment of ground targets. Up to now, information acquired by the SAS patrols had been used mostly for intelligence purposes; now it was to be used as the basis for an attack, to be carried out on the night of 14/15 May.

The SAS were to raid Pebble Island off the north-east coast of West Falkland. The airstrip on the island was the base for Argentinian-manufactured Pucara ground-attack fighters, which were capable of carrying a wide range of ordnance – and a lot of it. These aircraft posed a threat to ships close to shore and would also menace troops deployed after the landings; therefore they had to go and D Squadron were given the task of disposing of them. It was to be an operation in much the same mould as the sorties carried out by David Stirling's SAS in the desert.

Initial recce was carried out by members of Boat Troop, which, landing by canoe, established an OP close to the airfield and confirmed that there were eleven Pucaras parked by the strip; they also set up a mortar base-plate. The rest of the squadron, under the squadron commander, Major Delves, were then flown in three Sea Kings to an LS (landing site), approximately 10 kilometres from the airstrip. The 45-minute flight from *Hermes* passed without incident and all three aircraft landed safely. Once on the ground, the men were given an on-the-spot briefing before heading off cross country on the 6 kilometres tab to the mortar base-plate. Here each trooper dropped off the two 81mm mortar rounds he was carrying in addition to his personal weapon and ammunition. The squadron then marched a further 4 kilometres to the forward RV, where, now in their individual troops, they were led to their respective start-off positions by the members of Boat Troop who had previously recced the area.

The assault on the airstrip was led by Mountain Troop. When they reached the perimeter, they opened up on the Pucaras with small arms, M203 grenade-launchers and 66mm LAWs (Light Anti-armour Weapons). Illumination of the target area was provided by para-flares fired from *Glamorgan*'s guns and the squadron's own 81mm mortar. In the artificial light the Pucaras were easily identifiable and the troopers were able to get in close to rig them with explosive charges and hit them with LAW rounds.

Their mission accomplished, the troopers withdrew from the airstrip under cover of mortar fire and with naval gunfire support from *Glamorgan*. The enemy had been caught completely off guard and it was not until the SAS were on their way off the airstrip that they attempted a counter-attack. This came to nothing, however; the officer leading it was felled by a well-aimed burst of SAS gunfire and that was that. With the exception of one NCO hit by shrapnel and another slightly injured when a command-detonated landmine exploded, the SAS raiders got safely away. In addition to destroying all eleven aircraft, D Squadron had blown up ammunition stores and had cratered the airstrip's runway.

The SAS returned to *Hermes* aboard Royal Navy Sea King helicopters. Royal Navy aviation ably supported the SAS throughout the campaign: helicopters inserted and extracted patrols, carried supplies and evacuated wounded. They also transferred personnel from ship to ship at sea, and it was during one such operation that tragedy struck.

On 19 May, just two days before the landings at San Carlos were due to take place, a Sea King helicopter took off from *Hermes*. On board were twenty-seven passengers, mostly from D Squadron, who were being cross-decked to *Intrepid*. The two vessels were only about a kilometre apart, and the flight, which took off around two hours after last light, should have taken about five minutes. On arriving at *Intrepid* the Sea King found another helicopter on the flight deck and it was therefore necessary to stay aloft and complete a second circuit. The airborne Sea King was circling off *Intrepid* when something went wrong.

Flying at a height of approximately 90 metres above sea level, the helicopter suddenly dived and plunged into the water, seemingly after suffering a catastrophic loss of power. The post-crash report suggested that this may have been caused by a collision with a large seabird, which was sucked into an engine intake. Whatever the cause, there was no warning for the passengers, most of whom stood little chance of survival. Having hit the surface of the sea, the helicopter immediately filled with water, and turned turtle and sank.

Inside the confined passenger compartment the SAS soldiers struggled to get out of the stricken aircraft. They were hampered by belt-kit and personal weapons – always carried by members of the Regiment when on operations – and few made it to the surface. In addition, the men wore only life preservers and not full immersion suits, normally mandatory for such flights, although it is debatable whether such clothing would have helped in their circumstances: the cumbersome nature of the immersion suits issued to passengers in helicopters may have prevented more soldiers escaping from the aircraft. In the event, those who did were picked up within thirty minutes.

As soon as the Sea King went down, rescue efforts began. The Sea King's two surviving crewmen, the pilot and co-pilot, managed to fire distress flares, and the automatic SARBE began to transmit its signal. Another helicopter was launched and began an SAR (Search And Rescue) sweep of the area, picking up one man. The remaining survivors were recovered from the icy water by a cutter launched from *Brilliant,* just as they were beginning to be overcome by hypothermia.

It was a black night for the Regiment and, in particular, for D Squadron, which lost many highly valued and experienced NCOs. Altogether eighteen members of the SAS perished and with them two 'outside experts' attached to the Regiment: Flight Lieutenant R.G. Hawkins RAF and Corporal D.F. MacCormack R Signals comprised an FAC team, specialising in guiding ground-attack fighter aircraft onto land-based targets.

The Sea King crash was the worst single disaster in terms of lives lost to strike the Regiment since SAS operations in the Second World War. Nevertheless, despite the severity of the blow, dealt by fate rather than by enemy design, D Squadron continued its operations. The survivors, now out of the battle, were returned to

Britain, and reinforcements sent to replace them were parachuted into the sea and picked up by the Royal Navy.

With Operation Sutton – the amphibious landing by 3 Commando Brigade and 2 Para – scheduled for 21 May, D Squadron's next task was to carry out one of a number of diversionary attacks designed to draw the enemy's attention away from San Carlos. Hours before the landing was due to begin, the heavily armed squadron was landed by helicopter on East Falkland from where it speed-marched to Goose Green and Darwin, later to be the scene of a famous victory for 2 Para. 'Shaking out' in line abreast to the front of the Argentinian positions they engaged them with every available weapon. Constantly moving their fire positions, the attackers created the impression that they were a far larger force than they actually were. The Argentinian defenders, thinking they were under fire from a battalion plus, did not once venture out to probe their attackers' strength, preferring, perhaps wisely, to stay put in their positions. The diversionary actions worked: at around 04.00 hours on 21 May British troops came ashore unopposed at San Carlos.

G Squadron, which was landed on recce operations on 1 May, had now been at large on the islands for three solid weeks, observing the enemy and sending out long-range patrols. It was now joined in its activities by D Squadron and over the next fortnight the two squadrons worked both East and West Falkland, sometimes inserted by helicopter, sometimes by Major Ewen Southby-Tailyour's LCVPs. Now the landings had been effected, it was less important that the SAS conceal their presence from the Argentinians and the Regiment was able to carry out more 'aggressive' patrolling: a number of enemy patrols were ambushed.

The land war was going reasonably well. On 27 May a patrol from D Squadron was landed on Mount Kent overlooking Stanley and the following day 2 Para attacked and took Goose Green and Darwin. Yet four ships had been lost since the landings began, including the Type 42 *Coventry* and the container ship *Atlantic Conveyor*, and reports were coming in that the Argentinians were moving troops onto West Falkland. Five four-man SAS teams were inserted onto the island on 5 June, one of which was led by Captain Hamilton, commander of D Squadron's Mountain Troop and a veteran of Fortuna Glacier and Pebble Island. On 10 June, while working out of an OP established near Port Howard, on the east coast of West Falkland, Captain Hamilton and his signaller were surrounded by a superior enemy force. They initiated the contact in an effort to force their way through the Argentinian circle and Hamilton was hit by enemy fire. Ordering his signaller to go on without him and make good his escape, the SAS captain continued to put down covering fire until killed. This was a selfless act typical of the SAS, where a close bond is formed between the members of a patrol. It was not the first time that the 'boss' had been killed covering his signaller's withdrawal, and it is unlikely to be the last. Captain G.J. Hamilton, an officer who had joined the Regiment from the Green Howards only five months before, was awarded a posthumous Military Cross (MC) for his gallantry. The war had only four more days to run.

Since 31 May pressure on the Argentinians had been mounting daily as British land forces bore down on Stanley. 42 Commando took up position on Mount Challenger west of Stanley, while 45 Commando and 3 Para converged on the beleaguered capital from the north, 'yomping' and 'tabbing' respectively. 2 Para advanced eastwards from Darwin towards Bluff Cove as the Gurkhas mopped up behind them. On 6 June 2 Scots Guards came ashore to join 2 Para at Bluff Cove with the Welsh Guards to follow. But two days later, as the Guards waited to land, calamity struck as the landing ship *Sir Galahad,* carrying half the battalion, was destroyed by aircraft with the loss of fifty-one lives. Nevertheless the battle for Stanley was scheduled to commence on 11 June and two companies from 40 Commando, held in reserve at San Carlos were brought in to replace the victims of *Sir Galahad.* Meanwhile artillery bombardment and constant airstrikes by the Task Force's Harriers attempted to further wear down the defenders.

But means other than the purely physical were being brought to bear on the Argentinians: the SAS had long since begun 'psychological' operations against the enemy. Lieutenant Colonel Mike Rose, CO 22 SAS, based aboard *Fearless,* had embarked on a plan to bring about an early Argentinian surrender. He was aided in his efforts by Captain Rod Bell, a young Royal Marines officer born in Costa Rica. Fluent in Spanish, Bell had spent most of his life in South America and was a unique asset to Rose as he tried to undermine the defenders' confidence in their leaders. Bell had spent much time speaking with Argentinian prisoners since shortly after the landings at San Carlos and, tasked with building up a psychological portrait of the enemy, he had gained a considerable amount of useful information. Rose used Bell's knowledge to compose signals and despatches to the enemy highlighting the discrepancies between the official Argentinian descriptions of how the battle was going and what was actually happening. The 'bare facts' were then broadcast or otherwise delivered to the defenders. In addition to their involvement in 'psyops', Captain Bell and Lieutenant Colonel Rose strove to negotiate terms of surrender with the Argentinian commander, Major-General Mario Menendez. Direct lines of communication were established and negotiations opened which may well have hastened the enemy's final decision to admit defeat.

While these complicated talks were in progress, the final push on Stanley began, with the battle for the mountains surrounding the capital. The Royal Marines assaulted Mount Harriet and Two Sisters on the night of 11/12 June and two nights later the Scots Guards took Tumbledown and 3 Para Mount Longdon. That same night, 13/14 June, 2 Para attacked Wireless Ridge with the benefit of a combined SAS and SBS amphibious raid as a diversion. Carried in high-speed rigid raiding craft, crewed by members of Major Ewen Southby-Tailyour's Landing Craft Squadron, the combined SAS and SBS force attempted to fire the oil-storage tanks outside

Stanley Harbour. Although driven back by heavy enemy fire, which damaged a number of the craft but only caused one minor injury, the attack served to underline the weakness of the Argentinian position.

The following day, 14 June, with a general cease-fire in effect, Lieutenant Colonel Rose and his 'delegation' (Captain Bell and a signaller) were 'choppered' into Stanley, where they discussed surrender terms with General Menendez. Within two hours a final agreement was reached, and before midnight on 15 June 1982, Major General Jeremy Moore, the land forces commander, and the Argentinian commander-in-chief signed the official instrument of surrender. This completed, the SAS group moved off to Government House, where they hoisted the small Regimental Union Jack which they had confidently brought with them from Hereford.

Later this flag was hauled down and replaced by a much larger version, which arrived with the Royal Marines some time afterwards. Filmed by a TV crew brought in specially to record the event, the lowering of the SAS Regimental Union Jack officially brought to a close the Regiment's occupation of Stanley, East Falkland. The SAS soldiers took the incident in their stride. Operation Corporate was over.

CHAPTER EIGHT

Preparing for Armageddon

Mission: a night infiltration by HALO [high altitude–low opening] parachute insertion. Aircraft type: a C-130 flown by SF [special forces] Flight 47 Squadron RAF. Jump Height: 20,000ft. Oxygen required. Opening height for main canopy to be pre-set for 3,000ft. DZ [dropping zone]: approximately 20km from the target. Target: an enemy radar installation comprising some half-dozen buildings. Aerial photo-reconnaissance suggests target has minimum security. On landing, regroup and move off towards target. Intelligence sources reckon little enemy activity in the area between the DZ and the target, although small, lightly equipped foot patrols have been seen close to the radar site. Suggest establish LUP [lying-up place] during daylight hours from which the target can be observed and move up to the perimeter under cover of darkness.

Approach and "eyeball". Study area for sentry schedule before entering compound and laying charges. Avoid contact with the enemy. Move out to PUP [pick-up point] 5km from target. LZ [landing zone]: unprepared grass strip running north-east to south-west. Layout IR [infra-red] lights for exfil by C-130 flying in with NVG [night vision goggles]. When aircraft lands, detonate charges at target by remote before boarding.

The above is an example of one of the many types of military operation for which the SAS regularly trains. Indeed this is the Regiment performing in its conventional war role, which is purely military, despite the general impression created in recent years by the media, of the Regiment as a unit dedicated to covert, clandestine and counter-revolutionary warfare. Precisely how the Regular Army Regiment, 22 SAS, and its Territorial Army counterparts, 21 and 23 SAS, would be used, is shrouded in secrecy. However, by analysing the potential threat, and by taking into consideration the specialist training and capabilities of the SAS trooper, it is possible to get a fairly accurate picture of how he would be employed.

In the Cold War SAS usage was closely integrated in NATO defence plans and the principles involved would be translated to other war zones. On the outbreak of an East–West conflict in northern or central Europe, the Soviet/Warsaw Pact forces would have launched an all-out offensive aimed at both devastating NATO's defences and destroying West Germany as a political entity. Such an invasion would have coincided with one of the major WarPac manoeuvres that are held just across the border, or with one of the biannual troop rotations of the Soviet forces based in East Germany. Soviet armoured thrusts into West Germany would have aimed at punching through the areas between individual NATO countries' corps boundaries, while at the same time a series of massive air strikes would have been launched with the intention of catching NATO air and land forces by surprise.

A surprise attack was the greatest threat faced by NATO, but logistical considerations on the Soviet side meant that there would have been some build-up to the assault.

Soviet military planners needed to inform their forward-deployed divisions of the decision to advance about twenty-four hours before H-Hour in order that these formations, together with their supporting arms and services, move up to their start-off positions. The second-echelon formations had even greater distances to travel to reach the frontier areas and relied on the road and rail networks. WarPac armoured vehicles would also have been loaded onto tank-transporters for road moves, and flat-cars for movement by rail.

Although it is considered possible that first-line elements of Soviet/Warpac forces would have deployed to their jump-off positions in twenty-four hours, a far more realistic timescale was a minimum of forty-eight hours. NATO maintained a sophisticated intelligence-gathering apparatus, including satellites and border signals-monitoring stations, and was able to receive the maximum degree of warning. The alliance's military planners would have had forty-eight hours to recognise the threat, mobilise reserves, and deploy troops. Among the first reinforcements to reach West Germany would have been the intelligence-gathering elements of the 21 and 23 SAS Regiments. This was because, in keeping with its tactical doctrine, NATO's armed forces required high-grade intelligence to maintain the 'Forward Defence' concept. While the various corps commanders had at their disposal modern satellite and remotely piloted vehicle systems to gather intelligence – in addition to the more traditional intelligence-acquisition assets, such as air and ground reconnaissance units – it was recognised that specialist close–reconnaissance units were required to provide the hard information that the commanders require.

Precisely what the SAS would have done in the event of an East–West conflict – what missions they would have conducted, and to where they would deploy – is something known only to the SAS and senior military planners, but some speculation is possible. A Soviet attack on the West would undoubtedly have been led by a concentration of Warsaw Pact armies in the East German transport system and this offered plenty of scope to Special Air Service units bent on disrupting the movement of enemy troops. For a start there were eight dual-tracked railway lines running from the Soviet Union to East Germany, each capable of transporting half a Soviet division a day. On top of this there were over 13,000 kilometres of single-tracked railway.

Other possible targets included the many major roads, which were also ideal for large-scale troop movement. There were over 1,300 kilometres of four-lane autobahn in East Germany, with innumerable bridges which could have been selected as targets. But bridges, both road and rail, would have been heavily guarded and difficult to destroy from the ground – as would their approaches –

but they could still have been vulnerable to air–ground and missile attack. The SAS task would therefore not have been sabotage. Small parties of SAS soldiers would have been inserted by means of HALO or low-flying aircraft, such as a small, high-speed helicopter. Their job was to identify a target and indicate the best method of taking it out. This was where 21 and 23 SAS came in; they were, and still are, Britain's Long Range Reconnaissance Patrol (LRRP) troops, or 'Lurps'.

Long Range Reconnaissance Patrol troops are capable of operating for long periods, with little or no support, in close proximity to the enemy. They work in small groups of between four and six men, often behind enemy lines, and are equipped with long-range communications facilities to allow them to keep up a flow of accurate, up-to-date information back to commanders at corps level. LRRPs provide these commanders with information on enemy movement, equipment and weapons systems; locations of headquarters, supply bases and airfields; and much more tactical and strategically valuable intelligence.

'Lurp' units have been developed by most NATO countries. Such specialist work requires highly trained soldiers, so LRRP troops are drawn from their respective countries' special operations force units. For example, Belgium has had members of its Para-Commando Battalion trained in LRRP duties while Holland has entrusted this work to the Army Commandos.

West Germany has LRRP troops, known as Fernspaehtruppen, and over the last thirty years or so, a bond has developed between these and the SAS, born out of mutual respect and a similar professional approach to their shared role.

The LRRP trooper's primary role is not one of a combat soldier. Indeed, he must avoid a confrontation with the enemy at all costs. His role is rather one of observation, identification and the communication of intelligence, and to do this he must avoid detection. His fieldcraft skills must be exceptional and he must be an expert in tactical movement.

The LRRP trooper moves – when he moves at all – primarily at night. Part of his job demands that he get into a position where he can actually see enemy troop movement. This may involve digging a hide location from which he can transmit information back to his base. Life in an underground hide can be extremely unpleasant, as described by a former member of the SAS:

> Spending four days underground with three of your 'oppos' can be incredibly boring. The main thing that actually came out of the exercise was how appalling this role really would be, because we were stuck down in this underground shelter for three solid days in pretty squalid conditions. It was the first time that this type of shelter had really been subjected to any serious testing by a full unit on a large-scale exercise, although small numbers of men, two or three at a time, had trailed the kit for short periods while on exercise in Zambia on an individual basis.
>
> But this was really the first time that the whole unit had gone down with all of the shelters as we

would do for real, and it was certainly the first time that the majority of us had to become familiar with the kit itself. We didn't realise how bad it was until the final stage of the exercise.

Exfiltration from the operational area was to be by air. The move out was undertaken by Royal Navy helicopters. They came in to pick us up and, as we moved to our helo and jumped in, the RN aircrew physically moved away from us and kept us at arm's length. We couldn't figure out why at the time. We had been out in the field for about five days, and underground in the shelters for about four. We had no idea how disgusting we smelt, because we were used to it. We smelt awful. In the shelter, we had to crap and piss into different bags which were then sealed together in a plastic bag. Do both together in the same bag and it is prone to explode. Before this exercise they tended to explode inside the shelter, a problem that has since been ironed out, but you could end up covered in the stuff, and with no real way to clear the mess up. We were also hot-bunking, using two sleeping bags between the four of us, surrounded by all our kit and with no room to move. The food was appalling and, probably because of the overriding stench, tasted awful. I'll never forget when we at last came out: the first gasp of fresh air after ninety hours underground – it was quite unbelievable.

Many of the techniques required by Long Range Reconnaissance Patrols are learned by the troopers at their parent units, but there is an advanced training facility in Bavaria available for LRRP troops – the International Long Range Reconnaissance Patrol School, at Weingarten. This establishment is commanded by a West German lieutenant colonel, and its instructing staff is provided by Belgium, Britain, Greece, Italy and the United States.

The school is divided into two parts: No 1 Wing, which is internationally staffed and conducts advanced training in LRRP techniques for NATO special operations forces, and No 2 Wing, which is purely for basic and intermediate training of Fernspaeh troops and is entirely German. The training conducted by both wings is of an exceptionally high standard and, in addition to LRRP training, the German hosts also run winter and mountain warfare courses for the other NATO nations. The school at Weingarten tests a number of LRRP skills and updates the students' knowledge in several areas. The school's courses are approved by an international working party which coordinates the curriculum. The courses are constantly evaluated, a flexible approach is adopted, and improvements to the tactics and techniques employed by LRRP units are continually introduced. One important aspect of LRRP operations is enemy recognition.

Troopers must be able to recognise enemy vehicle types rapidly and reliably. The make-up of enemy vehicle columns and their methods of deployment assist a corps commander in assessing the enemy force's strength, composition and, ultimately, its threat. With the information provided by the LRRPs, he can identify the enemy and deal with it.

In order to pass this vital information back to their headquarters, members of LRRP teams must be competent signallers. Great care is taken to train the patrols in the use of codes and ciphers, and to equip them with the most advanced communications equipment available. Messages are never sent 'in clear', but are always encrypted first. Using systems developed during the Second World War by units such as Britain's SOE, messages are translated into indecipherable numbers and then transmitted on high-speed morse radios. The introduction of 'burst-morse' radios has greatly reduced the chances of a message being intercepted. Additionally, this equipment lessens the likelihood of LRRPs being located by enemy DF (direction finding) units. The 'Lurps' are valuable assets, and great care is taken to protect them. Occasionally, however, techniques and training, camouflage and concealment, are not enough; and hides are located and patrols captured.

An officer with a combat supply unit recalls an incident:

> I was conducting a sweep to clear the area for my battalion headquarters to move into, when one of my men – never the brightest member of my platoon – came up to me and said, 'Sir, Sir, I've found a pair of binoculars.'
>
> Now this in itself wasn't unusual. Kit, even costly kit like binos, occasionally gets left behind when troops 'crash out' of a position. So I wasn't especially concerned, until I realised that this private had left them behind; he hadn't picked them up. However, it

wasn't until I started to bollock him that I realised that something was up. He told me that he'd tried to pick them up, but they were 'stuck'. He also mentioned that they were covered by a face veil. When he led me back to his 'binoculars', we found that one of the more switched-on members of the platoon had placed his beret over the binos, which, as you've probably guessed were in fact a periscope. Anyway, this was the first time I had seen anything like it. Of course, I'd heard rumours about SAS hides, but this was the first one I'd come across. They're pretty difficult to find.

Well, we looked around the area, sent for another platoon, and after shouting down into the ground 'Give yourself up!', or something like that, nothing happened until we started to dig. Then, all of a sudden, four guys appeared and took off. Of course, by this time the area was totally surrounded by members of my company, and all these guys were caught, but not without putting up a fight.

Anyway, we caught them and tied them up. None of them said a word, except one – their boss, I suppose, although none of them wore any badges, insignia or anything. And all he said was, 'Don't search us, we're carrying secret documents. Don't go into the hide, get hold of so-and-so' – at Brigade or Division, I can't remember which. Anyway, after waiting some time, this other guy pitched up, gave them a hard time for getting caught, picked up them and their gear, and took them off, saying to me, 'OK, they're mine now. I'll take care of them.' That was it. I must say, I'm

> glad I wasn't with them, as the guy who took them away didn't seem particularly happy with them.

Evasion techniques are among the subjects covered in 'Lurp' training. Students at No 1 Wing, for example, conduct long-range cross-country marches, often having to avoid troops out searching for them. Carrying heavy loads, the troopers encounter numerous natural obstacles during these marches. Mountains must be climbed, rivers swum, crevasses crossed and forests negotiated – often at night, and all in order to carry out the mission. To do this successfully, LRRP soldiers must be extremely fit. Not only must they cope with the long marches, but they must also be able to stay awake and alert for long periods, accurately reporting their observations back to base.

The LRRP courses at Weingarten are both tough and well attended, and the NATO allies send some of their best troops to the school. Here Belgian para-commandos, Dutch army commandos, German Fernspaeh troops, US Special Forces soldiers and TA SAS troopers rub shoulders. The latter traditionally do well on the LRRP courses, often coming in the top five per cent. One point should be noted at this stage. Out of all the special operations force units which comprise NATO's Long Range Reconnaissance Patrols, Britain's contribution (21 and 23 SAS) is the only non-regular group. This comes as something of a surprise to other nationals, as a former British student of the school recalls: 'We were some days into the two-week course when one of the American "Green Berets" from Bad Tolz [base of the US 1/10

Special Forces Group in West Germany] came up and asked us if it was true that we weren't full-time soldiers. It seemed to piss him off that we were doing ... well, better than the Americans on the course, and we weren't professional soldiers.'

There has always been an underlying but nevertheless deep-rooted belief within armies that the part-time soldier can never be as effective as the 'professional'. This is especially true of all-regular forces, such as the British, American and Canadian armies. All other NATO member nations have a professional cadre, but use conscripted soldiers, on compulsory military service, to make up the bulk of their armed forces, and consequently seem to be more understanding of 'civilians in uniform'.

Whatever the prejudices of the various armed forces, British TA units have vitally important combat roles, and their performance in recent years has proved that they are more than capable of performing their assigned combat roles up to the required level. For a number of years, the SAS requirement in Europe has been provided by the two TA regiments. The fact that, with the exception of the SAS, all of NATO's LRRPs are high-calibre professional soldiers, says much for the skills, dedication and determination of 21 and 23 SAS.

The international nature of the LRRP courses at Weingarten illustrates the spirit of cooperation that exists in NATO's special operations forces. New tactics and techniques are tried out, and ideas are swapped. Some of these methods are quite unusual. The British LRRP school graduate continues:

> Apart from the US Special Forces, there were Belgians and Dutchmen on our course. We all got on well together, and it was interesting to see the different ways we operated. SOPs weren't all that different, but you did pick up new points which were of value. One incident I remember happened at the end of the course, when we had our slap-up 'end-of-training' dinner. We had been promised a great meal, but in the event this consisted of us being given live animals to kill and cook. Two of the 'cloggies' [the Dutch army commandos] had this interesting technique of mesmerising chickens. First you hold the chicken down – this method requires two of you – then you counter-rotate a finger each side of its head in front of its eyes. It sounds crazy, I know, but what happens is the chicken concentrates on the fingers, gets confused, and just stops where it is. You can walk off, come back ten minutes later, and the chicken's still there, looking confused. The second method is to extend the chicken's neck with its head resting on the ground, and then draw your finger away from its beak in a straight line. Then it just lies there, wondering where your finger's got to. It sounds strange, and I don't know what practical application it's got, but it actually works. I suppose, by immobilising one chicken, you're then at liberty to do the same to other birds, eventually knocking out the entire coop. I've tried the same technique on women, but it only seems to work with chickens.

Living off the land is a skill which must be mastered. Without support, often behind enemy lines, patrols risk running short of supplies. Teams go out laden with special-to-task equipment – such as radios, weapons and ammunition – and rations take a back seat. In wartime a patrol might have to live for extended periods on what it could find in the surrounding countryside.

The LRRP courses and competitions are not the only opportunities that members of the SAS get to train alongside their NATO counterparts. The German 1st Mountain Division runs a demanding course at the Gebirgs-und Winterkampf Schule (Mountain and Winter Warfare School) at Luttensee, near Mittenwald in Bavaria. The Heeresbergführer (Army Mountain Guide) course is one of the longest and most arduous courses run by the Bundeswehr. Divided into a 17-week summer 'term' and a 15-week winter 'term', the course is open to suitable NCOs and junior officers, and is regularly attended by members of 22 SAS. The task of the qualified Mountain Guide is similar to that of the Royal Marines' Mountain Leader (ML). He must be capable of advising commanders at all levels on all aspects of mountain warfare. In addition, he must be an able instructor, capable of passing on his skills to other members of his unit.

The course begins at Luttensee with an initial selection week, followed by five weeks of intensive rock training at Oberreintal on the Wendelstein. Living in tents high up in the Bavarian Alps near the Zugspitze, Germany's highest mountain, the troops become acclimatised and spend up to ten hours a day on climbs up to Grade 5. From Oberreintal, the course moves to Chamonix in the French Alps, where they get to grips with the ice-climbing techniques before attempting a peak in the Mont Blanc area. This difficult ascent must be achieved if the students are to remain on the Heeresbergführer course. The summer phase culminates with a tour across the Dolomites and a traverse of Watzmann eastern face. By the 'end of term', the initial training intake of between twenty and twenty-five men will have been reduced to between ten and fifteen, and the ratio of instructors to pupils will be at least one to three.

After a brief break for Christmas, winter training begins in earnest. Skiing is one of the aspects which causes most difficulties for members of 22 SAS. Often skiing for the first time in their lives, they have to keep up with native Bavarians who have been on skis since the age of four. This disadvantage is realised by the DS (directing staff), and extra tuition is given where required. While getting to grips with the 'planks and poles', the members of the course are introduced to the tactical aspects of mountain-warfare operations. However, the German Mountain Guide course devotes less time to applied combat training than does the Mountain Leader (ML) course run by the British Royal Marines' 3 Commando Brigade Patrols Troop, formerly known as the Royal Marines Mountain and Arctic Warfare Cadre (M&AWC). The West Germans concentrate on the technical skills required for mountain operations, paying special attention to casualty evacuation, high-altitude medicine and mountain rescue, including avalanche rescue. This entails a volunteer being buried two to three metres (six to ten feet) under the snow, equipped with only a sleeping bag, radio, thermos flask and torch. Here the luckless 'victim' waits while his colleagues flatten the surrounding area to disguise the scent. Then, with the aid of a dog and poles, they set out to recover him. Officers and foreigners are the favoured 'volunteers' for this special treat!

After six weeks of ski training, all students must pass the West German Ski Association's Instructors test. This is particularly demanding, especially for relatively inexperienced skiers. But the standard of instruction is exceptionally high, and the students have already spent a month on skis, doing very little but going up and down mountains. Success in this test means a further three to four weeks on a high Alpine course in the Gran Paradiso region of Italy, ending with an extended ski-march patrol across a series of peaks of up to nearly 3,000 metres. From Italy it is back to Luttensee for the final test and, for the successful, the award of Heeresbergführer certificates and badges. Qualified Guides are respected throughout the international mountaineering community, civil and military. The Mountain Guide course is both difficult and demanding, but it enables 22 SAS to train high-quality instructors who can then pass on their hard-earned knowledge to the Regiment's mountain troops. Almost ten years on from the end of the Cold War, the SAS now has to be ready to operate anywhere in the world under British national, NATO or United Nations command. The Regular Regiment retains its counter-terrorist commitments in the UK, Northern Ireland, and around the world, wherever British citizens are at risk from terrorists. It is also assigned to support the newly formed Joint Rapid Deployment Force (JRDF) and sent troops to take part in Exercise Purple Star in North Carolina in the summer of 1996. This was the biggest UK–US airborne and amphibious exercise since the Second World War, involving almost all the British armed forces intervention forces: 5 Airborne Brigade, 3 Commando Brigade, and the SAS spearheaded the exercise, which simulated an Allied intervention to help a friendly nation threatened by a hostile neighbour.

The two Territorial SAS units participated in the operation, illustrating that they now have a more global area of operations alongside their Regular counterparts in time of crisis. They still retain their NATO tasking, but are now assigned to the British-led Allied Command Europe (ACE) Rapid Reaction Corps (ARRC). Although its primary ARRC task is LRRP, the new NATO force has to be ready to conduct a wide range of missions, including peace support, peace enforcing and peacekeeping. In December 1995, the ARRC was ordered to Bosnia to implement the Dayton Peace Accord. SAS troops went with the ARRC, but other members of the Regiment had been serving in the war-torn Balkans since the first British troops were sent there with the UN Protection Force (UNPROFOR) in 1992. Their role in Bosnia gives some idea of the type of operations the SAS will be called upon to perform in the 'new world disorder'.

In the summer of 1992 the former Yugoslav republic of Bosnia-Herzegovina was awash with blood from three months of civil war between Serbs, Croats and Muslims. The UN authorised UNPROFOR to begin escorting aid convoys to war-torn communities. British troops from the Cheshire Regiment set up bases at Vitez, Gornji

Vakuf and Tuzla to patrol central and northern Bosnia. Individual SAS soldiers went with them to act as liaison officers and interpreters with the warring factions, to negotiate the passage of UN aid convoys. The British Government was paranoid about British troops and aid workers being taken hostage by local warlords, so an SAS troop was kept on alert at the main British supply base at Split, in Croatia, ready to rescue anyone in danger. In the first year of Operation Grapple its services were not required.

When former SAS commander Lieutenant General Sir Michael Rose was appointed commander of UN forces in Bosnia, he gave the SAS a more pro-active role. Their first job was to cement the newly formed Bosnia–Croat alliance and they were dubbed Joint Commission Observers (JCOs). Small groups of SAS men moved between Croat and Muslim headquarters making sure they were not about to restart their bloody war. Their first major success was at Maglai in March 1994 when they negotiated the withdrawal of Croat HVO troops to open the besieged Muslim enclave to aid convoys. A JCO team was then sent to Gorazde where Serb troops besieging the Muslim town were threatening to attack. While on patrol the SAS team came under Serb fire and its forward air controller called in NATO bombers to retaliate on 10 April. The Serb attacks continued and more air strikes were called in the following day. It did nothing to stem the Serb offensive and four days later Corporal Fergus Rennie was killed while on patrol around the enclave. General Rose evacuated the SAS and the Serbs were forced to withdraw after NATO threatened major air strikes.

Around 400 British UN troops moved into Gorazde to police the town but they were far behind Serb lines. Their resupply convoys were constantly being harassed by the Serb troops and General Rose moved more SAS men to Sarajevo to stand by to rescue any convoys that were held hostage. Another JCO team was in the Bihac pocket in November when a Serb offensive threatened the town and they stood ready to call in NATO air strikes.

In May 1995, the Serbs seized several hundred UN soldiers, including almost forty British troops, after NATO air strikes on ammunition dumps at Pale. The British Government rushed reinforcements to Bosnia, including an artillery regiment and two squadrons from 22 SAS, to form the UN Rapid Reaction Force. Their job was to prepare to push through Serb lines to relieve the UN garrison besieged in Sarajevo and other enclaves. A JCO team was trapped in Srebrenica with Dutch troops when Serb forces attacked in July. They called in NATO fighters to try to hold back the Serbs but their advance was unstoppable and over the next week around 8,000 Muslim prisoners were massacred.

In August, the UN was ready to strike back. British and French artillery on Mount Igman blasted Serb positions around Sarajevo, and NATO aircraft roamed Bosnia destroying key Serb military assets. The SAS played a key role, infiltrating behind Serb lines to look for targets. From covert OPs they called down artillery fire and gave battle damage assessments of NATO bombing. Once the Serbs gave in to NATO demands, SAS teams were on hand to ensure their withdrawal from around Sarajevo went according to plan.

By December 1995, the warring factions had agreed to the Dayton Accord and British troops were ordered to join the new NATO Peace Implementation Force (IFOR) to separate the rival armies. In north-west Bosnia, British commanders had little information about the location of the frontlines or the position of the warring faction military units. The SAS was given the job of securing this vital information so that British troops could be positioned along the frontline. In freezing winter conditions, SAS teams infiltrated tense battle zones to keep the warring factions under observation until units of 4 Armoured Brigade were ready to move in.

Once the ceasefire lines had firmed up, IFOR began to supervise the demobilisation and return to barracks of Bosnia's three armies. SAS liaison teams were set up with key military commanders throughout Bosnia, to smooth over any problems. They reported to the ARRC commander, Lieutenant General Sir Michael Walker, in Sarajevo. Working in small teams, the JCOs would be making daily visits to barracks and arms stores to ensure the peace was holding. In November 1996, conflict flared near Brcko when Muslim refugees tried to reoccupy their old village in Serb territory. SAS men attached to US troops led them to the crisis point and Bosnian Army barracks, where 1,000 AK-47 rifles were confiscated to prevent things getting out of hand.

Operation Resolute, the British commitment to IFOR, involved large numbers of SAS personnel but it provided invaluable lessons on how special forces troops can contribute to securing peace in an uncertain world.

CHAPTER NINE

Keeping up to Scratch

Out of the mist staggered a lone soldier, bowed down under the weight of a 25-kilogram Special Air Service bergen rucksack topped with a bright orange marker panel. Soaked through, he made his way up the slippery trail – little more than a sheep track – until he reached the cairn. A pile of grey-white stones, contrasting sharply with the black, peat-like earth, the cairn was significant only because it was marked on the soldier's 1:50,000-scale map.

The soldier double-checked his map, studied his issue prismatic compass, and looked back the way he had come up the mountain. The visibility was worse now, down to about 30 metres, and the path he had taken over the crest and onto the small plateau had vanished in the mist. Soaked through from the damp air and the occasional, sudden rain squalls, the soldier shivered a couple of times before moving off downwind. There, in a slight hollow and scarcely protected from the elements, stood a hooped, green 'bivvi-bag'. The soldier walked across to the shelter and tapped on it.

Inside, a well-wrapped member of the SAS selection

course's directing staff (DS) finished pouring hot coffee from a thermos into a plastic cup before unzipping the front of his bivvi-bag. 'Name?' he asked. The soldier told him and the instructor checked his list until he found it. When he did he discovered that this man was an officer, a 'Rupert'. The instructor marked a cross beside the name, and then confirmed that the lieutenant knew exactly where he was and was capable of continuing the march, before giving him the grid reference for the next RV (rendezvous). The exhausted officer pointed out the next RV on the map with a blade of grass he had pulled up for the purpose. Then, after accepting a quick swig of the by now tepid coffee, he rose stiffly and shrugged his bergen into a less uncomfortable position. 'You'd better get going', suggested the man in the bivvi-bag; 'you've got some catching up to do if you want to make it.' With that, the Rupert set off back down the mountain, wondering why he had not been asked any demanding tactical questions; if he would make it to the next RV within the time; and what would happen then. Most of all, perhaps, he was wondering what folly had induced him to apply to join the SAS in the first place. For his current state of extreme physical exhaustion and mental confusion were all part and parcel of the Regiment's notorious selection process; a process which has been a major contributory factor in 22 SAS's many successes since its formation in Malaya in 1952.

The Special Air Service is made up of volunteers from all arms and corps of the British Army; it also has a small number of Royal Air Force personnel, who come mainly from the RAF Regiment. Unlike several of the world's special operations forces, it is impossible to enter the SAS directly, and each volunteer must have served with a 'regular' corps or regiment, and gained a good grounding in his corps or regimental skills, before he can offer himself for service. Most volunteers for the SAS are in their mid-twenties and the average age of soldiers serving with the squadrons is usually around twenty-seven – although commissioned officers can be accepted any time between the ages of twenty-two and thirty-four years and senior non-commissioned officers and junior ranks are eligible between nineteen and thirty-four. One stipulation is that volunteers must have a minimum of three years and three months left to serve from the date that, if successful, they pass SAS selection.

Gaining acceptance and then passing SAS selection and continuation training is a tiring and lengthy process that only the most determined candidates survive. Having expressed an interest in joining the Regiment, the man must first of all complete the relevant documentation at his unit. There then follows a short acquaintance visit to the SAS Regimental Headquarters at Hereford during which he will see the recruitment video explaining the Regiment's role, organisation and training. If he is still interested in going for selection, the candidate returns to his parent unit where he undergoes a check-up from his own Regimental Medical Officer (RMO). Assuming he is passed fit, the candidate then completes further documentation and then waits until there is a space on the selection course (run twice a year: one in the summer, one in the winter, regardless of the weather). When a vacancy arises, he will be called to Hereford.

When the prospective trooper or officer arrives at Hereford, he will have at least an inkling of what is expected of him over the next month, having already paid the short acquaintance visit to the Regiment. The programme commences with the customary course introduction, followed by the final round of documentation and the issue of required kit. The formalities completed, selection begins.

The modern SAS selection course is based on that designed by Major John Woodhouse when he returned from Malaya in 1953. His programme, in turn, owed something to the training devised by David Stirling in the Western Desert during the Second World War. This continuity is possible because the Special Air Service still requires the same type of soldier as it did in the desert and in Malaya. Like so many of the activities conducted by the Regiment, the selection programme is, within certain limits, flexible. What is not flexible, however, is the standard that must be achieved and maintained.

The programme is conducted by Training Wing 22 SAS, whose long-standing motto – 'Train Hard, Fight Easy' – still applies. Based at Stirling Lines, Hereford, Training Wing is a team of experienced Regimental commissioned and non-commissioned officers whose sole mission is to select and train the best men for the job. They make their choice on the basis of a man's performance during a build-up period – two weeks for officers, three weeks for soldiers – and a Test Week, a series of solo forced marches across the inhospitable landscapes of the South Wales mountains. The instructors look for particular qualities in a potential recruit, one of the most important of which is a high level of physical fitness and stamina.

Fitness is initially tested upon arrival at Hereford with a series of road runs. All contenders at selection must be capable of passing the standard Battle Fitness Test (BFT) in the time required for infantry/airborne soldiers. This involves a 2.5 kilometres group run in 13 minutes, followed by a solo run of the same distance in 11.5 minutes. But the BFT is only the basic requirement; a very high overall standard of fitness is required when the soldier first joins the course. This is then built up progressively during a number of group cross-country marches over the mountainous countryside. These marches gradually increase in difficulty as the weight carried becomes greater and the groups themselves smaller, until eventually the men are on their own.

To make sure that they are near the right level of fitness to start with, many candidates prepare themselves for the event for some months beforehand. They go out on hill marches and perhaps actually walk over the Brecon Beacons and Black Mountains, the area in Wales in which SAS selection is conducted. Some lucky volunteers will get time off for this; others have to take leave.

Most volunteers find SAS selection and continuation training the most physically demanding periods of their lives. Nevertheless, much more than fitness is tested and a man's physical capacity alone is not enough to get him through the course. Certain skills – map-reading and land navigation, for example – are absolutely essential to the aspiring SAS man, but more important still are the individual's personal qualities and character. The Special

Air Service requires soldiers who are self-confident and self-reliant and have the ability to endure extreme physical hardship and to carry on regardless.

This latter quality is to a large extent dependent on a soldier's motivation; something that is, in fact, sometimes put to the test when a man first decides to try for selection and informs his unit. Although a candidate's application for SAS selection has to be forwarded to Hereford, no platoon or company commander wants to lose a good officer, NCO or soldier with experience and potential. Infantry commanders are loath to lose their best men to the battalion's reconnaissance platoon (the traditional haven for the bright and fit infantry soldier), let alone to the SAS. The attitude of 'I've spent all this time training Private Jones and now someone else is going to reap the benefit while I have to train someone else to take his place' is all too common and understandable.

In the past, this view occasionally led to files being 'misfiled', letters 'lost' and messages 'mishandled'. The situation is reputed to be better now. A better understanding of the Regiment throughout the rest of the Army, together with a knowledge of the benefits that will be reaped when the SAS-trained soldier eventually returns, have led to a better rapport between the Special Air Service and other units in the British Army. When endorsing and forwarding an application for SAS selection, the candidate's colonel can look forward to the not-too-distant future when the soldier comes back a highly trained and experienced leader who can pass on his hard-earned lessons to others.

It is not merely the strength of a volunteer's motivation

that is in question; it is important that the SAS ascertain that he is correctly motivated. The Regiment was faced with a problem in this area in the wake of the successful hostage-rescue mission at the Iranian embassy in London in May 1980. Interest, both civil and military, was aroused following the live TV broadcast of SAS Counter-Revolutionary Warfare (CRW) troops storming the besieged building. Suddenly, the Regiment went from being a little-known military formation to being a household name, and both the regular and the TA regiments became besieged by budding SAS 'operatives', all of them aspiring to be black-suited siege-busters. The fiasco that followed was not of the Regiment's making, as a former member of the 21st SAS Regiment's Training Wing explains:

> Of course, we were all pleased about the achievement of the Regulars at Princes Gate. What we weren't expecting was the sudden influx of prospective recruits to the Duke of York's [Barracks in Chelsea, which houses the headquarters of 21 SAS]. There were what appeared to be mile-long queues outside the office. Suddenly, everybody wanted to join, but for all the wrong reasons. Very few people understood what our role was, and most thought we spent most of our time abseiling down the sides of buildings. Some very strange types came in. We had prospective recruits coming in with concealed weapons – knives strapped around their ankles, the lot. I felt sorry for the usual TA soldiers who wanted to take selection and transfer

> across [to the SAS]. They had really chosen the wrong time to come along.

However, despite the sudden interest in the SAS, and the surge of volunteers – most of whom were totally unsuitable – the two TA SAS regiments managed to maintain their high standards. Well over a hundred people attended the first cadre to be held after the Iranian embassy rescue, but only single figures passed through selection and went on to continuation training. One course actually had to be closed down because too many men dropped out. The regular SAS experienced similar problems, as a member of Training Wing points out: 'We had a lot of blokes volunteer, but for all the wrong reasons. Most dropped out because of the physical side. Some got through the early stages, but they obviously weren't suitable. If they didn't "jack it in", then they got "binned". Very few who are unsuitable get through the system, and those who do don't make it through continuation.'

Essentially then, the course is designed to be a test of the individual's mental as well as physical qualities, and it is conducted, under observation, in carefully controlled conditions. The series of 'beat-up' marches, which lead up to the final test, are intentionally hard, but graded to allow the candidates the best possible chance of success. After all, 22 SAS wants volunteers to pass the course, and while selection candidates are not actively encouraged, neither is there any longer any 'negative motivation'. This used to take the form of 'beasting', a practice whereby candidates were encouraged by 'well-meaning' instructors to take a short break, or even to give up completely – and 'RTU'd' (returned to unit), as they say in the SAS, if they succumbed. The will to win against the odds, and to overcome physical hardships through mental strength, is all important. Being neither encouraged nor cursed, a candidate depends solely on his own effort for success.

Much of the candidate's time during the early stages of selection is taken up with map-reading theory and practical land navigation. To many outsiders it may seem unusual that a soldier's map-reading skills may not be up to scratch, but many soldiers have only limited experience in this field, since, used to being led rather than leading, they are accustomed to relying on an NCO or officer to read the map and plot the course.

Practical map-reading is a vital SAS skill and it is tested to the full during selection. The Brecon Beacons, although undulating, lack the more obvious identifying features, such as buildings or roads. Also, visibility is often severely restricted, and students must become adept at marching on a compass bearing taken from a map rather than from a feature on the horizon.

At the start of selection the groups of candidates are divided up into pairs, but as the course progresses the men are deprived of the comfort of a partner and sent out on their own – and the stress levels rise. Each man sets off with a bergen, a map and a compass. He is given the grid references of the first RV, and he must make it there in the best way that he can.

Speed is important on these marches and there are

time limits, but these are known only to the DS; nobody tells the candidate, who is therefore unable to pace himself reliably. Neither is he told beforehand how many RVs there are, or where they are. All he knows for sure is where the next RV is, and only on reaching it does he find out where the one after that lies. This uncertainty serves to induce stress, which is further increased by special mental tests introduced by the DS.

For those few who make it through to Test Week, life only gets worse. By this time, the numbers on the course have thinned out considerably, giving the directing staff more time to concentrate on the individual. By now, the weight of the bergens will have increased from the original 11 to 25 kilograms, the maximum the men will carry during selection. Although fitter now than when they started, they are also very tired. Some will be completely exhausted, seemingly working on willpower alone.

The men and their abilities are constantly being observed and assessed. As they arrive at the various checkpoints SAS instructors evaluate their condition. Does this man have the ability to continue? Is he likely to become disorientated or collapse? If the answer is 'yes', the man is pulled off the course. Should this happen and the soldier has been doing the best he can, the Regiment may give him another chance on a later selection course. However, if a man 'jacks'– gives up – he is unlikely to get a second bite at the cherry.

The last hurdle for those who have got this far is a 60-kilometre march. Known as 'Long Drag', or the 'Fan Dance' – after Pen-y-Fan, the highest peak in the Brecon

Beacons – it is the last in the series of day and night land navigation exercises that make up Test Week. Regardless of weather conditions, the volunteer – who by now will be wondering why he is doing all this—has to complete the course within a set period, usually twenty hours. The route for 'Long Drag' is chosen to encompass some of the highest peaks in the Brecons. As one SAS man ruefully recalls, 'Now that mountain [Pen-Y-Fan] is a big, big bastard. You look up at it, and you know it'll be like running up the side of a house – and it is.'

However, with the end now in sight, most men who start 'Long Drag' finish it. They have come too far to turn back now, and failure after all they have gone through is not an option to be considered. To reach the final RV in the time allotted, almost any amount of pain is bearable, for when 'Long Drag' is over, so is selection.

With selection successfully completed, the volunteers are past the first obstacle but are not yet in the SAS; they have three further phases of training to complete before they are 'badged'. The first of these is continuation training, which teaches the soldiers basic SAS skills. Up to this point, the men have been very much on their own. They began selection as strangers, coming as they did from different units of the British Army, and relationships between them have since been little more than nodding acquaintances. This is due to the nature of the training, with much of the candidate's time being spent on solo 'tabs' across the Beacons, and the rest in trying to grab some rest in between. Once on continuation training, however, the pace changes and the stress eases.

Although it is still possible to fail to gain entry into

the Regiment at this stage, the course members now feel more confident. They have a shared experience, having been through selection and proved themselves capable of withstanding its rigours; they also have a common goal. The attitude of the SAS instructors has changed as well. They become more approachable and less of an apparent threat; the DS are still testing the men, but they are teaching them too.

Over the next fourteen weeks, the prospective SAS troopers are involved in detailed, realistic training that is specifically designed to enable them to become part of a four-man patrol – the basic SAS operational unit. Operating as part of a four-man patrol is likely to be different from anything the men have done during their previous military service. The closest they will have come to it is if they have served in an infantry battalion's reconnaissance platoon, but even then there will be a marked difference in Standing Operating Procedures (SOPs).

During 'continuation', the potential SAS troopers are introduced to SAS SOPs, a term with which they will become increasingly familiar. Training is both theoretical and practical. Instruction is given in the basic skills vital to the SAS soldier: small patrol tactics, elementary signalling, first aid, demolitions, combat survival, jungle warfare and static-line parachuting.

SAS patrol tactics differ from those used by other branches of the Army. In a four-man patrol, as opposed to an eight-man infantry section, each man has his own specific, individual role, and his own arc of fire, for which he is responsible while the patrol is on the move. The man in front, the lead scout, covers an arc of 180 degrees to the front. The man behind, usually the patrol commander, covers an arc to the left or the right, while the man behind him covers the area on the opposite side. The final man, or 'tail-end Charlie', is responsible for the arc to the rear of the patrol. In this way, the four-man patrol is able to move with maximum security. While undergoing continuation training, the members of a team are swapped about, each man getting the opportunity to take his place in a different position within the patrol, until all the men are conversant with the roles and responsibilities of each member of the team.

The four-man patrol is a close-knit group. First devised by Stirling when he formed the Regiment in the Western Desert, it has withstood the test of time and become the model for many of the world's special forces. It is small enough to move undetected, but large enough to put down sufficient fire to enable it to escape a contact. It is not designed to be an aggressive fighting unit, but rather to be self-sufficient. Should a fighting patrol or an ambush party be required for a particular operation, patrols are joined together either into eight-man teams or complete troops of sixteen men, depending on the tactical situation and the mission. Nevertheless the four-man patrol remains the basic operational unit, the cornerstone of the SAS, as its founder intended.

As the continuation course continues its tactical training, it is introduced to signalling. Communication is a skill vital to the SAS. Without the ability to maintain contact with their operational base, SAS patrols would be unable to provide the higher authorities with the all-important information gleaned by their reconnaissance missions. Patrols would be unable to call in artillery and air strikes, or aircraft for exfiltration once a mission was completed. Over recent years, the ability to communicate has become increasingly important. Nowadays, all SAS soldiers must achieve Regimental Signaller standard, which involves, among other skills, transmitting and receiving morse code at a minimum of eight words per minute. In addition, all troopers must be conversant with the codes and ciphers used by the SAS.

Signalling within the SAS is a skill that must be mastered to a level of proficiency far greater than that required by communicators within infantry battalions, and indeed to a level higher than that of all but the most specialised operators within the Royal Corps of Signals, the British Army's communications experts. An indication of the professionalism required by the SAS in their field is illustrated by the number of different systems they have to operate. Most units employ a maximum of six different types of radio; the SAS use at least thirty different sets. During the course of continuation training, potential SAS troopers are also introduced to first aid, SAS style. The medical skills taught by the Regiment are pitched at a number of levels. Initially instructed in basic first-aid techniques, such as how to resuscitate a casualty or how to stop bleeding, the troopers go on to learn about casualty-stabilisation and how to splint broken bones for medical evacuation. After getting to grips with the basics, the students learn more advanced techniques, such as how to set up an IV infusion (drip), how to administer drugs – both oral and injected – and the basics of casualty-handling and care.

In addition to signalling and first aid, basic demolitions techniques are also taught during continuation training. The soldiers learn about the handling and care of explosives, how to construct charges and, most importantly, where to place them. It is no use getting the explosives to the target, making up the charges, and then placing them where they do little or no damage. Prospective SAS troopers are instructed in identifying exactly the right spot to put the correct type of charge. An engineer explains:

> If you want to take out, say, a railway line, you probably wouldn't lay charges on the track itself. Blown tracks are easy to repair – a couple of hours and you can lay new lines. So the only reason that you'd destroy the track itself would normally be if you wanted to derail a train. You'd find somewhere where the target, either the train or the railway line, passed through a tunnel or culvert, or across a bridge, then you'd blow the bridge, for instance. There is a picture taken of, I think, the Royal Marines in Korea. They are laying charges on a railway line, and in the background there is a tunnel. If they had taken out the tunnel, it would have caused maximum damage to the target. The photo serves as a good example of how not to do it.

After successfully negotiating this section of the continuation phase, the students move on to Combat and Survival Training, which lasts for about a week. During this part of the course, the prospective SAS troopers learn how to live off the land, how to evade capture and, in case they do get caught, how to resist interrogation and how to escape.

Surviving in the wild is a skill which must be mastered by all. Initial theoretical instruction is given in the identification of food sources; the students are taught, for example, which plants are edible and where they can be found. The men learn how to build shelters using the materials to hand, how to lay snares to trap wild animals, and how to light fires using little more than their imagination. These skills are then tested when the trainees are dropped off in a remote part of the British Isles and left to fend for themselves. Wearing ancient battledress and old army greatcoats, the men have to use the limited resources available to them to their best advantage. A group of three or four men might, if they are lucky, have a knife, a watch and a box of matches between them.

The combat and survival phase culminates in an escape and evasion (E&E) exercise in which the students are pursued by an 'enemy force' – which is usually a local infantry battalion, bent on proving themselves by capturing the trainee SAS men. The object for the trainees is of course to avoid capture, but even if they do, for the purposes of this exercise they suffer the same fate as those who are caught. Those still at large at the end of the exercise must make their way to a 'compromised' RV, where they will either be captured, or required to give themselves up within a certain period of time. Once captured, the men are blindfolded, often with their hands tied behind their backs, and led off to an interrogation centre for the next stage in their training – Resistance-To-Interrogation (RTI).

For many, the RTI phase is the worst part of their training so far, even worse than selection. It is an unnerving experience. A soldier who got this far describes how his RTI experience began:

> I was picked and led to a 'Rover where there was an SAS captain I knew quite well. I was blindfolded by him with one of my puttees – this was in the '70s, before the boot (combat, high). I was then placed face down in the back of the 'Rover with my hands tied behind my back. There were a couple of bodies underneath me, which was useful, as we were then driven off cross country and they absorbed most of the shock. There was quite a lot of swearing going on, but I didn't recognise the voices. Somewhere along the line to the holding centre, we were transferred to the back of a four-tonner. Getting into the back of a wagon with your hands tied behind your back and blindfolded is an interesting experience. The guards helped. I remember thinking at the time that I owed someone in the Royal Green Jackets [the regiment providing the search force] a couple of bruises.

On arrival at the interrogation centre, each man is interviewed by a doctor, who gives him a once-over to check him for any physical problems, before being passed on to his interrogators. Each soldier signs a release form, but there is little actual physical abuse of the captives –

and certainly no torture – during these RTI exercises, and the condition of those being interrogated is carefully monitored by experts.

Exactly what happens during the interrogation phase cannot be discussed in great detail, but the aim, as one would expect, is to coerce the men into giving away information. A soldier is required to state only his name, rank, service number and date of birth. All other questions, regardless of their apparent insignificance, must be responded to with the phrase 'I cannot answer that question'. Experienced interrogators rely on maintaining high levels of both physical and mental stress to break down their subjects' resistance. Despite the fact that treatment complies with the rules laid down in the Geneva accord, the situation of the captives is anything but comfortable. For the twenty-four hours that the exercise lasts, the men on the course endure a gruelling series of interrogation sessions, between which they spend their time standing spreadeagled or squatting in various stress-inducing positions.

Getting through the RTI phase requires a great deal of self-control and commitment. Being constantly bombarded by questions and having to endure considerable discomfort when already exhausted does take its toll. The most common reasons given for 'jacking it in' at this stage are 'I didn't see the point in going on' and 'If my own guys could do this to me, I didn't think it was worth finding out what the opposition might do'.

In fact, putting up with being interrogated 'by your own side' is, in many ways, more difficult than being questioned by the enemy, even should the latter use physical force. In continuation RTI, all the soldiers have to lose if they crack is a little pride and a place in the SAS; in an operational situation, there is a real need to keep silent, a real risk involved in imparting any information, however insignificant it may seem. The period of mock Tactical Questioning (TQ), as resistance-to-interrogation is known by the 'professional interrogators', is a severe test conducted under conditions which are as realistic as possible. For the captives it is twenty-four hours of purgatory that reaffirms the individual's commitment to avoid capture at all costs.

Success during the RTI/TQ phase effectively marks the completion of continuation training and the prospective SAS soldiers' attention now turns to the Far East and the jungle warfare phase. Jungle operations have been an important part of 22 SAS's role since the unit's formation in Malaya and the Regiment takes this aspect of its work seriously. For the next four to six weeks the men will be on location in the exotic surroundings of, for example, Brunei, learning the ins-and-outs of what will be, for the majority of them, a totally unfamiliar environment.

After a period of acclimatisation, the students are given instruction in basic jungle survival skills. These include how to make use of the local flora and fauna for food – the trainees learn how to kill and cook a snake without being bitten or poisoned – and how to construct a jungle 'basha'. Students are also taught how to navigate and move in the restricted visibility of the jungle. Only when they are fully conversant with the skills, techniques and procedures necessary for successful operations in what is becoming for them a more familiar environment, are the men let loose in the jungle itself.

The jungle phase builds up to a demanding final exercise in which the candidates are divided into four-man patrols that have to complete a series of realistic tasks successfully. Once deployed, the patrols are on their own, and their only contact with the outside world is by radio. Should a real emergency occur, the patrol's only recourse is to their training, experience – and SOPs. There is no instructor with them to offer advice or assess their performance. The measure of success or failure in this final test of their ability is whether or not they achieve their objectives. Recently, one patrol became lost during the final exercise in the jungle phase. All four men were 'RTU'd'. A severe penalty for failure at this late stage, but one demanded by the uncompromising standards of SAS.

Those who pass the jungle training phase are through the last major barrier between them and joining an SAS 'Sabre' squadron. All that now lies between them and their ultimate goal is the basic static-line parachute course. In fact some of the students, such as those from the Parachute Regiment if there are any, may already be para-qualified and therefore over the finish line. The remainder face four weeks at No 1 Parachute Training School (PTS) at RAF Brize Norton in Oxfordshire.

All military parachute training is in the hands of the RAF and all Britain's airborne forces learn their parachuting at Brize Norton. Members of the Parachute Regiment and 5 Airborne Brigade, both TA soldiers and regulars, train alongside Royal Marine commandos; Navy personnel attached to the Marines work alongside RAF Regiment and RAF Parachute Jumping Instructors (PJIs) under training; and included in this all-arms, multi-forces mix in the PTS hangar are members of the SAS, usually small in number, doing exactly the same course as everyone else.

Over the four-week period, the students are introduced to the PX1 Mk4 and PX1 Mk5 main parachutes, and the PR7 reserve parachute. The Mk5 is only used for the first jump, the Mk4 – commonly referred to as the PX4 – is used for the remainder. The PR7, hopefully, will not be used at all. The students make a total of eight descents, including one, the first jump, from a balloon, one at night and one operational descent.

The operational descent, the final jump on the course, was introduced by 5 Airborne Brigade in the mid-1980s. Instead of simply taking the soldiers up to 300 metres and despatching them from the aircraft, on this eighth descent the RAF add in certain extras. Once airborne and in clear airspace, the aircraft descends to around 100 metres for a minimum of an hour of low-level flying. It may, for instance, go up to Wales and fly along the valleys, which is good experience for the aircrew, but not for the less fortunate parachutists. An SAS trooper explains:

> The operational descent is a bit of a sickener, both in the classic and literal sense. It's designed to give you an idea of what an actual combat deployment by air would be like. As far as I know – and I've had

experience of French, German and US systems – we are one of the only countries to do this. The Americans, for instance, jump from high-flying C-141s and usually exit the aircraft from 1,200ft. Neither their aircraft, nor most of their crews, are capable of the type of flying required for an operational jump. It differs from normal training sorties and jumps in a number of ways. It entails servicing and stacking your bergens, which are containerised for parachuting, inside the aircraft before take-off. Normally, you carry them onto the aircraft with you and stow them between your legs . . .

So you're being thrown about in the back of the aircraft as it weaves its way down the valleys, probably the same ones you spent hours walking over during selection. You're hot and sticky, because the temperature is difficult to control after coming down from altitude. Anyway, that's the excuse the RAF gives out. Actually, conditions are pretty bad for them too, and I've seen RAF PJIs and 'loadies' [loadmasters] throw up like the rest of us. I actually saw one PJI float off the ramp for a couple of seconds once, because the aircraft was pulling negative 'G' or something. Poor bastard went as green as his flight suit.

In addition to the discomfort of low-level flying, the men have other problems to occupy them. On an operational descent, the sticks – the number of men parachuting at one time – are larger than normal, with fourteen or more jumpers on each side of the aircraft. This means that there will be more people in the air at one time immediately after the exit and therefore more chance of a collision. Also, the dropping zone (DZ) for this descent, although longer, is much rougher than the one at Weston-on-the-Green that they are used to, and the likelihood of injury is therefore greater.

Around P-Hour minus 40 – that is, 40 minutes before the jump is due to take place – the bergens are handed down and hooked onto the parachute harnesses. It is difficult to do this in the cramped, confined conditions, but the RAF PJIs are excellent instructors and the drills are simple and easy to remember. Checks are then carried out on equipment, the parachutists hook up their static lines to the overhead cable, and the side doors are opened. By this time, it's approximately 'P' minus five.

The parachutists are now lined up along the sides of the aircraft and the PJIs take their positions at the doors. After what seems like an eternity of discomfort and anticipation the green light goes on and the first parachutists, one on each side of the aircraft, exit from 250 metres. They are followed in quick succession by the next pair and the next, while inside the plane their colleagues, their heavy containers held before them, shuffle towards the door and freedom. Within moments the whole course is out of the aircraft and enjoying that great feeling of relief which is rivalled only by that felt on a safe landing – one you walk away from. No one likes an operational descent.

This final jump marks the end of the SAS trooper's training. The following day there is dekitting and the course debrief in the morning, and the 'wings' parade in the afternoon. The SAS contingent are awarded their

'Sabre' wings, while the remainder of the course receive the normal parachute wings, worn by all Britain's airborne forces and para-qualified commando forces. The style of 'wings' awarded does not reflect any difference in parachute training; rather it reflects differences in the training the men have undergone before arriving at PTS. On completion of the 'wings' course at Brize Norton, the men return to Hereford, where they are 'badged' SAS and join one of the Regiment's four 'Sabre', or fighting, squadrons. Each of these is divided into four troops of sixteen men, and each troop is divided in turn into four patrols of four men each. Additionally each troop within a squadron has its own specialised role: Boat Troop – amphibious warfare; Mobility Troop – Land Rovers and motorcycles; Air Troop – freefall parachuting; and Mountain Troop – mountain and winter warfare.

On assignment to one of these troops the new arrival starts training in the particular specialisation. The trooper in Boat Troop, for instance, will learn combat swimming and the handling techniques of small assault craft and two-man canoes; in Air Troop he will be taught military free fall (MFF) parachuting; in Mobility Troop he will learn how to drive and maintain Land Rovers and other vehicles; and in Mountain Troop he will be instructed in special climbing skills and high-altitude movement.

The newly badged SAS soldier serves a probationary period of twelve months, which starts from the date on which he was first selected for training. During this phase, in addition to beginning to learn the role of the troop to which he is assigned, the SAS trooper learns a personal, or patrol, skill. In a four-man patrol each member has one primary speciality – medicine, demolitions, communications or languages – with the result that each of the four specialities deemed necessary for successful SAS operations is represented at a high standard within each patrol. As the trooper spends more time with the Regiment, he will pick up a second, or even a third, patrol skill. Cross-training is vital in a unit that operates in four-man patrols, where 25 or even 50 per cent casualties as a result of a contact with the enemy is an ever-present threat. Were troopers not trained in other specialisations, such losses would automatically doom a mission to failure.

At the end of the probationary year, SAS soldiers take their place as fully fledged members of a four-man patrol within their particular troop and go on to advanced training in the SAS disciplines mentioned. Those who display an aptitude for languages may be sent to the Army School of Languages at Beaconsfield, where popular courses include German and Russian. Learning a language properly takes time and the advanced Russian language course alone lasts eighteen months. Advanced courses for medics are shorter, but no less interesting. All SAS soldiers receive some medical training, but some troopers opt to further their skills. These men are assigned to selected hospitals in the UK, where they work and train in casualty rooms and operating theatres. It should be pointed out that training at all levels and in all skills is a continuous process for the SAS trooper – a fully trained SAS soldier does not exist. Specialist skills such as medicine and foreign languages enhance a patrol's ability to operate independently, but troop skills are no less important: reaching a target can often depend on the use of more than one troop skill, just as the ultimate success of a patrol may depend on an SAS soldier having more than one individual skill. For instance, should an operation call for a freefall parachute drop into a mountainous area, the obvious personnel to conduct it would be those with experience with both a Mountain Troop and an Air Troop. The SAS training system endeavours to ensure that these people exist.

The standard tour of duty with the SAS, for both officers and men, is three years. At the end of this period, non-commissioned ranks may opt for a further three years; officers must return to their units at tour-end. This is not as unfair as it may appear. Quite simply, officers' promotion requirements are different from those of NCOs and soldiers. Officer promotion depends on experience in a number of fields, and 22 SAS is limited in what it can offer in this respect. However, officers are not barred from the Regiment after one tour; indeed a number who serve with the SAS as troop commanders return later as squadron commanders, and may even come back again in a more senior post.

The SAS training schedule is punishing and unrelenting; it has to be if the Regiment is to remain capable of fulfilling the variety of tasks to which it is committed. From selection through continuation, jungle training and the 'wings' course, there is no let-up. And it does not end there. Once qualified, the members of the SAS can expect to spend around six to eight months away from Hereford every year; about half of this time will be spent overseas, usually on a squadron detachment. The Regiment lives up to the motto 'Train hard, Fight easy'.

Yet the SAS is not for everybody. Many volunteer; few are selected. This does not reflect on their competence as soldiers. The SAS is different from other branches of the Army. It specialises in small-unit operations where great emphasis is necessarily placed on the individual. This is in contrast to most other units, where soldiers work in larger groups in which teamwork is important and individual responsibility is less heavy at the lower levels. To join the SAS requires enormous self-confidence and motivation plus fitness, determination and outstanding military proficiency. But for those cut out for it, there is no doubt that the Regiment offers the ultimate in soldiering.

CHAPTER TEN

Special Forces on Trial

The SAS have close links with many units around the world. These ties may be historical, as they are with certain French and Belgian units which fought in the British SAS Brigade during the Second World War, and which still wear SAS badges and insignia as part of their uniforms. Or they may be working relationships with special forces of other nations, whether they be multi-role military organisations, such as US Army Special Forces, or specifically tasked units, like GSG-9 and GIGN – the West German and French counter-terrorist groups respectively.

Special forces are inclined to be similar in many respects. Their activities are generally cloaked in secrecy and the very nature of their work dictates that they must be teams of highly trained specialists. In addition, in much the same way as airborne troops worldwide, special operations forces tend to share a common bond. Nevertheless differences do exist – in size, in structure, in training, in methods and in role. A comparison of some of the major organisations shows just where the SAS fits into the world of special forces, and how its members operate in conjunction with or sometimes as part of these units.

The increase in international terrorism in the early 1970s led to the appearance of a number of anti-terrorist units in the West. Close links now exist between these organisations; intelligence and information on the development of equipment, weaponry and tactics is continually exchanged. The SAS is a leading member, perhaps the leading member, of this 'fraternity', and has been particularly important in training other units.

Counter-terrorist units tend to fall into one of two broad categories: they are either military or paramilitary. Organisations of the first category themselves come in different types. The SAS – along with its Commonwealth relatives – was an established unit which then underwent training in CRW (Counter Revolutionary Warfare), while the US 1st Special Forces Operational Detachment was raised especially for the job. The BBE (*Bizondere Bystand Eenbeid*), the counter-terrorist arm of the Royal Netherlands Marines Corps, is slightly different again. For though it is part of the Dutch Marines, candidates must volunteer for service with it and if successful are posted to the unit for two years, rather than serving in the counter-terrorist role on rotation as the SAS squadrons do. With a strength of around a hundred men (compared with eighty in an SAS squadron), the BBE is, like its British counterpart, a tried and tested group. Its most well-known operation was the June 1977 rescue of hostages from a train held by South Moluccan terrorists at De Punt in northern Holland.

Many Western nations, however, have chosen to draw

their hostage-rescue teams not from the armed forces but from the police and related arms. Italy has done this in developing the NOCS (*Nucleo Operativo di Sicurezza*), the 'Leatherheads', from the police force, and the GIS (*Gruppo di Intervento Speciale*) from the Carabinieri. Both are units of around fifty men and both have successful operations under their belts – the NOCS freed US Brigadier-General James Dozier from the hands of the Red Brigades in January 1982 and GIS smashed the Trani 'superprison' siege in December 1980.

Another country with a paramilitary anti-terrorist unit is Spain, which has the GEO (*Grupo Especial de Operaciones*). Paramilitary is not quite an accurate term to use for this group, however, because although it is run by the National Police, it contains Spanish Special Forces officers. In 1981 GEO successfully ended a siege at the Banco Centrale in Barcelona, where customers and staff were being held by gunmen demanding the release of imprisoned army officers. The methods GEO used in clearing the bank of terrorists were reminiscent of SAS Killing House tactics and, as the SAS did at Princes Gate, GEO checked everyone as they were brought out of the building in order to try to prevent terrorists escaping by posing as hostages. It is believed that some of the Spanish terrorists may still have escaped, but only one person – a gunman – was killed in the rescue operation. These similarities in operating procedures are not coincidental, as the SAS had a hand, along with the German GSG-9, in setting up the Spanish training programme.

The dedicated anti-terrorist units of France and West Germany owe their existence to the 1972 Munich

Olympics massacre. This incident, in which operatives of the Palestinian Black September group raided the quarters of the Israeli athletes in the Olympic village, ended with a disastrous shoot-out between the terrorists and the West German army and Bavarian state police at Munich's Fürstenfeldbruck Airport. The massacre was a turning-point in Western attitudes to counter-terrorism, highlighting as it did the need for specifically trained, specialist anti-terrorist units.

After Munich, the French set up the GIGN (*Groupement d'Intervention de la Gendarmerie Nationale*), which is part of the Gendarmerie, in November 1973. The decision was vindicated in February 1976 when the unit swung into action to rescue successfully all but one of a busload of thirty French children held captive in Djibouti by members of the Somali Coast Liberation Front (FLCS). The basic operational unit of the fifty-four-man GIGN is the twelve-man team, a large unit when it is considered that the SAS use four-man teams while the West German GSG-9, the Spanish GEO and the Dutch BBE favour five-man groups.

As mentioned above, another CRW unit which came into being as a result of the Munich massacre was, naturally enough, the counter-terrorist group of West Germany itself – *Grenzschützgruppe* 9. More commonly known as GSG-9, it belongs to the *Bundesgrenzschütz* (Border Police) and has a strength around 210 men. There are a number of reasons why West Germany chose to develop a paramilitary rather than a military unit, among them the postwar reluctance of the authorities to create an elite within the armed forces. Since its formation GSG-9 has achieved a number of successes, the most spectacular of which was the rescue in October 1977 of passengers held hostage aboard a hijacked aircraft at Mogadishu, the capital of Somalia.

The SAS link with GSG-9, which started with the latter unit's formation and continues to this day, is built on mutual respect. At Mogadishu it was the SAS's turn to help by sending two CRW experts armed with stun grenades; before Princes Gate the boot was on the other foot as the SAS sought advice from Ulrich Wegener, then commander of GSG-9. The SAS has even taken the lead from the Germans in the sphere of weapons on occasion: the Heckler and Koch MP5 machine pistol was already in service with GSG-9 when the SAS adopted it for counter-terrorist operations after seeing it in action at Mogadishu.

The skills required by anti-terrorist organisations are similar to those needed by military special forces. Physical fitness and marksmanship are given great emphasis in training programmes – with some units having their own version of the SAS Killing House. Mobility is also very important – a hostage-rescue team is useless unless it can get to wherever the captives are being held – and parachuting is taught by most units as a matter of routine. (One unit outside the military with little need to do this is Italian GIS, which recruits mainly from the para-Carabinieri.) Other mobility skills may be learned. In the GIGN training programme, for example, skiing, mountaineering and Scuba-diving figure prominently.

One reason, of course, why military special forces are so suited to CRW duties is because they have many of these skills already; the SAS certainly did when they set up their CRW wing at the end of the 1960s. They were very much the pioneers in this field and soon attained such a level of expertise as to be regarded as the doyens of CRW. The SAS's first full-scale hostage-rescue was not until May 1980, at Princes Gate, but before that, as the acknowledged experts, they had been called in to 'advise' on other operations. Besides taking part at Mogadishu, they were at De Punt, and the Italians requested SAS advice when Aldo Moro was seized by the Red Brigades.

What all the paramilitary units have in common is that they are dedicated counter-terrorist organisations and can concentrate on hostage-rescue and allied operations. The Dutch BBE is similar (though it would have some responsibility for reconnaissance in wartime), and although members usually only serve two years with the unit, for this period they eat, drink and sleep counter-terror. The SAS, on the other hand, has only one 'Sabre' squadron on CRW duties at any one time. The SAS soldier trains for anti-terrorist operations for six months before moving on to other aspects of the Regiment's work. In the Australian SAS it is a little different, with soldiers being assigned to CRW for a year, but the idea is basically the same.

Thus to volunteer for the SAS is to commit oneself to a much wider role than counter-terrorism – it is to enter the world of military special forces, a world in which the SAS have been as influential as they have in that of CRW. In the Commonwealth SAS forces they have spawned a number of like groups around the globe. Two of these units which are now firmly established branches of their respective nations' armed forces are the Australian and the New Zealand Special Air Services. The latter is the elder of the two; it was formed in 1954 to fight against communist terrorists (CTs) in the Malayan Emergency. Originally composed of 138 volunteers from civilian life and a regular cadre of 40 officers and NCOs, by the time the 'home-grown' selection programme was over, this number had been reduced to less than 100 all ranks. One point of interest regarding the background of those who were accepted is that one third were Maoris. They, like the Fijians who served in the British squadrons of 22 SAS, proved themselves to be exceptionally good soldiers.

The 'Kiwi' squadron deployed to Malaya in 1956, replacing C Squadron 22 SAS. (This was another Commonwealth unit, having been raised in Rhodesia; it now went home to become the Rhodesian SAS.) Commanded by Major Frank Rennie, the newly arrived New Zealanders undertook their parachute and jungle warfare training in country, and then worked as part of 22 SAS. They were deployed against CT guerrilla groups operating deep in the jungle and played no small part in gaining the initiative over the communists. At the end of its service in Malaya, the squadron returned to New Zealand and was disbanded, only to be re-established in 1958 as a company. Four years later one troop deployed to Thailand where, together with US Army Special Forces, it trained local army and police units in counter-guerrilla warfare in support of the South East Asia Treaty Organisation (SEATO).

During the Vietnam War the New Zealand SAS returned to the region to conduct special-forces operations.

Now based near Auckland, the squadron consists of five 'Sabre' troops and a headquarters troop, and while it maintains links with 22 SAS, its selection, training and equipment, because of its archipelago area of operations, are based on those of its near neighbour – Australia.

The Australian Special Air Service Regiment (SASR) was formed in Western Australia in 1957, beginning life as the 1st SAS Company. It was based at Perth, at the former base of a wartime special operations force unit known as 'Force Z', a highly successful outfit which conducted SBS (amphibious and shipborne) and sabotage operations against targets in Japanese-occupied territory. The SAS Company, originally raised to carry out long-range reconnaissance, was part of the Royal Australian Regiment (RAR) until the Borneo Confrontation, when it was detached and expanded to regimental size. Today it comprises a headquarters squadron, three 'Sabre' squadrons, a support squadron and a signals squadron, making it marginally smaller than 22 SAS.

The Regiment is still stationed in Western Australia, a part of the country where it has ready-made training areas in the form of the state's deserts and tropical rainforests. Selection is based on the British SAS system of a series of timed navigation marches, but takes place in the dry, featureless bushlands of the north-west of Western Australia, a far cry from the wet, windy mountains of Mid- and South Wales. SASR selection also boasts certain added refinements to the usual hardships of hunger, thirst and exhaustion: the Australian volunteer has to contend with poisonous snakes and salt-water crocodiles (the latter are renowned for ambushing the unsuspecting with all the stealth and cunning normally associated with an SAS patrol!). As in the British SAS, parachuting, tracking, patrolling and survival techniques all have to be mastered before the volunteer is 'badged' SAS, and further training in communications, demolitions and amphibious operations then follows. The SASR pays particular attention to amphibious skills because it also acts as a marine commando unit. Scuba diving, combat swimming and canoeing are an integral part of life in the Regiment.

All these courses and exercises are tough in the extreme and a point worth noting is that the Australian SAS have lost more men in training than in combat, despite the fact that the unit served in Vietnam from 1966 to 1971. Indeed, the 'diggers' lost only one man directly to enemy gunfire during their five-year involvement, and he died as a result of wounds suffered in the first year of operations. The SASR tally for that year, on the other hand, was forty-six confirmed enemy dead.

The SASR started their Vietnam campaign on surveillance operations and went on to become acknowledged experts at fighting reconnaissance and ambush techniques, using the five-man patrol as a basic unit, rather than the four-man team favoured by the British SAS. The US forces, with whom the Australians worked on occasion, were very impressed with their methods and the establishment of the US Army's Long Range Reconnaissance Patrols (LRRPs) owes much to the SASR's outstanding performance; the Americans also invited the Australians to instruct at the MACV Recondo (Reconnaissance Commando) school at Nha Trang. Links between the SASR and the US forces are still strong and exchange programmes exist with the US Navy SEALS and the US Special Forces. The Australian SAS as part of a Commonwealth army also has cross-postings with the British 22nd Regiment and SASR men also attend courses run by the Royal Marines Mountain and Arctic Warfare Cadre and by the Special Boat Squadron.

The New Zealand, Australian and British SAS units are all similar in structure; they are also, all three, small, especially in comparison with the special forces of the USSR and the USA. Spetsnaz, the Soviet special forces group, is a truly massive organisation with a peacetime strength of around 30,000 men and women. Naval Spetsnaz, an organisation somewhat akin to the SBS but bigger, accounts for part of this figure, but the bulk of the manpower is concentrated in sixteen Spetsnaz brigades attached to particular formations and to the Soviet military districts. Each brigade has a strength of between 1,000 and 1,300 troops divided among three or four parachute battalions (depending on the type of formation to which it is attached), a headquarters company and various integral support units. In wartime one parachute battalion would be detached from the brigade and assigned to 'specialist' tasks (for example, target reconnaissance or attack); the remaining battalions would either fight as a single formation or, more likely, divide into sub-units to a maximum of 135 such teams. The headquarters company, consisting entirely of professional soldiers, is specially trained to conduct sabotage and assassination missions.

Assigned to each of the three Soviet operational

theatres, including, it is believed, the Western European Theatre, there is a full Spetsnaz regiment, comprising six to seven companies and with a total strength of 700 to 800 men. In addition, independent Spetsnaz companies are attached to each Soviet army. A company consists of a headquarters detachment and three parachute platoons, plus communications and logistical support elements. The strength of each company depends partly on the manpower available and partly on its particular specialised task, but normally they consist of nine officers, eleven warrant officers and senior NCOs and some ninety-five men. Although capable of operating as a single unit, the independent Spetsnaz company will normally deploy in small groups of up to fifteen men.

The Red Army is often considered by outsiders to be unwieldy and unimaginative, but it has been innovative in a number of areas of warfare. It was one of the first armies in the world to realise the potential of airborne shock troops. As early as 1930 a Russian airborne platoon executed a successful parachute assault on a corps headquarters during a training exercise. The idea for special forces, however, came later, growing out of Soviet experiences during the Great Patriotic War (Second World War) against Germany. During this conflict, Soviet military leaders recognised the success of partisan groups in disrupting Axis lines of communication and in the postwar period they therefore set out to develop this concept. Their aim was to work out effective methods of coordinating armed clandestine groups and of supplying fifth columnists operating in potentially hostile countries. Spetsnaz grew out of this work.

Like the SAS, Spetsnaz keeps a very low profile. It is in fact essentially a military formation, drawing its recruits, both men and women, from all Soviet arms and services. Initial selection begins early, usually many years before conscription age. Apart from possessing the physical and mental attributes normally associated with membership of a special forces unit, Spetsnaz recruits must, of course, be politically reliable. Most of those chosen will have parents who are members of the Communist Party, will have excelled at school, and will be prominent members of DOSAFF (the Army, Air Force and Navy Voluntary Co-öperative Society). This organisation is open to those aged fourteen and over, and is designed to foster close links between the military and the young.

Although likely Spetsnaz candidates are initially viewed by 'headhunters' while in DOSAFF, the final decision is not made until they are categorised for military service. Spetsnaz, together with the KGB, gets first choice from what is available. A short but intensive basic training course weeds out all but the fittest potential leaders, who are then sent on an NCOs cadre. Those who pass then return for further training with Spetsnaz companies as private soldiers. Here they receive full special forces training; that is, instruction in parachuting, sabotage, small-unit tactics, infiltration techniques and suchlike.

This system is of course quite different from the SAS selection process. The latter draw their recruits from volunteer professional soldiers with a minimum of three years' service behind them; the Red Army, on the other hand, is a mainly conscript force and the Soviet special forces candidate is therefore younger and less experienced. In addition the turnover is higher – conscripts complete their two years' military service and leave – and there is not the same continuity as there is in a unit manned solely by professionals.

Spetsnaz's wartime roles are diverse and highly specialised, but its primary task is the destruction of the enemy's command and control structure. This may take the form of the assassination of military leaders or key political figures, and, in the case of the latter, may involve combined operations with KGB agents. Other targets are of the type that the SAS would be called upon to raid, and include headquarters, communications centres, naval and air bases, and air-defence networks. Power supplies and nuclear facilities are also considered prime Spetsnaz prey. In addition Spetsnaz might be used to guide in airborne or airlanded troops to conduct partisan operations in the enemy's rear areas.

Spetsnaz troops are even more difficult to recognise than their NATO counterparts. The SAS at least have a known headquarters at Hereford; Soviet special operations forces do not. Indeed Spetsnaz do not have the same 'corporate' identity as organisations like the SAS and US Special Forces. Rather than having identifiable barracks and HQs, small groups of Spetsnaz troops tend to be co-located with airborne and air assault units, despite the fact that there is no direct connection between them – and little fraternisation. Also Spetsnaz have no special uniform, although it is thought that they wear the blue vest, epaulettes and berets of the airborne forces, but without the Guards Division badges, which only the airborne are entitled to wear.

This last point does not hold true when Spetsnaz are operating in Warsaw Pact countries, for here they wear the uniforms and insignia of the nearest unit in the area. It is also claimed that in time of war, Spetsnaz operatives would seek to cause confusion by wearing the uniforms of the enemy countries in which they were operating and that assassination squads would be at large in plain clothes. Some commentators claim that reconnaissance of potential target countries is undertaken by these assassins while touring as members of high-level sports clubs; this is not out of the question, as a prerequisite for entry into the organisation is a high level of athletic proficiency.

Soviet special forces had every opportunity to put their diverse skills to the test during the Soviet occupation of Afghanistan from 1979 to 1989. After finding that traditional motorised warfare was getting them nowhere against the Mujahedin hillmen (in fact it was bringing them heavy losses), the Soviet military leadership opted for a less conventional approach, sending their Guards Airborne Divisions off the roads and into the mountains after the rebels – and also into the mountains went Spetsnaz on deep-penetration operations into Mujahedin-held territory.

The switch from conventional to special forces is reminiscent of that made during the British campaign against rebel tribesmen in Oman in the late 1950s. In this conflict, the SAS were called in to take the fight to the enemy after airpower and battalion infantry assaults had failed to have an impact on the hill tribesmen holed up on the seemingly impregnable Jebel Akhdar (Green Mountain). In much the same way as Spetsnaz were to do twenty years later in Afghanistan, the SAS had to rely on their first-rate physical fitness and endurance to survive the extremes of temperature and to move in difficult, and unfamiliar, terrain. The Omani rebels and the Mujahedin both knew their mountains intimately and were remarkably agile, something which the SAS and Spetsnaz discovered to their disadvantage; both units on occasion found themselves surrounded and outnumbered by wraith-like rebels.

Nevertheless the high calibre of special forces troops and their training inevitably brought successes: the SAS took the Jebel Akhdar by climbing up an extremely steep and almost undefended wall of rock – an operation beyond the scope of conventional troops. The guards atop the cliff, thinking their emplacement inaccessible, were not manning their machine-gun when the SAS turned up. A report has come out of Afghanistan of a similar operation in which a Spetsnaz team scaled a seemingly impossible cliff to eliminate a Mujahedin position.

The taking of Jebel Akhdar ended the first Oman campaign, but the SAS were back in the Sultanate in the early 1970s, and once again fighting rebel tribesmen. This time, however, the SAS were not concentrated against a particular target such as Jebel Akhdar, but were charged with bolstering the Sultan's Armed Forces (SAF) against Dhofari rebels. Under the title of British Army Training

Teams (BATTs), SAS men were providing military training, but this was a cover story and only part of their task. Unofficially the SAS were taking groups of recanted rebels – firqat – on operations, a job similar to that carried out by Spetsnaz in leading local militia groups on missions in Afghanistan. Nevertheless there was a fundamental difference in approach between the two forces. Whereas the SAS led their firqat charges against identifiable rebel targets, it is alleged that Soviet special forces, in an attempt to increase friction between the resistance factions, dressed up as Mujahedin and raided villages and bombed mosques. Spetsnaz also reportedly deployed assassination squads, also in Afghan dress, to take out key rebel figures, but one of these squads was unmasked and publicly executed by the Mujahedin.

The use of terror is only one way of dealing with insurgency; another approach is through a 'hearts and minds' campaign. Instead of attempting to frighten the population out of helping the terrorists, this type of operation aims to build up a rapport with the local populace by providing aid such as medical services, thereby gaining both their support against the rebels and a steady stream of intelligence. This was a technique first used during the Malayan Emergency by the British and it was a feature of the second Oman conflict. It also became the central doctrine of the second largest special operations force in the world – US Army Special Forces.

The emphasis of US Special Forces operations is quite different from that of the SAS, despite the fact that the two organisations have historical ties and a close present-day relationship. The Regiment, in addition to undertaking

CRW work, specialises in behind-the-lines intelligence and offensive operations, primarily reconnaissance and target attack. US Army Special Forces, on the other hand, tend to concentrate their efforts on training the troops of friendly governments, and, on occasion, the training of indigenous guerrilla groups across the borders of unfriendly regimes, although it is believed that the Green Berets do have Spetsnaz-style assassination squads. The Special Forces motto is *De Oppresso Liber*, or 'Freedom from Oppression', and this reflects the fact that they were originally created to raise and train resistance groups in enemy-occupied (that is, communist-occupied) territory.

The Green Berets are still heavily committed to providing military assistance abroad. During the period 1975 to 1983, for example, 532 training teams – known as MTTs (Mobile Training Teams) – were deployed to 58 different countries. These detachments are similar to the British Army Training Teams (BATTs) set up in the past by the SAS and their provision is on the rise. This step-up in activity came at the same time as an increase in world unrest and an intensification of political problems in Central and South America. Interestingly the US Army's second language is Spanish and many Special Force personnel speak it fluently; some as their mother tongue.

An increase in the deployment of MTTs also coincides with a revival of Special Forces. In 1986 legislation was passed increasing the Special Forces budget. This legislation was enacted in 1988 and a two-phase expansion programme was begun. At the time of writing, the Green

Berets consisted of four Special Forces Groups (Airborne) – numbered 1, 5, 7 and 10 – with each group roughly equating to a US regiment in size and with its own geographical area of responsibility. The 5th Special Forces Group (SFG) is based at Fort Campbell, Kentucky, and is responsible for South-east Asia and the Indian Ocean, while the 7th SFG with its base at Fort Bragg, North Carolina, covers Latin America and has its third battalion (3/7 SFG) stationed in the Panama Canal Zone. The 10th SFG (Eastern Europe and Africa) is based at Fort Devens, Massachusetts, with its first battalion (1/10 SFG) permanently stationed in Bad Tolz, Bavaria, and a detachment in Berlin. The 1st Special Forces Group (Pacific and north-east Asia) was reactivated at Fort Lewis, Washington, in the early 1980s with its first battalion deployed to Okinawa and a detachment in Seoul, South Korea. In addition there is the 3rd SFG which was scheduled to be reactivated before the end of 1989 with its base at Fort Bragg. There are also a number of Reserve Army SFGs, including the 11th and 12th Groups (Army Reserve) and the 19th and 20th Groups (National Guard).

One major criticism levelled at large special forces organisations is that, because of the sheer weight of numbers in play, it is impossible to match the exceptional standards maintained by small and highly manageable units like the SAS. Nevertheless, although the US Special Forces are larger now than at any time since the end of America's involvement in Vietnam, many observers believe that the Green Berets are becoming increasingly effective.

Although the mainstream of US Special Forces are different in role from the SAS, there emerged in the late 1970s a US CRW unit which closely resembled the Regiment – the 1st Special Forces Operational Detachment (better known as Delta Force, or simply as 'Delta'). Made up of former US Special Forces personnel and some Army Rangers, it was modelled, both in its selection procedures and in its methods, on the British Special Air Service. Delta was commanded by its creator, Colonel Charles A. Beckwith, a Special Forces officer since 1958, and a para officer with 82nd Airborne Division (the 'All Americans') for three years before that. Beckwith had served on attachment with the SAS as part of an exchange programme set up in the late 1950s by Colonel I.A. Edwards, then commanding officer of the 7th Special Forces Group, and Lieutenant Colonel John Woodhouse SAS. Under this system both countries exchanged an officer and an NCO for a year; in 1962 Beckwith and a Special Forces sergeant named Rozniak were chosen as the programme's American representatives, and the former, then a captain, became a troop commander with A Squadron 22 SAS.

Captain Beckwith took some time to adjust to the Regiment's way of doing things, but he soon got to grips with his new job; in fact he became hooked on it. He was particularly impressed by the stringent SAS selection process, the Regiment's no-nonsense professional attitude and its effective SOPs (standing operating procedures). While serving with 22 SAS, Beckwith, against the advice of his US Army liaison officer, took up the invitation to deploy to Malaya with A Squadron. Although the

Emergency had officially ended in 1960, there was still limited guerrilla activity along the Thai–Malay border. Beckwith took his troop deep into the jungle, where he lived, worked and learned with his men under operational conditions until been 'casevaced' out with a severe case of leptospirosis. He recovered from his ailments, but the experiences he shared with the SAS never left him.

By the time he left A Squadron at the end of his one-year attachment, Beckwith had become a vociferous advocate of SAS methods – and still was when he retired in 1981. In the following years he continually tried to persuade those responsible for formulating US Special Forces doctrine to adopt the Regiment's techniques. Beckwith's one-man crusade met with little success. The US Army Special Forces was a 'home-grown' force and was, in the eyes of many, the best in the world. For this reason, and with perhaps an element of national pride thrown in, American military leaders were reluctant to borrow another country's concept. It was not until the late 1970s that Beckwith was given the go-ahead to create an American unit along the lines of his SAS ideal.

Acquiring recruits of the right calibre was a problem for the US Army Special Forces, and the Green Berets themselves knew it. In the late 1950s and early 1960s, when admission to the SAS was already governed by the now familiar series of tests, such was the shortage of officers going into US Army Special Forces that there was little or no selection. In fact Beckwith himself was assigned to the 'Green Berets'; he did not volunteer. These difficulties became more acute during the organisation's expansion during the Vietnam War. Therefore, when he established SFOD-Delta, Beckwith set out to achieve the highest possible standards through his induction programme, based on what he had seen of Special Air Service methods of selection.

Besides implementing his own selection process and an SAS-style training programme (Delta has its Killing House which is known variously as the 'Haunted House' or 'House of Horrors'), Beckwith moved away from the established Green Beret unit structure. The organisation of US Army Special Forces dates back to their involvement in the Vietnam War. In South-east Asia the Special Forces Groups operated in what were known as 'A', 'B' and 'C' detachments. Each 'C' detachment, based on a Special Forces company headquarters, was designed to control up to nine 'B' detachments in a particular area of operations. In turn the 'B' detachments were essentially responsible for command and control of 'A' detachments within a specific area – each 'B' detachment would control three to four 'A' detachments. The 'A-Teams', as these latter detachments are commonly known, are the fighting units of the US Army Special Forces.

Each A-Team originally comprised eight men, each with his particular Military Occupational Speciality (MOS), but the size has since increased and today an A-Team consists of twelve men: an officer, a warrant officer and ten NCOs. As a fighting unit, especially for special operations, a team of twelve is far more unwieldy than, say, a team of four – that is, than a unit the size of an SAS patrol. This fact was recognised by Beckwith and when he formed SFOD-Delta he incorporated the basic four-man patrol principle.

But Delta was far from what Beckwith had in mind as the finished product when he was ordered to lead it into Iran. A total of fifty-six US nationals were being held captive by Iranian 'students' in Teheran; negotiations were making little or no headway and US President Jimmy Carter, increasingly concerned for the safety of the hostages, turned to the military.

The advisers came back with a plan for a complex operation 'Eagle Claw' – involving, at various stages, the Army, the Navy, the Air Force, the Marine Corps, and a number of intelligence agencies. The rescue force itself comprised a party of Rangers, a Special Force A-Team – and Delta. In phase one of the operation, Delta would fly from the USA to Mazirah in a C-141 Starlifter. At Mazirah they would transfer to three MC-130 Hercules transports and be flown at low level, by USAF Special Operations Wing crews, to 'Desert One', the point in the Dasth-e-Karir salt desert where the assault teams and the 'choppers' which would carry them on to phase two would RV.

The choppers, which were due to arrive at 'Desert One' thirty minutes after the rescue force, were to be RH-53Ds, the Navy variant of the HH-53 'Jolly Green Giant'. Crewed by US Marine aviators, they would fly in from USS *Nimitz*, which would be lying off the coast in the Arabian Sea. This type of helicopter was chosen ahead of the HH-53 for its increased payload and performance.

At 'Desert One' the helicopters were to land and refuel from bladders carried in a small fleet of C-130s. The rescue force would then fly out in the RH-53Ds to a forward landing zone. Here they would meet intelligence operatives who would then provide transport to the target area. Once at the embassy complex, Delta would divide into three groups before storming the buildings and releasing the fifty-three hostages there. At the same time the Special Forces A-Team would attack the Foreign Ministry and free the remaining three captives. Delta would then secure a landing area for the helicopters, which, having spent the intervening hours concealed in a remote wadi, would airlift the hostages and their rescuers to a staging point. This would be at Manzariyeh airfield – some 55 kilometres south of the capital – which would be secured by a Ranger company. All personnel, rescuers and released hostages alike, would then board C-141 Starlifters for the journey home. Or at least that was the plan.

Initially the operation went smoothly, but disaster was looming even before the rendezvous at 'Desert One' as two choppers dropped out with technical problems during the 80 kilometre flight from *Nimitz*. Another developed difficulties at the RV and the force commander was left with no option but to abort the mission. But even at this stage fate had one more blow left in store. While one of the remaining serviceable helicopters was moving clear of a fuel-laden C-130, it lurched out of control and collided with the plane, exploding in a ball of flame. The aircrew of both aircraft died instantly; 'Eagle Claw' had ended in catastrophe.

Post-operation investigations into the reasons for the failure of 'Eagle Claw' continued for many months. Without doubt the whole enterprise had been plagued by a series of misfortunes, yet it seems that some of these might have been prevented had certain items been taken into account before the mission started, and certain advice heeded. The major area of concern was the suitability of the type of helicopter chosen for the operation. UK sources – there were two SAS observers with Delta during the planning, preparation and rehearsal stages – consistently maintained that the helicopter type was unsuited to 'Eagle Claw'; they also stated that they thought that too few machines were being used. Other critics generally agreed with the second point, most saying that there should have been a minimum of ten helicopters available. The Israelis who, with the South Africans, probably have more experience than anyone in mounting external heliborne operations, went further still, maintaining that such a mission required a minimum of a 100 per cent safety margin; that is to say that at least twelve helicopters should have been deployed from *Nimitz*.

It is perhaps surprising that the Americans were not swayed by the strength of opinion against them on these points – particularly considering Colonel Beckwith's respect for the SAS. Yet in 1982, during the operation to retake South Georgia in the South Atlantic, the SAS were warned by a mountain expert that their proposed helicopter landing on Fortuna Glacier would be very unwise. The Regiment saw fit to ignore this advice and in the ensuing abortive attempt two helicopters were lost and the SAS men had recourse to all their ingenuity and powers of endurance to stay alive in the appalling weather conditions.

Certainly no blame can be attached to the troops on the ground. Neither Delta, nor the Special Forces personnel, nor the Rangers, nor the Marine and Air Force crews, could have done more than they did. Unfortunately they had never been given the opportunity to prove themselves. Delta was especially hard hit. After months of intensive training its members had been denied the opportunity to show what they could do.

In the wake of 'Eagle Claw' the US Army, in October 1982, set up the 1st Special Operations Command (Airborne), or 1st SOCOM, as an umbrella organisation to coordinate all its special operations forces. Delta plays a major role in this as the unit responsible for all CRW training. And not only does Delta provide direct instruction to other special operations forces, such as the Green Berets and the Rangers, but under a new programme it is tasked with supervising the provision of basic CRW training to the combat troops of conventional units of the US Army. Far from being destroyed by the Iranian débâcle, Delta has become established as one of the leading anti-terrorist units in the world and boasts a strength of 400, of which around 200 are assigned to combat duties.

Comparisons between the special forces of one country and another are difficult to draw. They differ in size and structure and their roles vary. They also recruit different types of soldier with different reasons for joining; indeed in the Special Air Service Regiment itself it is said that there are as many reasons for joining as there are members. But attempts at comparison aside, one fact is certain: the SAS is unquestionably the most widely experienced organisation of its type in the West (since its inception in Malaya in 1952, 22 SAS has had little time without operational commitments); it is also arguably the most effective. Stringent selection procedures, an exceptionally high standard of training, and a capacity for self-criticism have made the Regiment a unique organisation – and a model for other special operations forces. But more than anything else it is the dedication, determination and self-motivation of the men themselves that make the SAS what it is.

CHAPTER ELEVEN

Watching for Scuds

The Iraqi invasion of Kuwait in August 1990 saw the SAS committed to action in its largest operation since the Falklands War. Advance elements flew out to Saudi Arabia in August as part of Operation Desert Shield to stop any Iraqi advance southwards into the oil-rich eastern province of the kingdom. At first the SAS was unemployed because the overall Allied commander, US Army General Norman Schwarzkopf, was deeply suspicious of 'snake eating' special forces after a number of bad experiences of them in Vietnam. It was not until January 1991 that the British commander in the Gulf, Lieutenant General Sir Peter de la Billière, persuaded his American counterpart to include the SAS in Allied battle plans to liberate Kuwait.

The SAS was to be given the mission of infiltrating into western Iraq to create so much mayhem that the Iraqis would think a major attack was coming and pull troops out of Kuwait. On the night of 16/17 January, the SAS was moved by air from the United Arab Emirates to begin setting up a forward operating base (FOB) at Al Jouf in western Saudi Arabia. As the RAF Hercules carrying the SAS flew into the desert, they had to dodge the thousands of Allied war planes heading northwards into Iraq to begin Operation Desert Storm.

Within hours of the war opening, a grave danger began to threaten the Allied Coalition. Iraqi dictator Saddam Hussein started to fire off salvos of ballistic missiles into Israel, causing considerable damage to Tel Aviv and Jerusalem. The Israeli Government was demanding the right to retaliate and destroy the Scud launch sites in western Iraq. Such a move would have been unacceptable to the Arab members of the Coalition, so US President George Bush ordered Schwarzkopf to do whatever he could to destroy the Scuds and head off Israeli intervention. These were desperate days.

The SAS was now ordered to search out the Scuds in western Iraq. In the space of a few days, the Regiment had gone from having a fairly minor part in the war to having the responsibility of keeping the Coalition together. It approached its task in its usual stoical manner. The days before they were sent into Iraq had been frustrating for the men of the Regiment, who were itching to get at the enemy, and, in their more idle moments, wondered what was becoming of their adversaries.

The SAS would tackle the Scud threat in three ways. First, static road watch patrols would be mounted to report the movement of Scud traffic, and then direct F-15s onto the convoys. Second, fighting columns would roam western Iraq to hunt for the missile launchers. Third, SAS parties would cut Iraq's concealed communications links to prevent orders being sent to the launch teams.

The road watch patrols would be made up of three patrols of eight men each, and would monitor the three main supply routes (MSRs) that went from the Euphrates valley to the Jordanian hills in the west. The men were to be drawn from B Squadron. After the teams had been assembled, a major from the Intelligence Corps gave them a briefing concerning mobile Scuds and the morale of the enemy troops. Then the men were issued with a warning order, a military term indicating they should be prepared to move at a moment's notice. After weeks of uncertainty and unhurried activity, B Squadron was suddenly plunged into a fevered state. The men checked their equipment to make sure they were ready to 'rock and roll'. This included the main patrol radios, tactical beacons (TACBEs), plus the usual bergen checklist: water purification tablets, demolition charges, nuclear, biological, chemical (NBC) suits, Polaroid camera (for photographs that could be used for intelligence evaluations), night vision scope, and glucose tablets for energy.

The TACBE was an old piece of kit and caused the Regiment serious problems in Iraq. They were originally designed for use in Europe against the Russians by transmitting short, encoded bursts of information on a high frequency, but in the desert interference from the ionosphere crippled their capability. After the war the Ministry of Defence procured new radios for the Regiment, after it carried out a major review of available 'emergency comms systems', including the satellite units used by the US Special Forces during the war. Each patrol carried other essential equipment.

SAS soldiers are given quite a lot of leeway when it comes to personal equipment, and this was reflected in the way each man 'tooled up' before the road watch patrols. Some had chest rigs that incorporated a belt order, while others wore a standard '58-pattern yoke, which supported a massive belt order of pouches carrying water, ammunition, survival kit, emergency food, TACBE, and a global positioning system (GPS) navigation aid. The patrol medics carried equipment pertinent to their duties.

As the time for the men to deploy neared, each patrol received its Orders Group (O Group) briefing. During this they received the facts and figures for the job, after which they would be deployed. This is SAS standard operating procedure (SOP), and ensures that no one has the chance to talk about the mission before they go. In the majority of cases this means that once a team has been briefed, it is simply a matter of them waiting for the aircraft and vehicles.

The three road watches were to be inserted by Chinook helicopter. The thoroughness of the SAS was matched by that of the RAF helicopter crews, who had spent a considerable time at the briefings going through procedures in the event of something going wrong on the ground. If it did, the helicopter crews advised the SAS teams to stay with the aircraft – the chances of getting out alive were apparently greater. However, SAS soldiers like to be in control of their own destiny.

Everyone tried to get some sleep, though it was

difficult with the deafening noise in the fuselage. Within what seemed to be no time at all, the loadmaster was waving his illuminated wand to get the occupants' attention – five minutes to the refuel stop. The fuel stop consisted of a unit containing British and American personnel at the Iraqi-Saudi border. The Chinooks took off and headed into enemy territory. When they reached their drop-off points, the aircraft disgorged their occupants. The commander of the South Road Watch team decided to abandon his mission almost immediately. The ground he and his men would have to operate on was a gravel plain. There was no cover and they would have been quickly compromised. The men left in the Chinook they arrived in. The story of the North Road Watch is told in the next chapter.

The Central Road Watch team was on the ground for four tense days in a hide close to a road that was regularly being used by Iraqi military and civilian traffic. Wearing NCB warfare suits, the men boiled in the hot sun. The position was very exposed and the team was paranoid about being compromised. Eventually the risk was too great and they arranged to be extracted by helicopter. They had a 7-kilometre march to the pick-up point and along the way they had to dodge Iraqi convoys. Four Iraqis were killed and two captured by the patrol as they made their way out from their hide. A Chinook picked up the SAS team and its prisoners on time.

Thus ended the road watch patrols, an audacious plan but one which ultimately failed. All special forces operations are high risk, and some have to be aborted. That they failed was no reflection on the men concerned or their equipment. They simply could not perform their task in the terrain. Better to live to fight another day. In any case, only one of the Regiment's strategies for finding the Scuds had failed. Another, the mobile fighting columns, were on their way. They would be much more successful in searching out the elusive foe. The lessons learned from the road watch patrols could be digested – future operations would benefit from their experience. There it should have ended. But the experiences of the North Road Watch team, codenamed 'Bravo Two Zero', ensured that this particular part of the SAS's campaign in the 1991 Gulf War will always be remembered.

It is not the intention here to paraphrase or summarise in detail the book written by Sergeant Andy McNab, the commander of the North Road Watch patrol, which describes the exploits of his SAS team, nor the book written by another team member, Corporal Chris Ryan, entitled *The One That Got Away*, which describes his thrilling escape to the Syrian border; rather, we will examine the tactical decisions taken by McNab and his men, as well as the choices they made regarding personal equipment and SAS methods of insertion.

The story of the team, *Bravo Two Zero*, is now, thanks to the best-selling book of the same name, probably one of the best-known SAS operations ever. It is the enthralling story of eight SAS soldiers, landed 300 kilometres behind enemy lines, who were compromised when an enemy force set up camp almost on top of them. They made frantic and heroic efforts to escape, but only one, Corporal Chris Ryan, managed to flee to Syria. Of the other seven men, three died and four were captured.

McNab was one of those captured, and half his book is devoted to his experiences at the hands of the Iraqis. Needless to say, it makes for grim reading. Mentally and physically abused, he was lucky to live to tell his tale. When he was eventually released a medical check revealed a dislocated shoulder, ruptured muscles in his back, scar tissues on his kidneys, burns on his thighs, and the loss of dexterity in his hands. Worse, he was also diagnosed as having hepatitis, no doubt a result of being forced to eat his own excrement. The treatment of McNab and other captured British and American servicemen by the Iraqis during the war was absolutely appalling, and it is to the eternal shame of the United Nations (UN) in general that no war crimes charges were brought against the Iraqis who administered this treatment.

The story of Bravo Two Zero is one of heroism, stoicism and courage in the face of adversity. That said, it should not blind people to the fact that the mission was a complete failure. It failed not because the men were ill-trained or unprepared, but because they were inserted into an area that was crawling with enemy forces, in addition to a hostile population that had been told to be on the lookout for 'infidel' soldiers and airmen.

It was not quite the same for the men of Bravo Two Zero. In McNab's book it is stated that the team later learnt that there were two Iraqi armoured divisions between the border and the team's first position. This is not quite true. The Regiment does all it can to ensure the success of missions. It had sent reconnaissance teams into the area, and they had reported the presence of Iraqi forces. Nevertheless, Riyadh, and specifically the Americans, insisted that the SAS be sent in. It was a small price to pay, it would seem, to keep Israel out of the war. The same view was not held by the commander of B Squadron, who got into a series of furious arguments over sending his men into an enemy-infested area. However, he was overruled and the mission went ahead. There was also another major problem, which does not seem to have been impressed upon the patrol members at all, and that was the fact that the local population were very keen-eyed, even more so than enemy soldiers. SAS teams spent weeks and months living among the native people.

Soldiers and civilians living in the West, who come from mostly urban, socially mobile environments, often misunderstand the mentality of Third World rural peoples. The latter tend to live in closed, tight-knit communities where outsiders are viewed with suspicion, even hostility. It is a lesson that was learned by the SAS in Malaya during the 1950s, Borneo during the 1960s, and Oman during the 1970s. In those instances, SAS teams spent weeks and months living near or among the native people. Slowly, the soldiers gained the trust of the local population, although it was a very painstaking and fraught process. Cultural and religious practices had to be respected, and individual troopers had to learn the indigenous tongues. These procedures now form part of the Regiment's 'hearts and minds' procedures (patrol medics often have to learn midwifery and veterinary skills to treat the wives and animals of the local men). In Iraq this was not possible for two reasons.

First, the campaign was not one of counter-insurgency. The SAS was part of a UN force waging conflict against

The remains of the gunpit beside the Dhofar Gendarmerie Fort at Mirbat. The adoo attack against Mirbat on 19 July 1972 marked the turning point of the Dhofar War. The nine-man SAS team, supported by a handful of local troops, beat off 250 adoo. The gunpit, containing an old 25-pounder field gun, was the focal point of the battle. It was held by the SAS in the face of repeated attacks, which allowed time for reinforcements to arrive. (private collection)

As the Regiment has found to its cost, Northern Ireland is a political minefield. Military successes, such as the 1987 SAS ambush of an IRA team at Loughall and the stopping of three IRA terrorists planting a bomb in Gibraltar in 1988, have been propaganda triumphs for the terrorists. The sentiments etched on the gravestone of Danny McCann, one of those shot dead by the SAS in Gibraltar, are widely held among certain sections of the British and Irish populace. (Photo Press)

Republican West Belfast. Northern Ireland has been the SAS's longest war, fought in the countryside of the six counties and the town and cities. It involves painstaking intelligence gathering on terrorist suspects, their movements and arms caches, with the occasional spectacular ambush. (Photo Press)

Above: The SAS's most famous operation to date created an image of the Regiment in the public imagination that has proved enduring. Black-clad troopers storm the Iranian Embassy in London in May 1980 to free hostages from armed terrorists. Five of the six terrorists were killed in the operation which was played out in front of the world's media. (TRH Pictures)

Below: The interior of the Iranian Embassy after the SAS attack. The success at Princes Gate propelled the Regiment into the spotlight, which it neither liked nor wanted. Selection courses after the siege were packed full of hopefuls who wanted to don a black assault suit and abseil down buildings. They were quickly weeded out by the instructors. (TRH Pictures)

Right: The SAS maintains a special building at Stirling Lines, its UK base at Hereford. Known as the 'Killing House', it is used to train troopers in hostage-rescue drills. Only hundreds of hours of training in the 'House' can bring an individual's speed and reaction times up to the required standard. (Photo Press)

Below: The Argentinian submarine Santa Fe lies crippled in Grytviken harbour, South Georgia, following the combined SAS, SBS and Royal Marines attack on 25 April 1982. The SAS campaign on South Georgia began badly, when D Squadron's Mountain Troop had to be evacuated from Fortuna Glacier after adverse weather prevented the men establishing observation posts around Leith. (TRH Pictures)

Above: A shot-up Argentinian Pucara ground-attack aircraft on Pebble Island. The aircraft stationed on the bleak island to the north of West Falkland presented a danger to the proposed British landings at San Carlos. The SAS was therefore ordered in to destroy them, which D Squadron did on the night of 14-15 May. (TRH Pictures)

Below: Typical Falklands terrain – wet and peaty. Before the British landings on the Falklands, SAS teams were sent in to collect intelligence concerning enemy movements and strengths. This entailed living in covert observation posts in the ground, lying in wet, cold 'hides' for weeks at a time. (TRH Pictures)

Above: The 1991 Gulf War. From 20 January onwards, the SAS sent mobile fighting columns into western Iraq to hunt for mobile Scud surface-to-surface missile (SSM) launchers. Saddam Hussein was targeting Israel in an attempt to bring it into the war, which would have split the UN Coalition. (TRH Pictures)

Below: The SAS Land Rover columns that were sent into western Iraq were drawn from A and D Squadrons and comprised around 12 Land Rovers each, plus motorcycle outriders. Each vehicle was armed with machine guns, Stinger surface-to-air missiles (SAMs) and Milan anti-tank weapons. (TRH Pictures)

A wrecked Iraqi convoy after the war. As well as hunting for Scuds, SAS patrols behind the lines called in air strikes on Iraqi vehicle columns and communications centres. (The Military Picture Library)

Above left: A lone figure is dwarfed by the peaks of the Brecon Beacons in South Wales, the area used by the SAS for its Selection Training course. Selection lasts one month, and is composed of arduous timed navigation marches. The culmination of the course is the 'Fan Dance', a solo 60km (37-mile) march over the highest peaks, which has to be completed in under 20 hours. (The Military Picture Library). *Above right*: After Selection comes Continuation Training. This lasts 14 weeks and is designed to teach SAS recruits the skills required to be a member of a four-man patrol. The combat and survival phase includes learning to live off the land. (The Military Picture Library)

Above: The SAS has a long association with the jungle, so recruits undergo six weeks of jungle training in the Far East to learn basic jungle survival and tactics. (The Military Picture Library)

Below: Each SAS 'Sabre' Squadron contains four 16-man troops, each one having its own speciality. Members of Air Troops learn all aspects of airborne insertion. Though freefall parachuting is taught as standard (as shown here), increasingly helicopter transport is becoming the favoured method of aerial delivery in the Regiment. (The Military Picture Library)

Above: SAS Boat Troops specialise in all aspects of amphibious warfare, including dropping troops into the sea from helicopters, a tactic known as helicasting. (Photo Press)

Below: The Regiment is continually testing different types of weaponry and equipment, but it tends to stick with tried-and-tested hardware. Land Rover vehicles have served the SAS well, one of the latest models being this Defender 90 Multi-Role Combat Vehicle. (Photo Press)

Iraq, so it was not there to subvert the Iraqi populace against Saddam Hussein (contrary to popular opinion, the UN did not have a remit to change the regime in Iraq). Second, the Iraqi population was hostile towards soldiers, sailors and airmen of the Coalition, especially its Western members (the governments of the Allies, and their representatives at the UN, liked to maintain the façade that the war was solely against Saddam Hussein and his henchmen; inhabitants of towns and cities who were bombed daily, and had their sewage, water and electricity facilities knocked out, thought differently).

This being the case, remaining hidden from prying eyes can be extremely difficult. Locals are very 'switched on' when it comes to their immediate environment. In Iraq, the discovery of strangers would result in wild shouts and hollering, and the certainty of the authorities being alerted. This is what happened to Bravo Two Zero: the members of this team were discovered by a small boy tending a herd of goats. In addition, the nomadic Bedouin who roamed the region were on the lookout for Western servicemen – partly, no doubt, to claim the rewards that were being offered.

If the planners in Riyadh had known of the concentration of enemy forces in the area – so the official line goes – the road watch patrols would not have been sent in. General Norman Schwarzkopf himself admitted as much to McNab after the latter's release from captivity. But by then the damage had been done and three of his team were dead. However, as stated above, Riyadh did know, and still the SAS was sent in (the role of sacrificial lamb is not one the Regiment likes to assume!).

McNab's team was given two tasks: to locate and destroy the Iraqi communications landlines in the northern Main Supply Route (MSR), and locate and destroy mobile Scud missile launchers. They were told that the landlines were the way that Saddam was getting orders to the mobile launch teams – all other communications methods had been destroyed. Allied aircraft had done an effective job in destroying the pylons and transmitters above ground, which was ironic since it had been the Americans who had helped build them in the first place. In 1985, for example, during the Iran–Iraq war, US military specialists advised Iraq on establishing 'electronic walls' along the Iraqi–Iranian border. Later that year the Americans concluded a cooperation agreement with Iraq, part of which concerned help with communications.

If the landlines could be destroyed, so went the theory, then the Iraqi leadership would have no way of contacting its Scud launcher units. Without direct orders from Saddam himself, the commanders on the ground would not fire the missiles (initiative among junior commanders was not a feature of the Iraqi armed forces, especially since any unauthorised decision making was likely to result in the perpetrator being executed for treason).

B Squadron's logistical backup left a lot to be desired at that time. The conditions at the SAS forward operating base (FOB) were appalling. McNab's team was forced to sleep on the ground round their Land Rover vehicles because there was no shelter available (the squadron sergeant-major had been instructed to ship the squadron tents to Saudi Arabia, but had decided against it because he thought the weather would be very warm and they wouldn't be needed!). Therefore, the men were forced to use the camouflage netting on the Land Rover vehicles for cover. In addition, there were not any tables or chairs, and so the men were forced to take their meals sitting on the floor. For supposedly one of the world's premier elite units it was a sorry state of affairs.

The decision where to insert the team was left to McNab and his men. This was the subject of a 'Chinese Parliament', a practice that is peculiar to the Regiment. In such a meeting anyone is free to offer suggestions or criticise the plan of action, regardless of rank or experience. It is a recognition that ordinary troopers within the SAS often possess considerable military experience, despite their lowly regimental rank. It also relates back to David Stirling's original thinking about the SAS: that it tolerates no sense of class. The team pored over maps of the MSR they were to watch. Like most highways, it was dotted with built-up areas. There were also four airfields and pumping stations for water in the area. They picked a location where the MSR was at its narrowest, a place midway between an airfield and the town of Banidahir, roughly 30 kilometres from each. Reaching that decision was relatively easy. The next one was how to get there – this was more difficult.

There were three ways to get to the destination: by walking, in Land Rover vehicles, or by aircraft. Walking (tabbing) was discarded almost immediately. It would be impossible for each man to carry his equipment load over such a distance (each team member would be carrying over 100 kilograms of kit – a back-breaking load). Land

Rover insertion was not so lightly dismissed. There were several advantages. First, vehicles allowed a quick evacuation to be made in the event of being discovered or ambushed. Second, to travel in vehicles meant more firepower, such as General Purpose Machine-Guns (GPMGs) and M19 40mm grenade launchers mounted on the vehicles themselves could be taken into enemy territory. This would increase the firepower of the patrol significantly, as would the additional ammunition and explosives that could be carried on the vehicles.

However, there were also disadvantages to using vehicles. First, and most importantly for a covert team, two vehicles substantially increased the danger of being compromised; after all, they make more noise and are bigger than a group of men, and thus more difficult to conceal (if it is dry they can also throw up clouds of dust). Second, the vehicles would undoubtedly need to be resupplied with fuel. This would mean a Chinook helicopter flying in the replenishment, again risking the team being compromised. As they were going to stay in the location for at least a week, anything that increased the chances of being discovered was to be avoided. Third, the vehicles would have to be guarded at all times. If the team left them alone they might be discovered by the locals, who would then report them to the authorities, after which they might be booby-trapped by the enemy. To avoid this would mean at least one man staying with them at all times, thus reducing the overall effectiveness of the team.

The third method of insertion was by aircraft, specifically the RAF's Chinook helicopter. This was chosen for two reasons. First, it was the fastest way in which to get to the location. Second, the team would have had to be resupplied by helicopter anyway, so why not fly in by chopper in the first place? In his book, Ryan admits that it was a mistake to go in by helicopter. He now believes it would have been better to drive in and hide the vehicles under camouflage netting. In addition to the mobility and extra firepower that the Land Rovers would have given, the team would not have been saddled with the back-breaking loads they were forced to carry. However, the decision at the time was to leave the vehicles behind. Having agreed on the method of insertion, the members of the team now had to decide how they would knock out the Scuds and landlines. This required examining in some detail the layout of the missile and its mobile launcher. Since the Gulf War the Scud has become an almost mythical weapon, and it has been accredited fearsome capabilities. The truth, as ever, is slightly different; indeed, the Iraqi missiles should not even be called Scuds.

Scud was the NATO codename for the Soviet R-17 short-range surface-to-surface missile. The initial SS-1 Scud-A had a range of 130 kilometres, was armed with a nuclear warhead and was transported on an elevating launcher attached to the chassis of a modified Josef Stalin tank. The Scud-B and Scud-C followed, the latter having longer range and a wheeled launcher, though less accuracy than its predecessors. The Scud-A and Scud-B versions were exported to Egypt, Iraq, Libya, Syria and South Yemen. The missiles were delivered to these states with conventional warheads, though several, notably

Iraq, have been developing chemical warheads. It was this potential that made the Iraqi Scuds much feared. The missile itself is a single-stage, liquid-fuelled model, with four fins to provide stabilisation and control. These supplement the control vanes at the nozzle end of the missile. The Scud in Iraqi service is properly called the Al Husayn, and is slightly different compared with its Soviet counterparts. The first Al Husayns were constructed from cannibalised Scuds, but then the Iraqis began building their own missiles. In the so-called Project 124, Iraq began to construct the missiles, again with West German help. Under the same project, Iraq tried to build a longer-range missile, codenamed Al Abbas. Test-launched in April 1988, it was apparently in production by the time the Gulf War broke out in 1990. Because of the secrecy that surrounded much of Iraq's space and ballistic weapons programmes, intelligence could not confirm how many Al Husayns and/or Scuds the Iraqis had (this is still unknown). However, there were thought to be between 200 and 1,000 missiles, with 30 to 40 mobile launchers (American estimates before the war insisted that the Iraqis possessed only 18 launch vehicles, but this figure was quickly amended to 36 when the Gulf War broke out). The latter, called transporter-erector-launchers (TELs), travel with the missile stowed horizontally on a launcher arm that is raised to the vertical position off the rear of the vehicle for launch purposes.

McNab and his men studied the information about the missiles and their launchers carefully. It soon became obvious that the men who prepared the missile for its launch were crucial players in the scene. TELs were usually escorted by a command vehicle carrying the commander and a surveyor. In the TEL itself were the crew (two in the front and the others in the back), with the missile command position in the centre of the TEL. The surveyor is the key player, for it is he who chooses the site and targets the missile. Once a site has been chosen, it takes approximately one hour of surveying, targeting and pumping propellants before the missile can be fired.

The SAS team talked about killing the TEL's crew. If the commander, surveyor and the TEL's command centre operators were killed it would obviously stop the launch of the missile. But they could be replaced. What about calling down an air strike? In the popular imagination this is what the SAS did during the war, and to a certain extent the perception is correct. However, there were several problems with this. First, the missile might be fired before it could be hit from the air (again, contrary to popular opinion, there was not a Coalition warplane flying over every square kilometre of Iraq and Kuwait during every hour of the day during the war). Second, the Regiment had not had the time to practise ground-to-air coordination of air attacks with the Americans. A member of the Regiment later lamented: 'By mid-December 1990 we had been rehearsing for every scenario, but the demand on other units to meet their own training package meant that we had little time to work up drills with American strike aircraft.'

There was another problem with regard to air strikes: the threat of being discovered by the Iraqis. The latter had very good direction-finding (DF) equipment: a series of listening posts around the country that provided bearings on radio sources. This meant they could target McNab and his team if they used the radio to call down an air strike. In McNab's words, they decided to use air strikes only 'if the Iraqis made us an offer we couldn't refuse – say, the world's supply of Scuds in convoy'.

Interestingly, neither McNab nor other SAS men who served behind the lines in the Gulf refer to taking laser designators with them on operations. There is a very good reason for this: the Regiment hardly used them, and none of the road watch patrols had them. The designators themselves are quite bulky and can weigh up to 20 kilograms. McNab's team was already carrying over 100 kilograms per man; the last thing they needed was bulky, useless equipment.

Having earmarked air attacks to be used only in exceptional circumstances, Bravo Two Zero decided to knock the Scuds out by destroying the control centre in the middle of the TEL. In this way the missile could not be launched. The missile itself was to be left well alone. The team did not want to blow up a missile that might contain chemical, biological or nuclear material (in its mad scramble to destroy the Scuds, the Coalition high command in Riyadh appears to have paid scant regard to aircraft destroying warheads potentially filled with agents of mass destruction; presumably better western Iraq be laid waste than Israel). What about the landlines? It was thought that the buried cables ran alongside the MSR and that every 10 kilometres or so there would be inspection manholes (this was yet another intelligence gap, which is really quite amazing considering that these landlines had been built with Western assistance). The team therefore decided to make four or six cuts along the cable and pack them with explosives, each timed to detonate at different times over a period of several days. The charges would be laid in one night, using small anti-personnel mines to booby-trap the manholes. In this way it was hoped that the cable could be rendered useless over a six-day period. Personal equipment was fairly standard, though tailored to the operation in hand. Each man carried two weeks' supply of food and water, plus explosives, ammunition and NBC clothing. The patrol had four TACBEs between them. Bergens were also filled with spare batteries for the patrol radio, intravenous fluids and fluid-giving sets. A glaring omission was sleeping bags. These were left behind because the 'weather would not be too bad'. As two of the team, Sergeant Vince Phillips and Lance-Corporal Lane, later died of hypothermia during the mission, this decision was probably regretted. Nevertheless, even the best make mistakes, and weight considerations were uppermost in the men's minds. Each man also carried a basic first-aid kit containing suture kit, painkillers, rehydrate, antibiotics and scalpel blades, plus two syrettes of morphine hung around the neck. Belt kit consisted of ammunition in pouches, water, emergency food, survival kit, shell dressings, knife and prismatic compass. As ever, the team carried the communal piss can. Four of the team were armed with M16 assault rifles with 40mm grenade launchers.

Other items of equipment issued to individuals included maps, though they were unsuited to the team's needs. In fact, they were designed for aircrews, and were therefore too small and showed few details. It is standard procedure to issue each team member with an escape map, but the ones the men initially received dated back to 1928! Fortunately, at the last minute the men were issued with up-to-date ones printed on silk. Indemnity notes were given to each man; these were written in English and Arabic and promised £5,000 to anyone who handed over a United Nations serviceman to a friendly power. Along the same lines, everyone carried twenty gold sovereigns to enable them to buy their way out of trouble or to facilitate a bribe. However, such measures did not work in the Gulf, and Allied airmen and soldiers who were captured were not able to buy their freedom. One suspects that though such inducements to the locals were undoubtedly appealing, the fear of aiding the enemy kept Iraqi civilians and soldiers firmly on the side of Saddam, and in any case, as mentioned earlier, the Iraqis themselves offered rewards for information leading to the whereabouts of Allied personnel in Iraq.

The team's choice of weapons was interesting. Four of the team were armed with M16 assault rifles with 40mm M203 grenade launchers. They carried ten magazines of M16 ammunition (300 rounds), plus 200 rounds of Minimi ammunition. One weapon that was not carried by any patrol member was the SA-80 assault rifle. This small arm is held in contempt by the men of the Regiment, who consider it to be unreliable, prone to stoppages and of poor quality. The other four members of the patrol were armed with 5.56mm Minimi light machine-guns and each carried 600 rounds of ammunition for their weapon. The weapons and equipment used by the SAS are studied in more detail in a later chapter, but suffice to say here that the Minimi is a versatile light machine-gun, and a definite weight saving on the larger-calibre (7.62mm) GPMG also used by the Regiment. That said, it has a rate of fire of 700 to 1,000 rounds per minute. In any firefight, even using controlled bursts as employed by SAS soldiers, the patrol ammunition would soon be used up. This is in fact what happened to the team, and is one of the disadvantages associated with foot-mounted missions. In addition, each man also carried one 66mm M72 anti-tank weapon. They would have liked to have had more than one each, but again weight considerations and a shortage of these weapons ruled this out. Other weapons carried were grenades, including those for the M203 grenade launchers.

Interestingly, patrol members also put in a request for silenced pistols, which are exceptionally quiet and deadly at close range, though they have to be reloaded manually after a round is fired. B Squadron was out of luck because there were none left in the stores. However, these weapons were issued to members of the other SAS squadrons in the Gulf. Mention should be made of the Claymore anti-personnel mines the team carried. Because of shortages these had to be fashioned by the men themselves from plastic boxes and nuts and bolts. This is an amazing state of affairs, and reflects badly upon British logistical efforts during the Gulf conflict.

There are other glaring anomalies with regard to equipment, and they reflect poorly on the logistical backup of the Regiment itself. For example, Chris Ryan endeavoured to draw some cold-weather clothing from the stores before he left, only to be told by the squadron quartermaster sergeant that he was going to the desert and wouldn't need it as 'it won't be cold there'. In another incident before they left, Ryan relates how the patrol could not practise its contact drills because of a shortage of ammunition. Again, this is an unbelievable state of affairs.

The shortages did not only relate to ammunition. For one thing, there weren't any M203 grenades to be had anywhere. This problem was eventually solved when another member of the Regiment donated some to the patrol. Yet another problem concerned the Land Rovers. Only A and D Squadrons had the 110 version. B Squadron was issued with short-wheel based 90s, which had to be worked on to get them ready for cross-border operations. Thus the doors, tailgates, wing mirrors, windscreens and hessian tops were removed. However, such improvisation could not compensate for the lack of the proper vehicles. This obviously had a detrimental effect on the men's morale, as Chris Ryan states: 'It was pathetic trying to operate with the wrong equipment, and altogether our training was poor.'

All their plans and preparations complete, it was time to mount the mission. The first trip to the drop-off point was aborted due to the intensity of Allied air activity – there was no room in the air. This was fortuitous, for when they got back to Al Jouf the men started to strip their bergens of anything that was considered a luxury. In the words of Ryan, the weight of the bergens had reached silly proportions: 'The only way we could get them on was to sit down, settle the straps over our shoulders, and have a couple of the other guys pull us to our feet, as if they were hoisting knights on to their chargers.' Unfortunately, one of the items they discarded would be desperately needed in the days ahead: warm clothing.

The second journey to the drop-off point was uneventful enough, apart from a scare from an Iraqi Roland surface-to-air missile, which the Chinook pilot managed to avoid. When the men were on the ground, though, it was a different story. First of all they were surprised by the amount of activity there was in their area. Eventually they found a lying-up position (LUP) in a cave located near the MSR. But then they failed to establish radio contact with the SAS's forward operating base. This in itself was not a disaster, as the men could go back to the landing site at their prearranged time and rendezvous with the Chinook, and there exchange radios. However, it was a foretaste of things to come.

The first detailed reconnaissance of the area they were in revealed that Bravo Two Zero was at its correct position, but that it was also in the middle of a populated area with plantations to the north and south, and an enemy anti-aircraft battery to the north-west of its LUP. As McNab himself states: 'From a tactical point of view, we might as well have sited our LUP in the middle of Piccadilly Circus.' To increase the difficulty of this initial situation still further, more enemy troops arrived and located themselves 300 metres from the patrol's position. It was obvious to the patrol that they would have to be evacuated straight away. However, attempts to talk to

Al Jouf via the PRC319 radio came to nothing. In fact, the team had been given the wrong frequencies – an amazing blunder that was to cost the lives of three of the patrol.

The first day of monitoring the MSR brought disaster: they were discovered by a boy tending a herd of goats. The patrol members tried to make it to the sanctuary of the Syrian border. In a series of desperate firefights and contacts with the enemy the SAS team used up all its ammunition. Nevertheless, the men acquitted themselves well, and the surviving team members estimated that they killed over 250 enemy soldiers in the firefights during their flight. When it is considered that the Iraqis deployed armoured personnel carriers against the SAS team, this is a phenomenal casualty rate, and also a superb testament to the weapons training of the Regiment.

Ryan's words about the battles with the Iraqis separates the reality from the myth regarding SAS men, and are worth repeating here: 'If anyone says he's not frightened in a firefight, I don't believe him. I was shit-scared, and so was everyone else. I know the SAS has a high reputation, but the guys are not superhuman: they may have enormous courage, but they are subject to the same fear as anyone else. The Regiment's strength lies in the fact that its members are highly trained to control their fear and respond positively to whatever threat they are facing.'

The tab to the border involved crossing 120 kilometres of harsh terrain, which was made all the worse by the freezing weather. All efforts to raise assistance via the TACBEs failed – the men were on their own. By this time the whole of the area was alerted to their presence, and soldiers and civilians eagerly hunted for the Western troops. The immediate concern of the team, though, was the weather. The rain, sleet and snow that lashed them was severely reducing their chances of survival. Dehydration and hypothermia became greater enemies than the Iraqi troops.

As the team scrambled west the inevitable happened: the group was separated. One man, Sergeant Vince Phillips, died of hypothermia and general exhaustion in the snow-lashed hills; another was captured, while a third, Corporal Chris Ryan, embarked on an epic lone journey that took him to Syria. He eventually walked more than 300 kilometres during the course of his escape and evasion. His description of his flight is certainly gripping, but it is also indicative of the mental and physical toughness of SAS soldiers.

By the third night on the run from his pursuers, for example, he was physically exhausted and alone. The next dawn he managed to find a hiding-place among some rocks, giving him an opportunity to examine his feet. He discovered that his blisters had burns, the skin was raw and bleeding, and his toenails were lifting. At this stage it had been five days since he had eaten a proper meal. Three days later, and after drinking poisoned water, Ryan's teeth were loose, his gums were bleeding, his feet and hands were cut to ribbons and smelt due to infection. Nevertheless, he continued with his journey and reached Syria after seven nights and eight days.

He had eaten nothing aside from two small packets of

biscuits, as well as having virtually nothing to drink. The effects on his body were brutal, including a severe loss of weight. It was two weeks before he could walk properly again, six weeks before sensation returned to his fingers and toes, and he had a severe blood disorder and liver problems due to drinking water from a source near a uranium-processing plant.

The other five initially fared better. They managed to reach the Iraqi town of Al Qaim, which was near the Syrian border, but then their luck began to run out. Their presence was discovered by the Iraqis, who gave chase. Throughout the confusion the SAS men were separated again, this time into one group of three and one of two. The enemy began to close in. To make matters worse, the men by this stage had used up all their ammunition and had thrown away their weapons. Members of the Regiment are trained in the use of foreign weapons. In theory this means they can use the enemy's firearms when conducting missions behind the lines. However, such a scenario is more pertinent to a counter-insurgency operation, i.e. a long-term mission behind the lines. McNab and his men wanted to get away from their pursuers as fast as possible.

Trooper Robert Consiglio was killed at this time, and McNab and his companion were captured soon afterwards. The two remaining members of the patrol managed to evade the Iraqis for a short while longer, but Lance-Corporal 'Legs' Lane was in a desperate state and died of hypothermia, and his companion was captured. The military exploits of Bravo Two Zero had ended.

Capture brought fresh perils for those who had been

caught. Initially all went well for the SAS soldiers, who were separated for interrogation. The Iraqis asked each man for the 'Big Four': name, rank, serial number and date of birth. As this is permissible under the Geneva Convention the men gave them. But the Iraqis wanted to know a lot more. An interpreter asked McNab what religion he was – he told them he was Church of England. However, they wanted him to admit he was Jewish; the interrogators were particularly keen to link them all with Israel. When McNab and his men started to say the things the Iraqis did not want to hear, they were beaten severely.

The SAS men tried to deceive the Iraqis, such as telling them they were from a search and rescue unit, but that only resulted in more beatings. Humiliations and more beatings followed, and McNab was subject to a mock execution as the Iraqis tried to make him confess to being an Israeli commando. If he had done so, then he would have undoubtedly been paraded on Iraqi television, where he would have been forced to repeat his 'confession'. Some of the Iraqi questions bordered on the sheer ludicrous. For example, the interrogators repeatedly insisted that McNab was Jewish. In a final effort to persuade his tormentors he was not, he informed them that he was uncircumcised, and proceeded to show them that this was so, causing much hilarity among his captors.

The relief was not to last long, for soon there were more beatings and vicious interrogation sessions for all of them. When they were finally released after more than a month of brutality, they were all very ill. One of the patrol members had a serious foot wound, but throughout his captivity had received no treatment for it. As a result his foot swelled to the size of a marrow, though this did not stop the guards giving him further beatings, mainly concentrated on his bad foot. The amazing thing is that the members of the patrol who were captured survived their ordeal. This was undoubtedly due to their physical fitness, allied to their mental strength. What comes across most strongly when reading McNab's book is that he kept his mind working even during the beatings, trying to think of ways to appease his interrogators and spin out time without actually providing any information. At the end of the day the Iraqis, for all their brutality, failed to get the SAS soldiers to say what they wanted them to say.

Ultimately those who had been captured were returned by the Iraqis after the cessation of hostilities. For those who had survived, plus Chris Ryan who had made it back on his own, the subsequent months were difficult. Each man was filled with different emotions as he tried to get back to 'normal' following his ordeal. For some, such as Chris Ryan, there were feelings of guilt. Recovering from trauma takes time, even for elite soldiers, and can put an immense strain on individuals and their families. Even SAS soldiers suffer from post-traumatic stress.

As an interesting footnote: when Chris Ryan returned to Al Jouf he discovered that B Squadron had been provided with tents and that the organisation side of things was much better. It was a shame that it could not have been so when the team set off. The failure of the patrol led to a lot of questions being asked at Stirling

Lines after the war had ended, questions concerning the Regiment's operating procedures and its logistics set up. Though there had been shortages of equipment and ammunition, the general consensus among patrol members themselves was that these things had not contributed to Bravo Two Zero's ultimate failure.

Far more serious had been the inadequate maps and the lack of intelligence concerning the nature of the terrain into which they were being inserted (the men were expecting to be landed into sandy terrain into which they could dig to build observation posts – not a rocky landscape). By way of a cruel irony, the accurate intelligence the patrol did receive was useless to them. For example, the men demanded to see satellite imagery of the area. At first there were none to be had, but persistent requests and demands eventually succeeded in some arriving. However, they were of extremely poor quality, and appeared to show that the operational area was very flat and open. This made the team quite happy because it confirmed the wisdom of leaving the Land Rovers behind (in flat terrain anything large, such as vehicles, can be seen for great distances, to say nothing of the dust clouds they would kick up). Unfortunately, the men's interpretation was completely wrong. What they had failed to realise, due to lack of tuition as to how to interpret satellite imagery, was that they were reading the transparencies upside down.

In addition, the TACBEs were revealed to be seriously deficient, and therefore should not have been relied upon to provide backup communications. The fact that the patrol had been given the wrong radio frequencies was a mistake, but it did illustrate the need to tighten up mission planning in general. If there were lessons to learn, there were also reasons for the SAS as a whole to be pleased with its procedures. Once again, the weapons training given to SAS soldiers had shown itself to be highly effective. The casualties suffered by the enemy during contacts with a small number of men illustrated that the Regiment's contact drills are just right (notwithstanding that the team members had inadequate ammunition to practise them at base before they were inserted). In addition, the Regiment's escape and evasion drills, as used by Chris Ryan on his epic journey, proved themselves to be spot on.

Perhaps what the mission illustrated above all is that, at the end of the day, SAS soldiers are only human like everyone else. They may be highly trained, but they can also make simple mistakes. For example, Chris Ryan decided not to take water-purification tablets with him, believing that he would be drinking from jerrycans. He knew that the team would not be taking water from wells for fear of them being poisoned. What he didn't realise was that he would be drinking from the Euphrates during his flight. In hindsight it appears a glaring omission, but we are all wiser with the benefit of hindsight.

Although the mission was ultimately a failure, it has left a lasting testimony to the physical and mental standards of members of the Regiment. Their ordeal has naturally left scars, notably the antipathy the patrol members felt towards their captors. McNab summed up the consensus of opinion when he said that if he met his captors in the street and thought he could get away with it, he would 'slot them'. Whatever the rights and wrongs of such a stance, he and the other members of the patrol can take pride in the fact that their conduct was a credit to the SAS.

CHAPTER TWELVE

Fighting Patrols

The failure of the road watch patrols and the continuing Iraqi Scud launches from western Iraq into Israel forced the SAS to rethink how it would deal with the Scuds. More effort would be put into sending vehicle-borne fighting columns into western Iraq to destroy Scud convoys and the communications links that sent them their orders.

Whereas B Squadron had undertaken the road watches, it was the turn of A and D Squadrons to mount the mobile columns. The Regiment gathered together its vehicles at its forward base at Al Jouf and assembled its columns. Each one would consist of approximately twelve Land-Rover vehicles plus motorcycle outriders. The vehicles, in true SAS tradition, were heavily armed. The Land Rovers bristled with General Purpose Machine-Guns (GPMGs), 40mm M19 grenade launchers, Milan anti-tank weapons and Stinger surface-to-air missiles (SAMs). In addition, most of the weapons had thermal-imaging night sights (passive infra-red sensors that convert detected heat into video images – used mainly for night work), and the drivers wore night-vision goggles.

There were four columns in all: two from A Squadron and two from D Squadron. Contrary to popular opinion, the SAS was not free to roam wherever it wanted. General Norman Schwarzkopf's SOCCENT had conferred with the Joint Special Operations Command and Washington to divide western Iraq into three areas. Colonel Massey and his SAS soldiers were to patrol the southern 'box', which straddled the Amman–Baghdad highway. The other two areas lay along the Syrian border, one being located near the town of Shab al Hiri, while the other lay near the town of Al Qaim, farther north-east. Clearing these two boxes would be the responsibility of the Americans, specifically the elite Delta Force. For this purpose a base was established at Ar Ar, located in northern Saudi Arabia some 50 kilometres from the Iraqi border. From there Delta Force could launch operations against the two northern boxes. After the disappointment of the cancellation of its hostage-rescue mission, Delta Force was delighted to have been given another task. It was also an opportunity to improve the unit's somewhat tarnished image among the special forces brotherhood.

In the first few days of the war the Coalition believed that the majority of the Scuds being fired against Israel were from Iraqi bases numbered H1, H2 and H3. The Coalition had targeted these bases from the beginning of the air war. For example, H2 and H3 were hit by US Air Force aircraft on the night of 16/17 January, and on the next night it was the turn of US Navy jets. Nevertheless, the Israelis were not satisfied. To the horror of the Coalition, they were planning their own strikes. They would hit the area with their own jets, they informed the

Americans, and would land their own troops in the area to hunt the Scuds. Frantic messages went to Israel from the Americans: we are doing all we can to destroy the Scuds, please do not use your own forces. For the moment, at least, the Israelis were appeased. But how long would their restraint last?

In Riyadh it was realised that speed was critical. Therefore, the first SAS mobile columns started on 20 January. But they were not just hunting Scuds. Iraq had deployed hundreds of artillery pieces and multiple-launch rocket systems capable of firing chemical warheads. They had a range of 30 to 40 kilometres, which meant they could hit Allied units in Saudi Arabia. And the Iraqis were quite capable of using them. During the war with Iran, for example, Iraqi units had fired many chemical artillery shells during the 1988 offensive in the Fao peninsula. The SAS teams were ordered to knock out the battlefield chemical weapons delivery systems, as and when they found them.

The first day, 20 January, was uneventful, partly because the SAS limited its incursion into enemy territory to 40 kilometres into Iraq. This was because the Israelis had threatened to invade the area, and no one in the Regiment wanted to be killed by Israeli jets. When the invasion failed to materialise, the SAS columns pressed deeper into Iraq. The urgency of the mission had been increased: on 22 January a Scud hit Tel Aviv, killing three civilians. The next day yet another was launched at Israel, though fortunately it fell into an uninhabited area. These launches did nothing to appease the Israelis, who were itching to send in their own forces.

In desperation, Lieutenant General Charles Horner and Brigadier General 'Buster' Glosson, chief targeter and commander of all US Air Force wings in the Gulf, hatched a plan for all the combat aircraft available to the Allies – some 2,000 warplanes – to be diverted to western Iraq. In a three-day campaign, the UN aircraft would completely flatten the area, particularly around Al Qaim, Rutba and other population centres. The enemy targets that faced destruction included police stations, service areas, and anything else that could support Scud operations. Also, bombers would sow mines on all the roads and destroy more than sixty underpasses (these were favourite Scud hiding places). The plan was presented to Schwarzkopf, who rejected it for two reasons. First, it would result in the deaths of many civilians; and second, it would not shorten the war.

Back on the ground in Iraq, the SAS initially had mixed fortunes. Its columns had not seen any Scud launchers for three days, and the men were becoming frustrated, especially since another missile had been launched against Israel on 23 January (though it caused no casualties). However, on 23 January the Regiment had a stroke of luck. One of A Squadron's columns was operating between Nukhayb and Karbala, south-west of Baghdad, when the men ran into a group of four Iraqis driving across the desert. In a brief firefight three of the Iraqis were killed. The fourth was captured and interrogated. Being highly relieved that he was not going to be killed by the SAS soldiers, he began to impart some valuable information. This took the form of a map he was carrying, which detailed the positions of a previously unseen enemy brigade in western Iraq. The SAS soldiers immediately relayed this information to the Tactical Air Co-ordination Centre, and within a few hours the brigade was being pounded by Coalition aircraft.

On 24 January the SAS began to push ever deeper into the 'Scud box'. The soldiers began to encounter the enemy more often, and there were frequent violent contacts. Whenever possible, SAS attacks were launched against the enemy at night. A Squadron itself suddenly became very busy: 'We had spotted the launcher two days earlier and had followed it, travelling at night over rough terrain until we had caught up with it and managed to plant explosives on it. The blast shattered the night's silence and sent a mushroom of flame high into the sky as our charges detonated, crippling the target and giving us the signal to kick off at anything that moved around the site.'

In the cold light of day the men discovered that it was not a Scud but a FROG surface-to-surface unguided artillery rocket. The two systems look very similar: the FROG has a cylindrical body, a conical nose and four large control fins. Ominously, Soviet FROGs were usually armed with nuclear warheads, but they could also be armed with chemical warheads. No one knew what the Iraqi warheads contained, but the worst scenario was feared. From their lying-up position (LUP), the SAS soldiers recognised the smaller rocket on its launcher, but no matter – they would destroy it: 'Scud or FROG, it had the capability to hit Allied targets and that was all that mattered to us.'

The SAS teams had been fully briefed as to the threat

of Iraqi chemical weapons, but they had to take a chance and knock the missile out, chemical warhead or not. This contrasts sharply with 'Bravo Two Zero', which specifically avoided damaging enemy missile warheads through fear of their contents. The FROGs could not hit Israel (they were battlefield weapons), but they could inflict damage on Allied units waiting for the ground offensive in Saudi Arabia.

A lot has been written about the Iraqi chemical threat, but how great was it? As far as is known (and even today no one knows for sure), Iraq possessed, and possesses still, all the main military chemical agents. These include blood agents, such as hydrogen cyanide, which disrupt the ability of the blood to absorb oxygen; blister agents, such as mustard, which cause skin burns and inflammation of the mucous membranes; and nerve agents, such as sarin, which disrupt the central nervous system and thus vital involuntary muscular activities, like circulation and respiration. With hindsight we know that the Iraqi commanders on the ground had no intention of using chemical weapons, but this was not known at the time by the Coalition High Command in Riyadh or the SAS in Iraq.

Despite the fact that they had immobilised the launcher with charges, the SAS soldiers from A Squadron stayed where they were. 'Nothing was said when the explosion erupted; it's not like in the movies where the good guys all stand around cheering.' Like many contacts between the Iraqis and the SAS, the special forces soldiers were often forced to fight off Iraqi attacks. So it was this time. But, as on so many occasions, bluff and audacity saved the day: 'Depending on the professionalism of the ragheads, they may have spotted us and mounted an anti-ambush operation, so we stayed low and quiet until it was clear what was happening and that our position had not been compromised in any way. Almost a minute later several trucks appeared from the rear of the site, all full of ragheads as they abandoned their position and tried to leg it.'

The one thing that is inadvisable when confronting the SAS is to present yourself as a target. Special forces troops have above-average weapons skills, and usually hit what they aim at: 'They were about 300 metres away and without delay we cracked off a couple of 66s [M72 66mm anti-tank weapons].' What the SAS soldiers had not realised was that there were several enemy trucks and armoured personnel carriers that lay undiscovered. They were about 100 metres from the FROG launcher, and had not been spotted by the team that had crept forward in the darkness to lay the charges. They now appeared, and around 150 Iraqi soldiers faced an eight-man SAS team. However, cool professionalism took over, and the SAS soldiers followed their drills exactly. First priority was to disable the first and last truck in the convoy: 'We banjoed the front and rear vehicles at the same time, but they had at least three armoured personnel carriers and they quickly opened up on us. The thud of their heavy calibre weapons seemed to get louder, probably because the rounds were ripping into the ground just in front of us. We knew we were on to a hiding, but the ragheads must have thought we were a much bigger unit. To our surprise they just raced away as quick as they could.'

The firefight had been fierce but short-lived – probably just a couple of minutes – and all that was left were two smouldering trucks. The SAS soldiers wasted no time. They left their LUP and sought their vehicles. Then they were away. As was standard operating procedure (SOP), they wanted to put as much space between themselves and the enemy as possible: 'It was essential to move fast. As far as we were concerned the Iraqi rank and file were a bunch of thick ragheads, but many of their officers had trained in the West, even at Sandhurst, prior to and during the Iran–Iraq War. They were aware of British tactics, and while we didn't think they had the balls, there was a possibility that they could turn around and ambush us during the day. If that happened we could have been well and truly fucked.' Fortunately the Iraqis did not pursue them, and the men were able to make good their escape.

As January came to an end, the Regiment had more success. A fighting column spotted two Scud convoys and ordered in an air strike. The Americans obliged, and several F-15E Eagles from the US Air Force's 336th Tactical Fighter Squadron totally destroyed the convoys. In addition, the SAS spotted a Scud launch site: once again the 336th TFS rendered it useless. The Coalition special forces were beginning to gain the upper hand, and the scales were tipped further in their favour by the arrival of Delta Force's 1st Squadron at King Fahd International Airport on 1 February 1991. The American elite unit was then rushed north to Ar Ar, from where it would be sent into the northern 'Scud box' to hunt for the Iraqi missiles.

The man responsible for Delta Force's operations,

Major General Wayne Downing, head of the US Joint Special Operations Command at Fort Bragg, went to see the SAS commander in Riyadh, Colonel Massey, about Delta Force's operations. Massey briefed Downing about the difficulties his men would face in Iraq. In particular, he warned him about the Bedouin, who would undoubtedly report the presence of any teams to the Iraqis. Nevertheless, Downing was confident his men could perform just as well as the SAS (to get these men into Iraq, Delta Force had the services of Task Force 160, a helicopter unit that flew Sikorsky CH-53 Sea Stallion, Boeing Vertol CH-47 Chinook, and Sikorsky UH-60 Black Hawk helicopters in a number of special operations variants).

When Delta Force was in the theatre, Massey's words proved to be true. Near Al Qaim there were many Bedouin, and they reported the American presence to the Iraqis. Very soon the American elite troops found themselves under attack. In early February, for example, nine Iraqi armoured vehicles pursued a Delta Force patrol across the desert. The special forces were on foot and would have been mown down were it not for the fact that an F-15 Eagle appeared and scattered the enemy. Then US helicopters managed to pick the men up. Two days later, another Delta Force team was chased by Iraqi helicopters, being saved only by the appearance of another Eagle, which destroyed one helicopter and chased off the rest.

Though Delta Force had a tough time of it, its missions in Iraq made a valuable contribution towards the Scud hunt, as well as repairing Delta Force's reputation. So pleased was Schwarzkopf with Delta Force's performance that he allowed another Delta Force squadron and an Army Ranger company to be deployed to Ar Ar. This meant the number of men operating in Iraq could be increased, and there were eventually more than 200 US elite troops in Mesopotamia. Though the number of confirmed Scud kills was small, Delta Force's efforts did limit the launcher teams' endeavours. With the aid of Eagles, Delta sowed hundreds of Gator mines on roads, underpasses and other suspected concealment sites. In this way the Scud launchers were forced into areas that could be more easily watched. But what of the SAS? By the end of January the Regiment's activities had provoked a vigorous Iraqi response. On 29 January, for example, the Iraqis attacked an SAS column, damaging two of the latter's vehicles beyond repair, although losing ten men and three of their own vehicles in the process. One SAS soldier was also badly wounded, but was evacuated to Saudi Arabia and survived the war. From 30 January to 3 February the SAS was extremely active in 'Scud Alley'. On the latter date an SAS team from 1 and 17 Troops ordered an air strike on a Scud convoy. This preceded a prolonged contact, when it was realised that the aircraft had destroyed only one of the launchers. The SAS attacked the rest with their vehicle-mounted Milans, scoring a direct hit on a Scud missile and its launcher. However, the Iraqis counter-attacked and drove off the SAS, though not before the latter had ordered a further air attack that destroyed almost all the convoy.

Most of the SAS patrols that were operating in western Iraq at this time were vehicle-mounted. However, some patrols were sent in on foot, as a member of D Squadron relates:

> We had clocked up four patrols into Iraq and the squadron had bagged about a dozen targets, but there was no time to relax. The pressure was increasing from Riyadh for more success, and just as soon as we had been debriefed and resupplied we were back on the road. Some of the mobile teams had already chalked up their Scud scores by painting silhouettes of the launchers on the wings of their Land Rovers.
>
> US intelligence had monitored recent launcher activity in our sector, and after just twelve hours back inside Saudi we were preparing to attend another operational briefing, at which the Americans would outline full details of the potential targets they had tracked. We were to fly into Iraq and check out two areas identified by the US Air Force as Iraqi operational sites and eliminate both by means of the explosives we would be carrying, or by calling down air strikes. The briefing was followed by an Orders Group (O Group), which was headed by our boss [troop commander] and the squadron commander. The mission was simple: find the two launchers and mallet them by whatever means possible and then fuck off out of the area as quickly as possible.

The sector was believed to be alive with Republican Guard units transitting through the region en route to reinforce Iraqi forces in and around Kuwait.

> After a night's sleep we packed our bergens and prepared our kits for another move into the field. For the trip we made sure we all carried tubes of ant-killer. The little bastards had earlier bitten us to bits, and came close to being more of a threat than the Scuds. I always shit myself when it comes to helicopter insertion – the actual point of drop-off is always the most dangerous, and you always think you're going to get bumped – but this time we were OK.
>
> Using the nearest main supply route (MSR), which as I recall was to our right, as our key reference point, we tabbed out of the area to a new location. Here we were able to put in an OP on the road while resting up for the next move. Moving across such open terrain was made easier due to GPS [global positioning system].

As ever, the weather and terrain had a debilitating effect on the men: 'At dawn I remember seeing several jets flying low overhead, probably on a photo-reconnaissance of the area to examine the damage we had inflicted the night before. At this point we had been in the field for just four days, and to be honest we were knackered. It was a cold morning. The sky was overcast, and I remember being surprised to see aircraft flying in such weather.'

Contrary to popular opinion, the desert is not always scorching hot. In fact, western Iraq in early 1991 was particularly cold: 'What really bothered us was the drop in temperature; it was so cold I had a bet with a mate over whether it would rain or snow.'

One of the most important aspects of operating behind enemy lines is resupply. Food and ammunition can be quickly used up by elite teams, and without proper logistical support a mission can be fatally compromised: 'Sleep and food are the most important things, and we had had little of either. We had cached a lot of our food on day two. This is SOP when you are operating in such a big area and need a reserve of stores at a later date. It also allows the team to cover more ground without carrying so much weight.'

A cache is also useful if the team is bumped by the enemy, because everyone is aware of where it is. While evading the enemy, team members know where there is a source of supply: 'The first thing to go off your back in a contact is your bergen, leaving you with minor supplies in your belt. Thus the cache is very important, although if you run with no GPS to locate the area you're probably fucked anyway.'

SAS field rations are basic. Liberal quantities of chocolate ('the best buzz food') are always carried to provide instant energy. The soldiers themselves also carry 'hexy blocks' – small, white tablets of hexamine fuel that burn well but without smell. However, they can only be used in daylight (the flames can be seen at night), and during the day they are dug into the ground to avoid any chance of being spotted. These tiny fires are ideal for cooking food and boiling water, and instead of the square standard-issue mess tins, the majority of SAS soldiers carry old '44-issue water bottles, which have a metal mug fitted to their base. The mugs are used to boil water, with a tin of food being boiled inside the mug.

The can is then pierced and the food eaten, with tea or coffee added to the remaining water for a hot brew. Masking tape is usually secured around the top edge of the mug to prevent lips being burnt. In addition, the hot water can be poured directly into boil-in-the-bag rations. A second mug of water may also be used to make a curry, though this depends on the area in which the patrol is operating, for smell can easily compromise a team. Often, though, because the men are too near the enemy, food will be eaten cold.

Despite the Coalition air activity, the Iraqis were often very careless and sloppy. An SAS foot patrol from D Squadron came across a Scud convoy in early February: 'We had just been on the comms net arranging a resupply for the following morning to bring in more ammunition and food when we heard the distinctive sound of a convoy nearby, but nobody could see anything. We were desperate for ammunition, particularly 66mm LAWs, and our immediate thoughts were that we would have to abandon our position.'

The team was well camouflaged ('out of sight among the rocky scrapes we had made') and its members just sat and watched. The Iraqis came into sight late in the afternoon. It was a sizeable target in the form of 'a column of about twenty-five vehicles in all, including two Scud launchers. In the main they were BMPs [Soviet-built infantry fighting vehicles] and BRDMs [Soviet-built armoured reconnaissance patrol vehicles], and they had all pulled into the side of the MSR.'

The SAS soldiers could not believe their luck: 'It appeared that one of the Scud launchers had broken down. Several mechanics or fitters were trying to sort out the problem while the vehicle crews stood smoking beside the road. As we monitored the situation through our scopes we couldn't believe what we were seeing.' The Iraqis made no attempt to pull any camouflage netting over their vehicles, they just parked them up on the side of the road in the open. They were a sitting duck. And yet the SAS team could do little by itself: 'Any question of mounting an attack was a non-starter. We were short of ammunition and would stand little chance against such a heavily armed unit. This was an opportunity for Uncle Sam to earn some brownie points and blitz the convoy.'

One of the reasons the SAS is so successful is that its members can realistically appraise a situation: 'If we tried to take them on, it could have been "game over" for us, and the prospect of being taken prisoner did not appeal to any of us, for the simple reason that we knew the Iraqis would ignore the Geneva Convention when it came to special forces.' (The Geneva Convention regarding the treatment of prisoners of war makes provision for the humane treatment of captured service personnel. The convention gives prisoners certain rights, such as to be kept in a place of safety, to be given medical care when necessary, and to have access to food and water. A prisoner is also allowed to keep items of sentimental value, and is entitled to a receipt for any other personal items, such as money, that are taken from him; prisoners are also allowed to write letters. All these provisions were blatantly ignored by the Iraqis.)

One SAS soldier was particularly succinct when it came to the prospect of surrender: 'All we were required to give was the "Big Four" – name, rank, number and age – but the moment they put a scalpel near my bollocks I feared I might start singing like a canary, and that was one of the main reasons that we were only told what we needed to know.'

As the Scud convoy was making no apparent moves to go anywhere, the SAS team radioed for an air attack. For some of the men this was the first time they would witness a combat air-patrol strike up close: 'I had only ever seen one from a distance in the past, during training in Scotland, but the attack would take place less than 500 metres from our position.'

The message was passed back to the SAS's forward base, then to American AWACS aircraft, who passed the targeting details on to the Eagles loitering over western Iraq. By this stage of the war the F-15Es were armed with GBU-12 laser-guided bombs, which were deadly effective, and recent research has shown that the Coalition's 'smart' munitions in the war had a 90 per cent success rate against enemy targets.

> An hour or so before last light an F-15E screamed over the target area, pulling high into the grey sky as it passed the convoy. I thought the pilot had taken a flypast as I couldn't see or hear anything – then there was a ball of flame and a thud as the high explosives detonated. It was strange to see it all unfold, it was just like being at the movies. Everything seemed to happen in slow motion. A second F-15 joined the attack, and as it swooped down to hit the convoy the Iraqis opened up with an anti-aircraft gun, but their

> efforts were wasted. After a third strike the whole convoy was decimated, and flames flickered from all the vehicles and smoke billowed into the darkening sky. Their war was over. Nothing moved – we presumed all the Iraqis had been either killed or wounded.

The other SAS columns were also experiencing good hunting in the desert. On 5 February, for example, A Squadron's Group 2 spotted a Scud convoy of two launchers and four escort vehicles, and immediately called down an air attack. The column later fought a gun battle with a force of Iraqis defending an observation tower, killing ten of the enemy with no losses. Three days later D Squadron called down an air attack on an Iraqi 'Flat Face' radar installation. On the same day a team from A Squadron destroyed a microwave communications tower, then had a 40-minute firefight with Iraqi troops before escaping into the wide expanse.

The worst encounter for the SAS occurred on 9 February, when a small patrol from A Squadron probed an enemy communications centre near Nukhayb. In a heavy firefight the SAS force was beaten off, though not before the patrol leader, a sergeant-major, was badly wounded. He had to be left by the other two and was captured. However, he survived the war and was awarded the Military Cross for his bravery.

The majority of SAS attacks upon Scud convoys were conducted at fairly long ranges – the teams did not want to get too close to an enemy who invariably outnumbered them. The preferred method of destroying the Scud convoys was by calling down an air attack, although if this was not available then the SAS Land Rovers would attempt it themselves. Typically, the attacks were conducted using vehicle-mounted Milan anti-tank missiles. The following is an account of one such attack: 'When we were within 600 metres we could identify the target ... The next moment several Milan missiles streaked across the desert and slammed into the enemy vehicles. A fireball engulfed the Iraqis as explosives combined with fuel to form a lethal cocktail.'

Such encounters, and the frequent firefights that erupted afterwards with pursuing Iraqis, naturally sapped ammunition and fuel supplies. The Regiment had to find a way to replenish those supplies. To service the vehicle teams, the SAS organised supply columns to drive into Iraq and liaise with its teams in the country. These columns consisted of ten four-ton trucks manned by SAS soldiers and Royal Electrical and Mechanical Engineers (REME) personnel. Six armed Land Rovers from B Squadron made up the escort, and the supply column was named E Squadron. It crossed the border on 12 February and met with the Land Rovers from A and D Squadrons 145 kilometres inside Iraq. By 17 February it had returned, though not before it had spotted an enemy observation post and had used a laser rangefinder to direct an air attack upon it – this was the first and only time the SAS used a laser designator in the Gulf War. The teams inserted by helicopter for foot operations inside Iraq were also extracted and supplied by helicopter. The conditions were often far from ideal, though:

> Ammunition, water, and radio batteries were quickly divided up and the sandbags tied. The weather was getting worse and our big fear was that we were going to tab a fair distance and then discover that the cab [helicopter] couldn't land. As we pulled on our bergens it started to piss down – terrific! There is nothing quite like rain and a strong wind to sap your strength. We had moved off on a bearing and had to use the GPS constantly due to the fact that we could not see a thing. After four hours it had stopped raining, leaving us with damp clothes, which had to dry out while we were wearing them.

To minimise the risk of compromise, all insertions and extractions were carried out at night where possible: 'We were to be picked up between 03.00 and 04.00 hours. The pilots would be flying at low level wearing night-vision goggles and with all lights off, requiring maximum skill to avoid unmapped obstacles in their way, such as pylons.'

To a team waiting on the ground, cold and wet and with the enemy all around, there is nothing quite like the sound of an incoming friendly chopper:

> We heard the 'clap clap' of the Chinook's twin rotors as it came in to land. No one said anything, but I think we all wished we could turn the noise down to avoid alerting anyone in the vicinity of our presence. We had a small strobe which could be held in the hand, and which transmitted a tiny but powerful flashing light. It

> was ideal in places like South Armagh, where there are plenty of hills, but in the flat Iraqi desert we were worried that the light might be seen. On each side of the strobe, two of us held torches with red filters. As soon as the aircraft came in a crewman flashed a green light from the right-hand door and we put our lights out. We raced to the crewman's door and grabbed the ammunition from him, as well as other stores all packed in sandbags. This is SOP, as the sandbags can be useful to a patrol and don't become just rubbish. The crewman wanted to know if we were OK. We gave him the thumbs-up, then we threw in a bag of rubbish from our early morning scoff, as well as the bulging shit bag. We knew someone would have to check the bags before they were thrown away and were they in for a shock! Ammunition, water and radio batteries were quickly divided up and the sandbags tied to the bergens. The most welcome was the fresh rats [rations] – the lads had sent out loads of sandwiches and fresh fruit, which we would trough later.

Resupplied, the SAS continued to enjoy success against the enemy. On 18 February, for example, a D Squadron patrol discovered a Scud convoy and called down an air attack to wipe it out. The next day another SAS-directed air attack hit a second convoy. However, tragedy struck on 21 February when a running battle developed between a group of Iraqis and one of A Squadron's fighting columns. As the SAS vehicles were pulling back, Lance-

Corporal David Denbury was shot and fatally wounded. Nevertheless, the SAS was making a valuable contribution to the battle against the Scuds.

What about the Americans? Delta Force had been concentrating its efforts on several hundred square kilometres of enemy territory around H2 and H3. Typically, the US elite teams would consist of between twenty and forty commandos, who would mount patrols of between ten and fifteen days in length. Their mission was primarily one of surveillance: watching for any military traffic and calling down air attacks. The results were excellent: by late February US intelligence had concluded that the Scud launchers had been pushed into a small area 16 kilometres in diameter around Al Qaim.

Farther east, the Americans had less success in their hunt for Scuds. A number of Green Beret teams were sent into enemy territory to hunt for the missiles. In early February, three were inserted near the town of As Salman. However, two were compromised and extracted almost immediately, while the third spent thirty hours in hostile terrain but failed to spot any launchers. The Green Beret A Teams were very similar to their SAS counterparts.

The A Team itself usually consisted of six to ten men, and had a skills blend of engineers, communications specialists and medics. In addition, as in the SAS, each man was a crack shot. During their surveillance missions the men lived in the ground in 'hides'. They covered the frames for their holes with hessian, which was then camouflaged. Human waste was bottled and bagged, and like the SAS the men carried bergens filled with loads weighing up to 100 kilograms. Although the Green Berets carried out valuable deep reconnaissance behind enemy lines just prior to the Coalition ground offensive, success eluded them in the great Scud hunt. The laurels belonged to the SAS and Delta Force; Major General Downing telephoned Colonel Massey at the end of February and they congratulated themselves for 'establishing Anglo-American dominion over western Mesopotamia'.

It was true that the SAS had not completely stopped the launch of Scud missiles from western Iraq against Israel, but it had made a major contribution in cutting them down severely. From an average of five launches per day during the first week of the war, the figure then fell to less than one launch per day. With the SAS fighting teams on the ground and the US Air Force in the air flying 75 to 150 anti-Scud sorties per day, the Iraqis found it almost impossible to set up and fire their surface-to-surface missiles. Above all, it had been the British special forces soldiers on the ground who made the biggest contribution to the anti-Scud war. The men who wore the Winged Dagger had once again proved that they were second to none.

CHAPTER THIRTEEN

Weapons and Equipment

As an elite special forces unit, the SAS fields an impressive armoury of weaponry and combat kit. It benefits from its own budget for research, development and purchasing of any kit it needs to do its job. As the Regiment is considered to be permanently 'on operations' its requests for funding go to the front of the queue when Ministry of Defence budget scrutineers are dishing out the dosh.

Small Arms

M16

Early versions of the M16 were first used by the SAS in the 1960s in Aden, Borneo and Oman, and were initially unpopular because of the weapon's tendency to jam in sandy and dusty conditions. The SAS was attracted to the American weapon because of its lightness; it was a full kilogram lighter than the L1A1 SLR (self loading rifle), and the 5.56mm ammunition weighed only half that of the NATO 7.62mm rounds. Its fully automatic capability was also an attraction for SAS troopers caught in a close-quarters firefight.

By the mid-1980s, the bugs on the M16 were finally sorted out and the M16A2 version was being used in large quantities by the SAS. It had only a three-burst rather than full auto capability, but this was found to be good for fire discipline and ammunition conservation. The attachment of an M203 grenade launcher under the forward stock also provided SAS troopers with a tremendous increase in firepower and few of them would go into action without one. In Northern Ireland, the Gulf and Bosnia, the M16A2 was the SAS's weapon of choice.

Heckler & Koch MP5 Family

Immortalised by the SAS in the 1980 Iranian Embassy rescue operation, the MP5 family of weapons has become synonymous with the Regiment. The German-made 9mm machine pistol became an instant hit with the SAS because of its close-bolt action. Unlike on many pre-1970s sub-machine-guns, such as the Sten and Sterling, the MP5's working parts are positioned forward when the firer first pulls the trigger. This releases the firing pin to strike the already chambered round; as there is no forward movement of its mass, the weapon is highly accurate and reliable.

The successful MP5 has appeared in a number of versions, customised for special forces and paramilitary users. The MP5K (k or kurz meaning short) is only some 32.5cm long (half the length of the standard version) and can easily be concealed under a raincoat or in a civilian car being used for covert operations, while the MP5SD is silenced and is ideal for taking out sentries.

Heckler & Koch G41

The G41 has been used by SAS snipers on inner cordon operations because of its high rate of fire and reliability. It is basically a German Bundeswehr G3 assault rifle, rechambered for NATO standard 5.56mm ammunition. The weapon's low-noise bolt-closing device and ejection port dust cover are popular features with the SAS, but its 850 rounds a minute rate of fire is the G41's main selling point. It can be fitted with a light bipod and telescopic scope to customise it for the SAS sniper role.

L1A1 Self Loading Rifle (SLR)

The British-made version of the Belgian-designed FN FAL was the British Infantry's issue personal weapon until the introduction into service of the L85A1 (SA-80) in 1984. It was always popular with SAS troopers because of its long range, accuracy, reliability and stopping power. Few enemies could get up and return fire after being felled by a 7.62mm round.

In Aden, Borneo, Oman, and in the early years in Northern Ireland, the SLR served the SAS well in numerous actions. Many SAS men were sad to see it go. The SLR had its drawbacks, principally its weight at 4.25kg and length of 1.09 metres, which made it unwieldy inside helicopters and vehicles.

L96A1

Introduced in 1986 as the British Army's standard sniper rifle to replace the L42 rifle, the L96A1 is basically a military version of the Accuracy International PM weapon. The SAS was very keen to get hold of a modern bolt-action sniper rifle and the L96A1 saw active service in Northern Ireland, the Gulf War and Bosnia. Its Schmidt and Bender telescopic sight can guarantee a first-time kill against targets up to 800 metres when used by a skilled marksman. The weapon's 7.62mm round provided plenty of killing power but the introduction of 12.7mm sniper rifles by the SAS's opponents has led to the SAS starting to field more powerful weapons.

Barrett M82A2

With the appearance of 12.7mm calibre sniper rifles in the hands of the Provisional IRA and Bosnian militias, the SAS has had to look to increase the firepower of its snipers. In early 1995 the British Army received funding to buy 12.7mm Barrett M82A2 weapons as part of a crash programme to upgrade the weapons of its troops in Bosnia.

The M82A2 is a real beast of a weapon, weighing in at around 12.24kg. However, it has tremendous punch and will literally cut a man in half, even if he is wearing body armour. Rounds will punch through light armour vehicles and bring down helicopters. The weapon has an advertised effective first-time kill range of 1,000 metres but in the Gulf War, US Army units were claiming kills at 1,800 metres.

9mm Browning High Power (L9A1)

Although some examples saw service with the commandos in the Second World War it was not until 1961 that the British Army officially adopted the Belgian FN version of the Browning automatic pistol.

Every SAS trooper tries to carry a side arm as a backup in case his assault rifle packs up at an embarrassing moment. In hostage-rescue situations automatic pistols provide close-quarters killing power in a compact and highly manoeuvrable form.

The 9mm Browning has been a favourite of the SAS for many years and the arrival on the scene of more modern rivals has not dampened the old weapon's popularity. It is a basic weapon but is reliable, easy to maintain and a true killer.

L85A1 (SA-80) Rifle/L86A1 LSW

The British Army's issue personal weapon and light support weapon (LSW) have never been popular with the SAS. Unlike the rest of the British Army, the SAS has had the chance to buy better weapons to use on operations. The main drawbacks of the weapon are that it is unreliable and lacks stopping power in the light support weapon role. A magazine-fed weapon just can't put down enough firepower.

Budding SAS soldiers use the 5.56mm weapon during

selection and Territorial Army SAS troopers also make extensive use of it. When SAS men are working with other units and do not want to draw attention to themselves, they nearly always use the SA-80.

Minimi

Not satisfied with the L86A1 as a fire team weapon, the SAS turned to the Belgian FN Minimi, which is designated the M249 in the US service. It can fire about 1,000 rounds a minute, and can either be belt fed from a 200-round belt or a 30-round box magazine.

The SAS used it to great effect in the Gulf War, where it provided SAS foot patrols with plenty of heavy firepower at almost half the weight of the old General Purpose Machine-Gun (GPMG).

Remington 870 pump action

This is a far from new weapon but has proved its worth with the SAS time and time again in close-quarters battle. This pump-action, 12-gauge weapon only has a range of 40 metres but it is almost guaranteed to kill if fired down range inside a building or aircraft. Shotguns are useful in hostage-rescue scenarios because their shot only causes damage in a very localised area, unlike high-velocity rounds that travel for long distances, even after going through walls, and can injure innocent civilians. Hostage-rescue teams love shotguns because they have a secondary role, blasting open locked doors.

Support Weapons

L7A1 General Purpose Machine-Gun (GPMG)

Considered by some to be the best weapon in the SAS armoury, the famous 'Gimpy' is considered a battle-winning weapon. Derived from the Belgian FN MAG, the GPMG provides long-range, sustained killing power. Every SAS trooper has to be highly trained in using the weapon in the light role, with bipod, and sustained fire (SF) role using a tripod and C2 sight.

The GPMG can hit out to 1,800 metres and will punch a 7.62mm round through a brick wall. It is belt fed and is designed to spread its fire around a beaten zone one metre wide and 110 metres deep.

Because of the amount of ammunition they eat up – a minimum (SF) gun team tactical load is 5,000, and that will be shot off in 20 minutes of fun-rate firing – GPMGs are rarely taken on covert observation missions by small teams. They are saved for full squadron jobs, where the guns and ammo can be mounted in Land Rovers, or there are plenty of troops involved to man-pack the ammo into the fire support base before the big attack. The GPMGs were used in the vehicle-mounted role during the Gulf War and in the Loughall ambush in 1987.

0.50 Cal Browning Heavy Machine-Gun

The big Browning has always been popular with the SAS because of its range and hitting power. With a range of around 1,800 metres the vintage American weapon can reach out across the battlefield to find its prey. The 12.7mm round will cut through brick and concrete. When fitting a special armour piercing round the weapon will also punch through light armour with ease.

With a rate of fire of 450 to 575 rounds a minute, the belt-fed weapon can put down an impressive rate of fire. Its main ammunition is a ball round and tracers are used to allow the fall of shot to be observed. In the ground-mounted role it is set up for action on a tripod.

The Browning provided the heavy firepower that drove off the *adoo* tribesmen at Mirbat and saw service again in the Gulf War, in the vehicle-mounted role. It was rushed back into service with the British Army in Northern Ireland in the late 1960s to counter large IRA truck bombs that were driven at security-force bases.

81mm Mortar

The L16A1 81mm Mortar is the largest calibre indirect fire support weapon in the armoury. It proved to be invaluable in Oman and the Falklands, where it turned the tide in a number of important battles. In Oman the SAS used the weapon to defend its desert bases. The battle of Mirbat was perhaps the most famous use of the weapon, where it played a key role in keeping the *adoo* tribesmen at bay. The defenders of Mirbat used the mortar's 4.47 kg high-explosive rounds to blast the ranks of the *adoo* human wave assaults. Also important was the weapon's ability to fire white phosphorus illuminating rounds, to protect perimeters at night and stop attackers sneaking up to positions under the cover of darkness.

While the mortar barrel, base plate, tripod and sight units are just about man-portable, at 37kg it is very difficult for small groups of men to carry worthwhile quantities of ammunition. So in the Falklands the SAS had to reserve the weapon for large squadron-sized operations where mortar ammunition could be shared out between everyone in the unit. The Pebble Island raiders had 81mm mortar support and the weapon was also used in the diversionary raid at Goose Green on the night of the San Carlos landing. In the latter attack around fifty SAS men were involved, but because of the weight of the firepower, including mortar fire, the Argentinians thought they were under attack by a full British battalion.

Putting mortar rounds accurately on target requires skilled observers to adjust the fire. Using radio communications, mortar fire controllers send back corrections to the mortar baseplate positions so the rounds can be 'walked' to the target. Essentially this is similar to adjusting artillery and naval gunfire, so it is not surprisingly a key SAS skill.

94mm Light Anti-Tank Weapon (LAW)

This is the British infantry's standard section level anti-armour weapon. It was first issued in the late 1980s to replace the 84mm Carl Gustav and 66mm M72 Light Anti-Tank Weapons (LAWs). It has yet to be used in action by the SAS but is extensively used in training. It is a throw-away weapon system, which is very easy to use. The fire has first to extend the weapon out of its plastic firing tube. It is aimed by a simple fold-up sight.

Before engaging with the main armament, three 7.62mm spotting rounds can be fired from an internal rifle to help ensure first-round kills with the 94mm HEAT warhead rocket. The weapon has an effective battle range against targets up to 500 metres range. It is able to penetrate the armour of most modern main battle tanks but is seen by the SAS as mainly a bunker-busting weapon.

M203

The M203 is an SAS favourite. It is installed under the fore stock of the M16A2 assault rifle and provides the SAS trooper with lightweight, close-range firepower. It can fire 40mm high explosive, smoke, CS gas and anti-personnel flachette rounds out to 150 metres range. SAS raiding parties in Iraq found the weapon invaluable. It is also used extensively in Northern Ireland to counter IRA lorry bombs, driven at speed towards security-force bases.

MILAN

The SAS uses the Anglo-German-French MILAN wire-guided anti-tank missile to engage long-range targets at up to 2,000 metres. It was first used in combat by the SAS during the Falklands War in the large diversionary raids at Goose Green and Port Stanley. In the Gulf War, the weapon was used in the Land Rover mounted role to shoot up Iraqi Scud missile convoys.

The MILAN comprises three main elements. The main element is the tripod-mounted missile firing post, which weighs around 16.4kg. The firing post can be fitted with a thermal-imaging night sight, called MIRA, which came into its own during the Gulf War, providing long-range night surveillance capability for SAS fighting columns. Individual missiles are prepacked in sealed plastic tubes, which are thrown away after use. Guidance commands are sent to the missile from the firing post by a thin wire cable that is fed out behind it in flight.

Stinger

This American-made anti-aircraft missile was first issued to the SAS immediately prior to the Falklands War. The Regiment's only qualified Stinger firer was unfortunately killed in the Sea King crash days before the San Carlos landings. His colleagues had to teach themselves how to use the weapon and used it after the Goose Green raid to shoot down an Argentine Pucara aircraft.

The Stinger is an infra-red homing (heat-seeking) missile that is attracted to the hot parts of aircraft. Later versions of the missile have been improved to allow it to engage head-on targets.

Mk 19-3 Grenade Launcher

This American-made weapon has also proved popular with the SAS. It saw combat service with the Regiment during the Gulf War, mounted on fighting patrol Land Rovers. Its big plus is its 325 to 375 rounds a minute rate of fire, so it can saturate targets out to 2,200 metres with a barrage of lethal 40mm grenade rounds. Usually the grenades are belt fed from a 20- to 50-round drum. Against point targets, such as armoured vehicles and bunkers, the weapon is accurate to 1,500 metres. It can fire a mix of high-explosive, armour piercing and anti-personnel rounds.

Demolition Kit

Explosives

The destruction of enemy targets with explosives planted by SAS sabotage teams has been a key skill since the Regiment was formed in 1941. SAS soldiers are taught how to blow up buildings, bridges, aircraft, ships and other structures vital to the enemy's war effort.

Explosives technology has advanced considerably since the Second World War, with smaller weights of explosives providing even bigger bangs. Plastic explosives are the main type used for sabotage missions, because of their light weight, small volume and power. Those used by the SAS include PE4, RDX and PETN. Electric initiating caps and time fuses are the main detonators used.

M18A1 Claymore mine

Claymore mines have been a popular SAS weapon since the 1960s when they were used extensively in jungle ambushes during the Borneo confrontation. The Claymore is an American-made weapon designed to kill or injure everything in a narrow beaten zone or impact area. Some 0.68kg of C4 explosive is used to blast around 700 small steel ball-bearings forward in an arc of 60 degrees. The projectiles are fired outwards some 50 metres and upwards about one metre. It is designed to take out a section-sized patrol moving along a track. The mine can be set to be detonated by a trip wire or a command wire. With an overall weight of 1.58kg, the Claymore is issued in large numbers to SAS patrols to protect their positions or set up ambushes. It is a very easy weapon to use, but operators must ensure they remember to point it in the right direction. Tired troops, especially at night, have been known to set it up the wrong way round and kill themselves.

Grenades

Hand grenades are used extensively by the SAS. The main high-explosive grenade used is the issue British Army L2A2. The egg-shaped grenade contains around 170g of RDX/TNT explosive, which turns the steel casing into shrapnel on detonation. It has a danger area of around 35 metres from the point of detonation. A good grenadier can throw one accurately up to 30 metres.

For generating smoke screens and marking targets for

air strikes and artillery observers, the SAS uses the No 80 (white phosphorus) grenade. Users have to be skilled at judging wind effects to get the best results from WP when trying to generate smoke screens. If the enemy is close to an exploding WP grenade he will suffer horrendous burns from the molten phosphorus.

HRT Stun munitions

Made famous during the Mogadishu hijacking and Iranian embassy siege, these weapons are now standard issue to SAS troops on counter-terrorist duties. They are essentially a development of the old training thunderflash.

On detonation they let off a very loud bang and then intense blinding white flash burns for up to 15 seconds. The effect on unprepared victims is to deafen, blind and disorientate. This shock effect provides just enough time for hostage-rescue teams to gain entry and get the first round off against the terrorists.

Signals/Navigation/Night Observation Kit

PRC319

While the rest of the British Army has to make do with 1960s vintage Clansman tactical radios, the SAS has procured the new PRC319 high-frequency radios. These are high-tech computer-based radios that use modern computer technology, including a data input device and a burst transmission capability. This allows long messages to be typed into a key pad and sent at the press of a button. The radio is a high-frequency set so it has almost unlimited range if the right antenna is used.

PRC320

Considered by many in the SAS as the finest radio ever to be used by the Regiment, the PRC320 is a high-frequency set that can be used with a wide range of antennas, from large antenna set up on eight-metre telescopic masts to pieces of wire attached to metal cattle fences. Given the right frequencies and antennas, PRC320s operating in the sky-wave mode have been able to send messages over thousands of miles. A morse key can be attached and is very popular with SAS signallers. All SAS men have to learn how to use morse code on the PRC320.

The set is designed for use in very primitive conditions and a hand generator is available for when a resupply of batteries is not possible. It weighs some 5.6kg and can easily be packed in a bergen.

Cougar

This is the British Army's secure radio system for use only in Northern Ireland. It is based on a series of hill-top repeater station sites and provides coverage throughout the Province. This means the size and power of the sets used can be dramatically reduced, which is a bonus for covert SAS patrols and observation patrols. Radio signals on Cougar are automatically encrypted so

SAS units do not have to waste valuable time encoding messages.

SARBE Beacon

The surface-to-air rescue beacon (SARBE) was designed for use by downed aircrew. It can either be used in beacon or voice mode to attract the attention of aircraft circling above. It is primarily for ground-to-air use and is therefore particularly terrain-dependent. An aircraft has to be almost above the user for the signal to get through and a mountain ridge or hills will block the signal. This proved to be the downfall of the Bravo Two Zero patrol in Iraq, who had great difficulty getting through to rescue forces with the SARBE when their main radio communications failed.

Spyglass

This is a man-portable, thermal-imaging sight system that can pick-up and identify targets up to 2,000 metres. It has a good reputation for reliability, but its drawback is that it needs regular resupplies of coolant bottles. Thermal sight systems detect heat sources and can see through low cloud, rain and forests.

Laser Target Markers/Range Finders

This specialist kit is used by the SAS to call in close air support and artillery fire. The laser target marker is designed to designate targets for strike aircraft. It reflects a laser light off the target, which is picked up by the inbound strike aircraft's targeting system, so laser-guided bombs can be guided to the target with pinpoint accuracy. It can be used against targets up to 10,000 metres away, and is fitted with the OTIS thermal-imaging night sight. The target marker is a very bulky and delicate piece of kit so the SAS tends not to use it unless on vehicle-borne operations.

Laser range finders are more compact and are more widely issued. They can be combined with Spyglass for night operations. SAS forward air controllers used them in Bosnia to pinpoint ranges to targets accurately before radioing their co-ordinates to NATO bombers, armed with laser guided and conventional iron bombs.

Common Weapon Sight

This is the British Army's standard night sight for its L85A1 Rifle, L86A1 LSW and GPMG. It uses imaging intensifying technology so it is not as capable as the thermal-imaging sights, identifying targets out to a few hundred metres. Imaging intensifiers amplify the ambient light from the moon and the stars, to produce a green tinted image in the sight. It has replaced the old Vietnam War era individual weapon sight (IWS).

GPS

The American-operated global positioning system (GPS) has revolutionised military navigation. Small hand-held devices are used to pick up the signals from a number of GPS satellites in orbit around the earth, the signals are processed by a small computer to produce a fix of the operator's location to within a few metres.

Commercial GPS receivers, called Magellans, were purchased for use by the SAS during the Gulf War and proved their worth when the fighting patrols were navigating through the featureless terrain of western Iraq at night. The ability to pinpoint their locations at night was particularly important for the SAS to call in air strikes.

GPS was also widely used by SAS forward air controllers in Bosnia to pinpoint their locations. They then used laser range finders to measure the distance to targets, to give the SAS men highly accurate targeting data on enemy positions.

Vehicles

Land Rovers

The principal tactical vehicle used by the SAS since the 1960s is the Land Rover. Its main use is as a desert raiding vehicle; in all other scenarios the SAS prefers to rely on the light personnel carrier (LPC) or helicopters to insert its patrols. The most famous version is the long wheel base Series II 15 cwt model, which became known as the 'Pink Panther' because of its pink paint scheme. This was based on the Second World War desert experiences, carrying extra fuel and water jerrycans, sun compasses, and numerous heavy machine-gun mounts.

By the time of the Gulf War the SAS had switched to

using the short wheel base Land Rover 90s and long wheel base Land Rover 110s. They followed closely in the tradition of the famous Pink Panthers. The small versions became known as 'Dinkies'. Photographs have shown various weapon fits, including 0.5 cal Browning heavy machine-guns, MILAN anti-tank missiles, GPMGs and Mk 19–3 grenade launchers. GPS devices and thermal-imaging sights were also fitted to many vehicles.

SAS troops working in Bosnia as Joint Commission Observers (JCOs) in hot areas were issued with ex-Northern Ireland armoured patrol vehicle (APV) versions of the Land Rover. These had armoured cabins, which provided plenty of protection from mines and mortar rounds, but Corporal Fergus Rennie was killed when his APV was hit by a heavy Serb anti-aircraft cannon inside the Gorazde enclave.

Light Strike Vehicle (LSV)

This much hyped vehicle was used experimentally by the SAS during the Gulf War. Two were flown out to the Middle East but proved unreliable in the harsh desert conditions and were not taken into Iraq.

Boats

SAS Boat Troops use a number of craft for amphibious assaults and patrols. The most easily used is the rubber-inflatable Gemini assault boat, which is powered by an outboard motor. Because it can be deflated it is used for operations from submarines. For more heavy-duty operations, SAS Boat Troops have Rigid Raiders – hard-bottomed craft that can carry up to eight men. Their 140 horse-power engine means they can reach very high speeds.

Since the 1950s the SAS has used the famous Klepper canoe for covert coastal insertions. It is made of ash and birch wood, covered with cotton woven with hemp for the deck, and polyester-reinforced rubber for the hull. It is around 5.2 metres long and can carry two men, along with their kit.

Uniforms and Personal Kit

SAS Smock

The famous SAS smock has a long and distinguished history dating back to 1942 when the British Army started to issue green, brown and pink camouflage smocks to any soldier who needed a wind-proof combat jacket. Many SAS men used the jacket during the war in north-west Europe, Italy and the Balkans. After the war, when the British Army decided to adopt green olive drab uniforms, the SAS decided to stick with the wartime camouflage jacket. It was used during the 1950s and 1960s, until the British Army decided to adopt disruptive pattern material (DPM). This was used in the design of a modern version of the SAS smock, which features a hood, large pockets and internal poachers' pockets.

SAS-PARA Bergen

In the 1950s, the British Army's issue '58 Pattern webbing system with its distinctive attachable large pack was the main load-carrying system in use with the British Army. During the Malay campaign the SAS found it far from ideal for carrying large loads over long distances.

When sent to Oman in 1958, it was necessary to carry heavy jerrycans of water up rough mountain tracks, so the SAS Operational Research Unit came up with the bergen rucksack design that is now known as the SAS-PARA. It features a metal frame and a detachable heavy duty fabric bag. The ability of the bergen to survive parachute drops led to it being adopted by the airborne forces during the 1960s; hence the name.

Hostage Rescue Team (HRT) Uniforms

The 'men in black' who stormed the Iranian embassy wore early versions of HRT kit that is now widely used around the world by specialist counter-terrorist units or police SWAT groups. The main element of the kit is black overalls made of fire-retardant material. Special fire-retardant underwear is also worn. A fire-retardant hood to protect the HRT operative's head from flames and the flash from stun grenades is worn, but at the Iranian embassy the SAS used dyed Royal Navy flash hoods.

In the 1980s the SAS also developed a special suede HRT vest to carry ammunition, radios, and other specialist kit. At the Iranian embassy special fabric body-armour outer covers were used, which had extra pockets sewn onto them.

Body Armour/Helmets

The SAS has been using body armour on its HRT operations since the late 1970s. However, the kit used then was the same surplus American flak jackets used by the rest of the British Army, but with a purpose-made black fabric cover. During the 1980s purpose-made Kevlar vests were bought from specialist companies in the UK.

For operations in Northern Ireland and Bosnia, the SAS wears Improved Northern Ireland Body Armour (INBA) because of its chest and back plates, which provide protection for the heart from high-velocity sniper rounds. When working in low-threat areas the plates can be removed to reduce the weight. Without the plates the body armour is only really good for protecting the torso from shell splinters. In the Gulf War, the SAS did not use body armour because of its weight and the reduction in mobility it caused.

During HRT operations, black-painted standard British Army Mk6 Combat Helmets are sometimes worn but were not used during the Iranian embassy situation because they restricted vision and head movement.

Webbing

The SAS has never liked issue British Army personal load-carrying equipment, which is universally known as webbing. The '58 Pattern webbing was made of fabric that soaked up water and doubled in weight after a dunking in a river, while the modern issue PLCE has too many pouches at the rear of the webbing and not enough ammunition pouches.

SAS troopers are keen to get hold of chest webbing and combat vests (or rigs) with many front pockets, so they can quickly get to their magazines during a firefight. British Army Northern Ireland issue chest webbing is much in demand and during the Gulf War, South African Army bush combat rigs were used in large numbers.

NBC Kit

The British Army issue nuclear, chemical and biological (NBC) warfare kit is used by the SAS whenever there is a chemical warfare threat. The first SAS patrols into western Iraq wore their NBC kit until the Iraq chemical warfare threat was reduced. This is one area where the SAS fondness for customising their kit has to be held in check. The current NBC kit was designed by the Porton Down chemical warfare centre and not even the SAS wishes to second guess their boffins.

The NBC individual protective equipment (IPE) consists of a two-piece charcoal suit with a hood, rubber gloves and overboots. The centrepiece of the IPE is an S10 respirator (or gas mask), which is also used during HRT operations where CS gas is being used to neutralise a terrorist threat.

Arctic/Jungle/Desert/Mountain Clothing

Due to the Regiment's worldwide role it has access to specialist clothing for a wide range of climatic zones. With few exceptions, the kit issued to the SAS is generally the same as that used by the British Army, whether it be jungle, arctic or desert. The main difference is that the SAS can get hold of its kit more quickly and in larger quantities.

SAS soldiers are notoriously impatient with the slow Regular Army logistic chain and are keen buyers of military kit from commercial sources. Much of the 'Gucci' personal kit used by the SAS has been bought by individual members to suit their individual requirements. There is no such thing as standard SAS combat uniform.

Aircraft and Helicopters

Lockheed Martin C-130 Hercules

The veteran C-130 or 'Fat Albert' has been the workhorse of the SAS since the 1960s. It is a four-engined tactical transport aircraft and serves for paratrooping, moving vehicles, cargo or personnel. The inside of the aircraft is very basic, but it can carry ninety-four troops or sixty-four paratroopers. Land Rovers can be loaded via its tail ramp.

The RAF's No 47 Squadron has its own Special Forces Flight and its aircraft are equipped with self-defence devices to allow them to penetrate through enemy air defences. The flight has built up a long relationship with the SAS and during one training mission, a Hercules pilot got so into the SAS role that he freefall parachuted out of the back of the aircraft with his SAS passengers. The RAF board of inquiry was not impressed with him leaving the aircraft in the hands of his co-pilot.

Boeing Vertol Chinook HC.2

Like the Hercules, the Chinook is the main helicopter used by the SAS. There is a Special Forces Flight of Chinooks, assigned to No 18 Squadron. The monster Chinook can carry around fifty-five troops, and when fitted with extra internal fuel tanks can fly more than 200 kilometres. Like the Special Forces Hercules, the customised Chinooks sport self-defence kit, Gatling guns and M60 machine-guns. The RAF has recently announced plans to buy special forces versions of the Chinook, which have improved navigation and communications, and an inflight refuelling kit.

Westland Sea King HC.4

As the Royal Navy's principal ship-borne assault helicopter, the 'Junglie' is the main mode of transport for the SAS when working alongside the amphibious forces. It can carry around twenty-eight troops inside its cabin and underslung loads outside.

The Sea King saw extensive service during the Falklands War, dropping off SAS observation patrols deep behind enemy lines, and one was lost when attempting to insert a patrol into Argentina. White-painted UN Sea

Kings were heavily involved in supporting SAS teams in Bosnia.

Westland Lynx AH.7

This is the British Army's main anti-tank and utility helicopter. It can carry up to ten troops inside its cabin and soldiers exit the cabin via two large sliding doors. The SAS has made extensive use of the Lynx in Northern Ireland because of its speed and flexibility. Its thermal-imaging anti-tank missile sight is also a great asset to the SAS in keeping IRA suspects under observation from long distances.

Two Army Air Corps door gunners are usually carried to man 7.62mm GPMG waist guns and there have been a number of air-to-ground firefights between Lynxes and PIRA teams along the border with the Irish Republic.

Westland Wessex HC.2

This veteran helicopter is still in service with the RAF in the UK and Northern Ireland. It can carry some sixteen troops and its robust features make it popular with the SAS.

Westland Puma HC.1

This Anglo-French helicopter is used by the RAF in the support helicopter role, moving troops and equipment around the battlefield. It can carry around sixteen passengers and is used extensively in Northern Ireland to support SAS operations, but it is generally not used to support special forces operations in general war because of its limited range and load-carrying capability.

Westland Gazelle AH.1

The British Army's standard light-observation and liaison helicopters are used by the SAS to move key commanders around and act as airborne command posts. The Gazelle can only carry a pilot and four passengers, so it is not used for assault missions. Some versions are fitted with closed-circuit television (CCTV).

Agusta A-109

During the Falklands War British forces captured two Italian-made Argentine Agusta A-109 utility helicopters, and they have since been pressed into service by the Army Air Corps to provide dedicated support to the SAS. They are used to move key SAS personnel around and in support of HRT assault operations. The helicopter can carry six passengers at up to 285 k.p.h., so they are considered superior to the smaller and slower Gazelle.

Index

Ranks: Military personnel are given their most senior rank mentioned in the book even though they may have subsequently attained higher rank.